HEALING HEARTS IN THE LITTLE VILLAGE

A cozy feel-good romance about second chances

ELLA COOK

Broclington Book 2

Choc Lit
A JOFFE BOOKS COMPANY

Choc Lit
A Joffe Books company
www.choc-lit.com

This edition first published in Great Britain in 2023

Cover art by Jarmila Takač

ISBN: 978-1-78189-540-5

To Alex — still my first reader. Thank you for putting up with me. And all the tea.

And to everyone who still believes in magic . . . or at least, those who haven't decided that they don't believe in it yet.

ACKNOWLEDGEMENTS

It's been a while since the last visit to Broclington. Unfortunately, real life got in my way for a while, so thank you — lovely reader — for bearing with me while I put my head back on straight long enough to visit there again.

And if you haven't visited Broclington before, thank you for taking the chance on this new book. I hope you enjoy your visit, and that you'll be back soon!

So, onto the many people who I owe thanks to for helping to bring this book to you:

Thank you to Sarah, my brilliant editor, for helping me keep my timelines straight (sorry, I will try to do better!). And to the rest of the Choc Lit family, and 'sister-authors' who offered me such support, encouragement and friendship when life got stressful. And another massive thank you to the Tasting Panel Readers and ARC team who pick and support all of our books — I'm so glad you were excited to return to Broclington with me! Special thanks to: Laura Sumner, Alan Roberton, Alma Hough, Deborah Warren, Fran Stevens, Gill Leivers, Honor Gilbert, Jenny Mitchell, Jo Osborne, Julie Lilly, Liana Vera Saez, Lorna Baker, Michele Rollins, Yvonne Greene, Alison Bilham, Cheryl Woodbridge and Kate Avetoomyan.

To Lu, who has the unenviable task of keeping us writers organised — thank you for always being so cheerful and supportive, and putting up with my 'stupid' questions and midnight ramblings. The biggest of thanks go to Lyn, who founded Choc Lit 1.0 and took a chance on my first 'marmite' book — I wouldn't be writing this if not for you.

And thanks to Joffe and everyone at Choc Lit 2.0 — from cover design, to project management to copy-editing and proofreading and marketing — because you wouldn't be reading this if not for them. Can't wait to see what we do together!

Keep looking for the magic and sparkle.

Love and light, Ella.

CHAPTER ONE

Liv pressed her hand against her hammering heart and fought to will away the anxiety that clawed at her throat, stealing her breath and threatening to choke her. Her fingers tingled and ached with adrenaline, and she tried to rub the feeling away through the cast that still wrapped around her left wrist, palm and forearm.

She closed her eyes and focussed on taking slow, calming breaths. She'd expected to feel anxious, so had left earlier than needed. Reassuring herself, she took another deep breath and tried to practice the mindfulness that so many people extolled the virtues of. Birdsong filtered through the open car window, joined by the laugher of children in nearby playing fields. The nearest thing to traffic she could hear was a farmer trundling his tractor through fields, doing whatever it was that farmers did with tractors on sunny spring days in March. There were no screaming sirens, no blaring horns and screeching brakes, and none of the roaring traffic and noise she associated with daily life. Or what used to be her daily life.

She didn't have to rush. She'd given herself plenty of time for the drive, overestimating to make allowances for getting out of the city and pulling over to rest her still-aching body. But the long drive had been easier than she'd expected, leaving her with plenty of time to explore the area and settle her nerves. If anything, she'd enjoyed watching the grey grime of the city slip away and fade into the rich browns, fresh greens and lacy blossoms of the countryside until she'd finally reached Broclington village.

Broclington. The name had been a beacon of hope for the last few weeks — ever since she'd been cajoled into accepting the position. She'd studied the place night after night online and virtually strolled through the streets that made up the large village. She'd seen pictures of the church, and admired the old stonework, the black-and-white gabled history and thatched roofs of the houses that people apparently lived in. She'd read the reviews left by day-trippers, seeking out a brief slice of quintessential British, edge-of-the-Cotswolds life.

It was worlds away from the busy city that had been her world until now. But even the sunniest, best staged photo on her laptop screen hadn't prepared her for the reality of being there. It was too quiet. Even in the middle of the night, her London apartment still hummed with the sounds of life going on outside. Here, in the middle of the morning, it sounded so different. It smelt different. Everything was too different.

The panic Liv had spent so much of her recent life fighting started to take hold again. The familiar nausea returning as the pressure built inside her chest, and she had to force herself to breathe.

Slowly she blinked and took another deep breath, reassuring herself. Yes, it was different here, and those differences were a major part of the reason she'd accepted the offer. She was safe here. There were no angry, violent patients more interested in hurting her than getting well. Different was good. Even if it was just a little bit scary.

She checked her reflection in the rear-view mirror. Tom Macpearson, her former professor and long-standing mentor, had promised her the job when he visited her in hospital. But the fact the job was already hers didn't mean she didn't want to make the best first impression possible — especially as Tom had already left on his sabbatical, and she hadn't met the other surgery staff.

After taking a moment to touch up her lip gloss and tuck a few errant blonde strands back into her ponytail, she readied herself to explore the village she'd agreed to help look after for the next few months.

* * *

Callum raced after Sarah as she zoomed through the recreation ground, her pigtails flying out behind her, matching the sparkly streamers on her handlebars as she laughed in delight. He'd only taken the stabilisers off her bike the night before, and his heart slammed against his ribs as he sprinted to keep up with her.

He was terrified she'd come flying off the bike any second and hurt herself. Obviously she was wearing a helmet and knee and elbow pads, but the problem with being a doctor was you got used to seeing the horrific injuries people managed to inflict on themselves, and he couldn't help but worry. In actual years his daughter was only six, but in attitude she was maturer, and her mother's independence and mile-wide stubborn streak were already getting her into trouble.

'Daddy, Daddy, look! I'm doing it. Look how fast I can go!' She squealed in excitement as she raced past him again.

'Be careful, sweetheart. Maybe slow down a little?' Callum begged.

'No way. This is too much fun!' Sarah pushed down harder on the peddles, speeding the bike even faster.

'All right. But just one more lap.' Callum checked his watch. 'Then I need to drop you off at Mrs Turner's and head into the surgery.'

'But it's the weekend.' Sarah's whine of complaint streaked past him as she tore up the recreation ground path.

'People still get sick and hurt, even at the weekend. And now I'm running the surgery, I have a lot more paperwork to

3

do.' Callum tried to reason with her. 'And I'm meeting the doctor who's covering for your grandad now.'

Sarah squealed to a stop in front of him, spinning the bike sideways like a pro. 'I miss Grandad and Grandma. I hope they come back from their samaticable soon. And I hope they stay home this time.'

'It's sa-ba-tic-al.' Callum sounded the word out for Sarah, yet again overwhelmed with the responsibility of being both father and mother to the incredible little girl in front of him.

'Sabbatical,' Sarah repeated obediently, watching for her father's approving nod. 'Sabbaticals suck.' She poked her tongue out.

'Little girls shouldn't say words like that,' Callum chided gently, while personally agreeing. He missed his parents, and all the support they gave him in bringing up Sarah. But he couldn't resent them the adventure of living in Africa and helping set up urgent care centres for some of the poorest people on the planet. They'd originally only planned to be there a few months, but that stretched into a few more, and as soon as they returned from one trip they were planning the next, and the next. It was over eighteen months since they'd regularly lived in Broclington, and he still hadn't fully gotten to grips with juggling his responsibilities to the surgery and managing his own life and Sarah's.

On their last visit, his parents had tried hard to hide their dismay at the chaos he'd wrought in the village surgery, and his mother — usually the practice manager — had blitzed through it with her usual ease in the weeks they'd been home before jetting off again.

At least this time his father had managed to source a semi-permanent replacement, instead of the different-al-most-every-day locums who'd been there, contributing to the general chaos.

'Hey?' Sarah looked up at him. 'If you're getting a new doctor, does that mean you can come home more early?'

'Yes, munchkin, hopefully I will be home "more early" more often.' He tweaked her nose.

'Awesome sauce!' She powered down against her pedals. 'Race ya!'

'All right.' Callum broke into a tired jog, before realising in horror where she was heading. 'Sarah! No! Stay inside the park.'

As he broke into a sprint, Sarah rounded the gate and disappeared. He prayed she had the sense to stay on the pavement. He heard the oomph, clatter and Sarah's cry as he reached the gate and flung himself through it.

* * *

Liv had already walked through the village centre and located the converted house that was the surgery. She was just strolling past the church, enjoying the fresh air and peace and quiet when a pink, sparkly fairy on an equally pink sparkly bike slammed into her.

Instinctively, Liv grabbed the little girl as she launched herself over the handlebars, and wrapped her arms tightly around her, protecting her from harm as they toppled backwards under the momentum of the bike that crashed painfully into her legs. Liv gritted her teeth and bit back a moan as the pink cycle helmet slammed into her chin, and smacked her head back against the pavement.

'Oh my God, Sarah, are you all right?' Strong hands pulled the little girl from Liv's arms. 'Does it hurt anywhere?'

'No, Daddy. The lady catched me.' The little fairy sobbed softly.

'I'm so sorry.' The man looked up from his daughter and Liv was struck by the intensity of his blue eyes. 'She's only just had the stabilisers off.'

'It's OK.' Liv sat up and ran her eyes over the little girl briefly, but couldn't see anything that instantly concerned her. Her side twinged painfully, and she grimaced and pressed her palm against the still-healing skin.

'Are you all right?' The man reached down to her. 'Are you hurt? Can I help at all? Did you bang your head?'

'No, no.' Liv shook her head, and instantly regretted the action. Hiding the pain, she seized his hand. 'I'm fine.'

He pulled her easily to her feet and smiled down at her, and she was intensely aware of the extra few inches he had on her as he looked her up and down.

'Is your hip all right? Are you in pain?'

Liv clenched her teeth and shook her head before answering. 'It's fine.' She took a deep breath. 'Old injury.'

'And you didn't knock your wrist?' He gestured to her cast.

'No.'

He watched her for a moment before kneeling to examine her knee. 'You're bleeding.' His large hand slipped around the back of the joint.

Liv gulped, and tried not to think about how good those warm fingers felt as they wrapped around her leg. Whoever this good-looking stranger was, she didn't have time to deal with him. Not when she was due at the surgery in less than half an hour and now had to deal with ruined stockings and a bloody knee. And she wanted to check her scar and reassure herself that she was really as OK as she said.

'I'm fine.' Irritated with herself, she pulled her leg away from him.

'Bleeding isn't exactly fine,' he argued, good-naturedly.

'Nope.' The little girl peered at Liv's knee from behind her father. 'It needs cleaning, and magic cream, and a plaster, and a kiss to make it better.'

Liv was horrified at herself as she focussed on trying really hard not to picture that kiss. 'Really, it's fine. It's just a scratch. I'm fine.' She shook away his concern and jiggled her leg, trying to convince herself as much as him. 'Look, perfectly fine.'

'If you're sure . . .' He didn't look convinced.

'I am.' Liv nodded and stooped to gather up the contents of her handbag which had — in the perfect demonstration of sod's law — exploded all over the street. 'Please, I just want to get on with my day.' Pain and worry made her terse, but she forced herself to flash a polite, professional smile his way, before hoisting her bag onto her shoulder, spinning on her heel, and striding down the street, trying to ignore her aching knee and side.

* * *

Callum watched the gorgeous blonde retreat, her ponytail bouncing back and forth as she strode down the street and back towards the village centre, only slightly favouring her injured leg. He felt a sudden pang of regret that he hadn't asked her name and was unlikely to ever see her again.

'Daddy.' Sarah tugged at his hand.

He gave himself a mental shake. He must be overtired to be distracted so easily. He had the surgery and his daughter to focus on. Speaking of which . . . He turned to glare down at Sarah. 'Do you understand now why I wanted you to stay in the park? You could have been hurt. You *did* hurt that lady.'

'I know. I'm sorry.' Sarah's eyes filled with tears, and Callum cursed himself for the hundredth time for not knowing how to deal with his daughter anymore. Things had been so much easier when she'd been smaller, and before her mother had abandoned them both.

'Daddy, are you very cross with me?'

Callum ran his hands through his dark blond hair, dishevelling it as he so often did when he was worried. 'No, munchkin, I'm not upset. I just worry.' He pulled her into a rough hug.

'So if you're not upset, then can I have an ice cream?' Sarah wheedled.

'I told you, I have to go into the surgery today.' He hesitated as her bottom lip stuck out, trembling with the threat of more tears. 'But if you hurry, we can stop by the bakery on the way to your sitter's and you can pick out a cake for lunch. Deal?'

'Can it be a Brockle cake?'

'Yes, I'm sure it can.'

'Deal.' Her face lit up, and Callum wished every problem in life could be solved so easily.

* * *

Liv darted into the pharmacy and ran her finger along the few options she had to replace her ruined stockings. She'd arrived in the village early to try and minimise her anxiety, but was quickly running out of time. She gave the girl behind the counter a brief smile, fully aware she'd likely be working with her in the future, but wanting to avoid striking up a conversation.

Clutching the new stockings, she raced back to her car and grabbed her black leather bag from the boot before nipping into the small café.

'Welcome to Brockle's Paws. What can I get you?' The woman behind the counter wore a black apron with a badger picked out in white embroidery.

'Just a medium tea to go, please.' Liv handed over a note and dropped the change into the tip jar.

'Thanks. Be ready in a minute.'

'Perfect. Where's the bathroom, please?'

'Round the corner' — she pointed — 'the one labelled "Sows".'

'Sows? Like pigs?' Liv was appalled.

'Dunno about pigs . . .' She laughed as she poured milk into a frothing jug. 'But it certainly applies to badgers.'

'Right. Bit of a theme in here, badgers.' Liv looked around, taking in the black and white décor, and pen and ink sketches of the furry woodland creatures.

The café was a cosy looking place, with a mismatch of tables, chairs, squishy couches and huge booths that could probably seat a dozen people each, and looked to be made out of huge old church pews. With yet more pictures of badgers decorating their wooden sides.

'If it is, it's one for the whole village. Broclington means Badger's Town.'

'Yeah, I think I remember reading something about that. But I hadn't realised they would be everywhere like this.' Liv was still smiling to herself as she headed to the bathroom to clean up her throbbing knee. She had less than quarter of an hour. It wasn't much, but it should be enough time to patch herself up, calm herself down and take the short walk back to the surgery.

She looked into the mirror and smoothed her hair back into place. She wasn't too dishevelled from the incident in the park. At least not outwardly. Internally, she felt much more shaken up. As much as she hadn't wanted to admit it, she'd been attracted to the tall, strong blond with the kind blue eyes and warm smile. The knowledge made her stomach twist.

She didn't *want* to be attracted to anyone — not when she was still healing from the abysmal way Mike had treated her. She'd thought they'd been in love and planning on spending the rest of their lives together — she certainly had. And when they moved into their rundown flat together — all they could afford at the time — she had loved every minute they'd spent making it into a beautiful a chic place to live — a proper city apartment.

When he'd abandoned her, right when she'd needed him the most, it hurt more than anything. Even more than being stabbed.

She shook her head to clear the ugly memories, and splashed cold water on her face. She'd already promised herself she wasn't going to waste any more time on Mike, or any other man, including good-looking strangers she probably wouldn't see again — except maybe in the professional doctor/patient setting.

Gingerly, she pulled her silky blue blouse up and examined her side carefully. The skin running parallel with the inside of her left hip, just above her underwear, was puckered and raised in an angry line, but there was no blood or signs of further trauma. Sighing with relief, she peeled off her ruined stockings and got to work cleaning her knee.

She was just straightening her skirt when the commotion started. Hesitantly, she peered around the door.

The cute little café had exploded in chaos centred around a small boy who gasped for breath on the floor, and an older woman by his side, begging someone to help.

For a moment, Liv was frozen by a flood of memories as the warm, welcoming café faded away and was replaced by the bright, chaotic, fast-paced noise of the A&E she was used to. She could almost hear the beeps and alarms, and smell the acrid disinfectant and antiseptics that permeated the place. Shock and worry held her feet to the floor as panic threatened to take hold. She was used to emergency situations, but she'd managed to avoid them recently. And before that, she would never have been in one by herself. There would always have been dozens of other people around to help — nurses, consultants, radiologists, anaesthetists, surgeons and other doctors — a veritable army to offer any backup she could possibly need.

Adrenaline shot through her veins, and her training kicked in. It didn't matter where she was, or who was around her, she had the skills needed. Before she'd even consciously thought about helping, she was on her knees by her new patient. The boy's swollen lips were already turning blue as Liv reached for the carotid pulse in his neck.

'It's all right. I'm a doctor,' she reassured the crowd. 'Let me have some room to work, please. Has someone called an ambulance?'

'Yes. But they're at least half-hour away. Maybe longer at this time of day.'

Liv looked up at the terrified woman. 'Has this ever happened before?'

'No. Never. Is he choking?'

'I don't think so.' Liv pulled the boy's T-shirt up to reveal the tell-tale hives that stood out bright red against his pale skin. 'It looks like an allergic reaction.'

'It can't be. He doesn't have any allergies. We eat here every weekend. He even orders the same thing. Please help him.' The woman dissolved into hysterical tears.

'I will, I promise. Could something have bitten or stung him?'

'I don't think so.'

Liv looked around for the woman who had taken her tea order as she rummaged through her bag. 'Is there any chance you've changed your recipes? Maybe a nut product?'

'No.' The woman was affronted. 'We're really careful here. All our products are . . .' She trailed off, turning pale. 'We've changed suppliers recently. They're supposed to be nut free but . . .'

Liv shook her head as her fingers closed around the tube she needed. 'I'm going to administer epinephrine to decrease the swelling, and help his heart and lungs work better.' She shoved the leg of the boy's shorts up to reveal his thigh, jammed the auto-injector against his leg, and clicked the top before rubbing the injection site briskly.

'Coats, jumpers or blankets please?' She didn't take her eyes off her patient as she rolled him into the recovery position and held the head of her stethoscope against his ribs.

After a few seconds she sighed in relief. 'His heartbeat is already returning to normal. He's going to be all right.' She patted the hand of the still-crying woman.

'Oh my God. Thank you so much.' The woman sobbed gratefully. 'He's my grandson. He's staying with me while his parents are at work. If anything ever happened to him . . .'

'He's going to be fine,' Liv reassured her again as she tucked coats and jumpers around the boy. 'If anything, this could be a good thing, because now we know about his allergy and can take steps to protect him from harm. What's his name?'

'Timothy Weston.'

'Timothy?' Liv leaned closer to her patient. 'Timothy, can you hear me?' She smiled in relief as he whimpered and started to stir. 'Timothy, my name's Dr Emery. You've eaten something that wasn't too good for you, but you're going to be fine. Can you open your eyes for me, sweetie?'

'What happens now?' Timothy's gran asked.

'Well, Timothy's coming around nicely, but he might be a little confused and scared. Just keep talking to him. He really should go to hospital still. It looks like he's over the worst, but there is a really small chance of what we call a biphasic reaction, or reoccurrence. When the initial reaction has been so severe, it's always better to be safe than sorry.'

'Of course.' Timothy's gran nodded worriedly.

'It really is a very, very small chance,' Liv reassured her. 'But also the hospital can arrange for tests to identify the exact irritant, and any other trigger-risk substances. I'll stay here with you both and hand over to the paramedics when they arrive.'

'What can I do?' the café owner wanted to know.

Liv glanced around the worried faces peering down at her. 'If you don't mind, I think a round of hot, sweet tea for everyone wouldn't go amiss.'

As spoons and china rattled together, Liv heard the distant church bells ring out, telling her she was now officially late for her meeting with the practice manager who'd be her boss for the coming months. Hoping he wouldn't hold it against her too much, she looked down at Timothy and smiled, grateful for being in the right place, at the right time, to help him.

And if her new boss had an issue with that, he'd just have to deal with it.

* * *

Callum Macpearson was not in the right frame of mind to deal with much of anything. Sarah had clung to his leg, begging him not to leave when he'd dropped her off at the sitter's, he was drowning in a pile of paperwork from the local clinical commissioning group, and he was stuck at work on a sunny Saturday morning waiting to meet with a locum who he had no choice in hiring, and who wasn't even polite enough to show up on time. And to make things worse, his thoughts kept wandering back to the image of a petite blonde with a bouncy ponytail.

He reached for another file and cursed as he slammed his knee into the open desk drawer. He was fed up and irritated with the whole world. With the commissioning group who were trying to cut the surgery's funding again, with his father for hiring a locum who, at best was rude and unprofessionally late, and with obnoxious, pain-in-the-arse women who couldn't be trusted to keep their promises.

He dragged his hands through his hair and stared at Sarah's picture on his desk wondering, for the millionth time, how anyone could ever leave such a sweet, beautiful little girl.

The buzzer sounded, letting him know that the late locum had finally deigned to grace him with her presence. He stalked into the reception, slammed his hand against the door release button and stomped back up the corridor without looking at the door.

'You're late.' He thrust open the door to the practice manager's office, waiting for her to follow, already irritated. Riffling through the paperwork on the desk that was so much better organised when his mother was in charge, he eventually found the file he was looking for.

'Olivia Emery, right?' He peered at the papers in front of him.

'Yes, but most people call me Liv.'

'First from Imperial College, good strong residencies in some major hospitals — including obstetrics in the Midlands and A&E experience in London, but lacking any real community experience. Any idea why my father recommended you so highly?' He finally looked up and gaped in shock at the last person he'd expected to see again. 'It's you.'

'Yes.' The blonde bit her bottom lip, and Callum had to drag his eyes away from the glossy pink mouth.

'OK then . . .'

'I'm sorry I'm so late. But I had to stop by the café to deal with my knee, and stockings are so much more difficult to put on when you're in a cast . . .'

Callum couldn't help but glance down at the knee he'd wrapped his hand gently around just that morning, now encased in silky black . . . stockings. The word conjured completely inappropriate images, and temporarily short-circuited his brain. He started guiltily when he realised he hadn't heard a single word she'd said since. He gritted his teeth, forcing his thoughts back on track, frustration making him tense.

'We're only a little village surgery, but we do appreciate professionalism and punctuality. If you're going to be late again, you should call ahead. Patient care is paramount. Even over external . . . concerns.' He gestured towards her legs, neatly crossed beneath her black suit skirt.

Her mouth hung open for long moments before she visibly swallowed. 'Understood.'

He pointed to the cast encasing her wrist. 'And your hand?'

'I'm fit to practice if that's what's worrying you.' She wriggled her fingers. 'The cast is due off in a few weeks, but I can manage fine with it.'

'Good. Then you can start on Monday?'

'I don't see why not.' She flashed him a brittle smile.

Callum groaned inwardly. This was not how he wanted this meeting to go. 'If you can be here before we start appointments for the day, I can introduce you to the rest of the team, our processes, and we can do a phased start. There's me, a community midwife and health visitor, two part-time nurses — though one is currently in America for a few weeks, and another GP — though we share his time with the next village over. We've got a part-time receptionist as well, though she's rapidly heading towards retirement.'

'Got it.'

'About eight thirty? That will give me and the rest of the team time to get in and set up.'

'I'll even try to be on time.' Her hazel eyes flashed dangerously at Callum.

'We'll see you on Monday then.' Callum hid a wince.

'Monday.' She nodded and stood. On reaching the door, she paused and turned. 'And in answer to your first question? Your father *hired* me because I'm a bloody good doctor. In *any* setting.' With that she stalked out of the surgery, heels snapping angrily against the floor.

Callum stared at the door and swore. He'd let his short temper get the better of him and irritated the doctor who was supposed to be relieving the pressure he was under. He'd nearly choked on his coffee when he'd looked up from his paperwork to discover the stuffy, city doctor his father had hired was actually the stunning blonde whose delicate hand he still felt in his from when he'd literally picked her up from the pavement.

But instead of acting like a normal human being, and asking how her knee was, or whether he could help her settle into the village, he'd snapped at her and insulted her professionalism.

Groaning, he rubbed his forehead, trying to dispel the headache already forming at the thought of working with her every day.

* * *

Liv threw her bag onto the passenger seat and slammed the car door so hard that the window rattled. She slumped down in her seat and tried not to cry. Tom had promised her a warm and friendly welcome, and a peaceful place where she could heal and take time to consider her future. But instead, the man she initially thought so attractive had been abrupt to the point of cold. He hadn't even acknowledged her explanation for being so late — he just stared at her knee, then lectured her on timekeeping.

It was so different from what she'd imagined and hoped for — and what she so desperately needed — that she struggled to keep the tears from her eyes.

She'd have to email Tom and tell him she couldn't take the job. Except she didn't know when he'd likely get online long enough to pick up her email and make alternative arrangements, and she didn't want to let him down. Plus, she felt like this was her last chance.

For the last year or so she'd been getting more disheartened and distressed by her job. Every day, the busy A&E she worked in seemed to attract more stress and violence, and she was exhausted at the thought of having to deal with more stabbings, shootings and road accidents. She'd started to think that all she saw most days was the worst side of people. More and more frequently she'd found herself fighting back tears of anger, frustration or just plain sadness at what she'd seen that day.

And then that man had attacked her. Her side ached, and the cast weighed heavy on her arm, giving her unnecessary reminders of the horrors of that last night shift.

The thought of going back to work in places like that made her blood run cold. She couldn't, wouldn't let Tom down. She had to find a way to make this work. It wasn't like she had anywhere else to go.

Groaning, she rested her head on the steering wheel and tried not to think about how she would handle her new grumpy colleague with the bluest eyes she'd ever seen. At least now, when he'd been such an arse, she wouldn't have to worry about any residual feelings of attraction she might have felt in her moment of vulnerability. She wasn't interested in anyone right now, and especially not an arrogant pencil pusher more interested in timekeeping than the health of a little boy. How the hell that man could call himself a doctor she didn't know.

A few minutes later, the sat-nav app on her phone cheerfully announced her destination was on the left, and she pulled into the driveway of the cottage that Tom's recommended agent had found her. She slipped her bag over her shoulder and headed up the garden path, lined with fragrant flowers. She didn't know enough about gardening to be able to name most of them, but did recognise the daffodils and hyacinths in amongst fluffy looking purple and pink tall blooms. She ran her fingers over the nameplate: "*Aosán Taigh*". She had no idea what the quaint name meant, but it seemed to suit the little golden stone and slate-roofed building that could have been lifted straight out of a fairy tale. She couldn't believe she was going to get to call it home for the next few months.

Tom had offered her the chance to house sit for him while he and his wife were away, but — as much as Liv had appreciated the offer — she'd really felt she wanted her own space to start finding her life, and herself, again. The apartment in London had been sophisticated, sleek and expensive — and filled with luxury marble, gloss and gadgets in every room. Very much Mike's home, and not hers — which he'd made abundantly clear.

Irritated at herself, Liv shook her head in the hope it would shake . . . him . . . out of her mind. He'd already had more space in her thoughts than he deserved, and she wasn't going to let him spoil this as well. Resolute, she knelt and stuck her hand through the letterbox. As promised by the agent, she found a length of string that, when pulled, produced a heavy key. She shook her head in disbelief as she let herself in to the small hallway — things were very different here to the alarms, video doorbells and multiple locks she was used to.

Smiling, she hung her bag over the banister and pushed the door shut. She'd bring in her suitcases and the couple of boxes of things she couldn't bear to leave in storage, later — now she wanted to explore her new home.

Opening the first door, she had to stifle a little giggle of excitement: the living room was small, but perfectly formed. Painted in pale yellows, with a squishy brown sofa facing a huge stone fireplace, it looked like something out of a holiday brochure. Liv could already imagine spending cozy evenings in there with a good book and steaming mug of hot chocolate — without Mike complaining about the smell or playing obnoxiously loud music. She shook her head, again banishing him from her thoughts.

The flagstone corridor led to another door, this one revealing a bright, typically country kitchen, clearly designed to be the heart of the home. A real kitchen with a solid wooden table that Liv thought was probably older than she was, matching countertops and cream wooden cupboards. It was exactly what Liv thought a *real* home kitchen should look like, without expensive imported marble and enough stainless steel to rival an operating theatre.

This time the excited laughter couldn't be held back when she spotted a cream Aga sited along one wall, in what was left of the old kitchen chimney. And there was a proper, stove-top kettle — instead of one of those soulless taps that spouted boiling water on demand, or a dreadful automated machine that beeped and hissed and spat. Yes, they were convenient, but to Liv there was something incredibly satisfying about the idea of taking her time to properly boil a kettle and make a nice cup of tea in the morning.

She peered out of the kitchen window, taking in the colourful, higgledy-piggledy garden and clapped her hands in delight. She hadn't even stepped foot on the second floor, and already she knew she was going to love living there, and that the kitchen was going to be the place she spent the most time. It was exactly what she needed.

If only her new — albeit temporary — boss had been as charming as this little home.

CHAPTER TWO

'How was judo?' Callum asked as Sarah threw her bag in the back of the car and clambered onto her booster seat.

'Awesome. We practiced falling and learned how to throw each other. It was really cool, even though I had to partner with Keith who has sweaty boy hands.'

'Well, I'm glad you enjoyed yourself. Even with sweaty boy hands. What happened to your usual partner?'

'Beth had to go to hospital to visit her brother.'

'Timothy? He's in hospital?' Callum was instantly concerned.

'Yup. He had annie lexus when he was with his nanny at the Brockle's Paws.'

'Annie lexus with his nanny at the café?' Callum tried to figure out what his daughter meant. Usually, he was good at interpreting her meaning, but sometimes she might as well have been speaking a foreign language.

'Yeah. You know. When you eat something bad for you, and your tongue gets all big and you turn blue.'

'You mean anaphylaxis?' He stared at Sarah in the rear-view mirror.

'Maybe. He was having breakfast with his nanny, and he got the annie lexus-thingy and had to go to hospital.'

'Is he all right?' Callum was already calculating how long it usually took an ambulance to arrive.

'Yup. There was a doctor lady there who gave him an injection and made him better.' Sarah paused in playing with her doll and stared at Callum in the mirror. 'Do you think it was the new doctor who is coming to work for you?'

'Yes, I think it probably was.' Callum grimaced and cursed himself mentally. He really had messed things up.

* * *

Liv paused at the surgery entrance, trying to mentally prepare herself for the day ahead. Once she had settled into her cottage — just thinking that made her feel warm and cosy! — and finished unpacking she'd spent the rest of the weekend trying to figure out how best to deal with Callum. But even though she'd wracked her brains for hours, she hadn't come up with the perfect answer she'd been looking for. That lack of certainty, plus a couple of sleepless nights, had left her feeling unsure and apprehensive.

After the attack in A&E she'd spent weeks recovering, with little else to do but think and question her life's decisions. She'd convinced herself the only way she'd really feel safe and happy again was to give up practicing medicine completely. She'd finally committed to that, only to have her former advisor, Tom, saunter into her hospital room like he hadn't just flown back into the country and beg her to change her mind. He convinced her that she was too good to leave the profession entirely, and that Broclington and its surgery was exactly what she needed, and the perfect place for her to heal.

She'd trusted Tom's judgement throughout the early years of her career, so she'd reluctantly agreed to give it a try. But after her first visit to the surgery and meeting with Callum, she was already questioning her decision.

She straightened her jacket and squared her shoulders before striding through the glass doors. The small reception room already had a young pregnant woman and older wheezing man waiting within. Liv smiled politely and made her way over to the empty desk. She stood there for a few seconds, trying not to let the anxiety take hold.

She rested her bag on the desk, and started to wonder if the practice manager was deliberately making her stand around waiting, to prove a point. She really hoped not, as she wasn't sure she could successfully work with someone who would be so immature and rude. She tapped her fingernails on the desk, starting to feel anxious again. Just as she was about to turn and leave, a woman rushed in, twisting her long auburn hair up into a clip as she looked around the waiting room.

'Sorry, Kerry.' She spoke to the pregnant woman. 'I got caught up at the nursery signing forms. Just give me a couple of mins?'

'It's OK. I'm early anyway.'

'Brilliant. Thanks.' The woman turned to Liv with a bright smile. 'Can I help you? Do you have an appointment?'

Liv couldn't help smiling back, instantly warmed by the other woman's friendly energy. 'Actually, I think I'm here to help you.' She held out a hand. 'I'm Liv Emery.'

'Right. Doctor Emery.' The woman seized Liv's hand and shook it firmly. 'Tom's old student. You're locum-ing for him while they're in Africa. Sorry for the chaotic welcome. The Macpearsons run the surgery together. With them both off adventuring, we're short on admin as well as doctor resource. I'm Millie. Mostly community midwife and sometimes health visitor, though I do a lot of work in the surgery as well.'

'Nice to meet you. And it's Liv.'

'Nice to meet you too, Liv.' She smiled cheerfully, before stepping behind the reception desk and grabbing some files. 'If Callum hasn't come out to meet you, he's either got a patient, or is running late with his daughter.' She shrugged. 'Struggles of being a single parent, I guess.'

'I've already met his daughter.' Liv smiled and reminded herself that she didn't care about the grumpy arse's marital status. Even if he did have warm hands and the bluest eyes she'd ever seen. 'Very memorable.'

'She's a real sweetie. Anyway, I can show you to your room, and you can get settled.'

'You're busy.' Liv's eyes flicked to the young expectant mother. 'I can wait.'

'Don't be silly. I'm a community midwife and nurse. Multitasking is par for the course. Kerry—' she turned to her patient — 'give me one more min, then come on in and I'll get you checked over. Liv, this way.' She headed down the corridor and held the third door open. 'Right. This is your room, at least temporarily. Give me a shout if you need anything, or have any questions.'

'Thank you.'

'More than welcome. We've been desperately waiting for you. There's been a flu bug making the rounds, and we've been run off our feet. Anyway, make yourself at home. Maybe we can have lunch later in the week?'

'That sounds good, thanks,' Liv agreed eagerly, already thinking she liked Millie. She might make a good ally in helping her to settle in and quickly learn more about the community.

'Perfect. I'll drop something into your diary when I've checked mine, and then I can fill you in on all the local gossip and everything you need to know.'

'I'll look forward to it.'

Millie paused at the door. 'Welcome to Broclington, Liv.'

Liv smiled to herself as she started to unpack her bag. If only everyone was so pleased to have her here. But she wasn't going to let one moody person ruin this for her. She'd just ignore him and focus her time on other people. Like Millie, and her patients. Resolved, she closed the door to her new, temporary office.

It swung open again a few seconds later. 'Damn. You beat me.' Callum's eyes sparkled at her from behind a tray of take-away cups, balanced on a white box, emblazoned with a black badger. 'I'd been hoping to leave these in here and

22

meet you at the front desk. I didn't know how you took your coffee, so I got one of everything. And pastries too.'

'One of each of those as well?' Liv eyed up the huge box.

'More than one. The others would not be best pleased if I didn't bring them some to share as well. And they wouldn't be shy in letting me know that. Especially our midwife, Millie. She'd make my morning miserable if I'd been to the café and forgotten her Brockle cake.'

Liv laughed. 'And is this a regular thing?'

'More of a special occasion or bribery type thing.'

'So, which is this?'

'This is a third, and hopefully not to be repeated, option.' He sounded somewhat sheepish. 'For when I've made an idiot of myself and need to apologise.'

'And does this third option happen often?' Liv found herself smiling at him, in spite of her earlier promise to herself.

'More often than I'd like to admit.' He set the box and cups on the desk. 'I was less than welcoming on Saturday. In fact, I was downright rude. I was busy and stressed, and then you came in late, and I took my frustration out on you. And now that I've come to understand the real reason you were late, I feel like I'd be a successful candidate for this year's "Village Idiot".'

'You heard about the little boy with anaphylaxis.' Liv wasn't surprised word had travelled quickly through the community.

Callum nodded, shamefaced.

'How is he?'

'He's going to be fine. Thanks to your quick actions. He should be coming home from hospital today. You've already made a big impact on the village.'

'Anyone would have done the same.'

'Anyone with medical training, a full kit, and the knowledge to use it, who just happened to be there to save a life,' Callum argued. 'You'd not even officially started and already there's a young boy alive because of you, and a grateful family wanting to thank you. But that's not what I wanted to talk to you about.' He took a deep breath, and Liv couldn't help but notice his broad shoulders move interestingly as he folded his arms and captured her with his bright blue eyes.

'What was it you wanted to say?' Liv's voice caught in her throat, and came out far more breathy than she had intended, or expected.

'Sorry. For being rude, and unfriendly. And, as my daughter would put it, "a total dumb dumb head". I know my behaviour was unforgivable, and I've totally blown my chances at a first impression with you, but is there any way you might give me a second chance? Well, a third chance.' He flashed her a mischievous grin that made her heart race. 'If it helps, I have Brockle cakes in here. They're a local delicacy. Chocolate, vanilla and cherry.' He tapped the top of the box. 'And I genuinely am sorry. What do you say? Have a cake and give me another chance to make a good impression?'

'Well . . .' Liv drew out the word deliberately. 'They do say "third time's the charm", and I have been known to be partial to cake.' She settled in her new desk chair, and took a few moments to adjust it to her comfort before giving Callum a shy smile. 'So, Mr Surgery Manager, do you want to get me up and running?'

Callum leaned over her shoulder to log the computer on to the surgery systems, and Liv was instantly warmed by his nearness, and felt her heart step up a few beats as she inhaled his warm, musky scent.

The reaction surprised and annoyed her. The last thing she'd expected — or needed — was the complication of a workplace attraction.

* * *

Callum shut Liv's door and leaned back against it. Tension zinged through his body and he felt the start of a headache building behind his eyes. He was grateful to have Liv arrive — the surgery was in desperate need of her medical services, and she'd picked everything up really quickly over the last few hours. He couldn't decide if he was more grateful or disappointed for that.

The cakes and coffee were probably a mistake. They'd shunted him across the line of professionalism, and into friend-liness. And he could so easily picture that leading further.

She'd accepted the gesture and apology with an easy, almost teasing, smile, and they'd slipped into easy banter that sparked the attraction for her he'd felt on Saturday when helping her off the pavement. And when he'd leaned across to show her something on the computer or how the supply and requisition system worked, the scent of her perfume had made his resolve crumble as his stomach tightened.

At one point he'd had to stop himself from leaning into her just to take another sniff of her honey-sweet hair. A woman he'd just met. What was the matter with him? He was acting like a kid with an infatuation when nothing could be further from the truth — he was a single father running a busy practice, not a teenager panting after a crush. Sarah and the village surgery were his priorities. And even if the surgery wasn't keeping him busy enough, there was no way he could risk bringing another woman into Sarah's life who would let her down again. Her own so-called mother had done more than a lifetime's worth of damage on that front.

He balled his hands into fists and took a slow, resolute breath, before striding back to his office. All he needed to do, he reminded himself, was make it through a few months until his parents returned from their adventures. Then Liv would be on her way, his mother could resume her role running the surgery, and he could go back to his normal, predictable life, where his biggest stresses usually involved trying to convince Sarah that fairy princess dresses weren't appropriate alterna-tives to school uniform.

All he had to do was remain completely professional, get through the next few months, and avoid any entanglements with unsuitable women. That was all. Piece of cake.

* * *

25

Liv kicked off her shoes and closed the front door — her front door — and sighed with relief. She'd made it through the first day without any major issues, embarrassing moments or anxiety flare-ups. She'd handled all her appointments with what she hoped was the right mix of friendliness, sympathy and professionalism, and Millie had already arranged the lunch she'd promised.

She dropped her bag and jacket on the sofa — feeling childishly gleeful that there was no one to complain at her for doing so — and sauntered into the kitchen. It all felt a little surreal: if she'd been on a day shift in her old life, at this sort of time she might just — emergencies allowing — have been heading out the hospital about now to fight her way through the crowds to the tube station. There she would have jostled with thousands of other commuters on the underground for an extra inch or two of space to get enough room to take a swig of her cardboard-encased take-out coffee and try to find enough energy to get herself home and cook whatever gourmet-esque meal Mike had wanted for dinner. Or get dressed up and go out when all she really wanted to do was collapse on the sofa.

If she closed her eyes, she could almost hear the rumble of the train and smell the heat of the crowds. But instead, she opened her eyes and the fridge. The chilled white wine glistened welcomingly. She hesitated for a moment, before opening it and pouring herself a generous glass. And why shouldn't she? She was an adult and finished for the day. She had every right to treat herself to a glass of wine, and she was going to take advantage of being home early and relax for a while. And she was going to do it in the garden — a far cry from the stainless steel and glass balcony of her last home.

She slid on her flip-flops, unlatched the heavy kitchen door, and wandered down the stone path. It was that magical time of day when the sun had just started its journey towards setting, turning the light to liquid gold. The whole garden had taken on the golden hue and seemed almost magical.

26

She took a seat on the curved stone bench that was set into the edge of the garden. It peeked out from beneath a riot of green leaves that had crept and twisted around and over it, leaving a space just big enough for her to comfortably sit down and rest her cup there. There were carvings over the stones, barely visible beneath the evergreen plants which had claimed the bench as their own. It looked and felt ancient, and Liv smiled as she let her fingers trace the barely visible carving. It had been worn almost smooth by the years and the many hands that had touched it before. The little seat was real and grounded in history, and it grounded her too.

She took another sip of her wine and let down her hair, leaving the tie on the edge of the seat. She looked around the beautiful cottage garden, feeling incredibly lucky — in London, the flat's tiny balcony was barely big enough for a couple of chairs and sad pot of geraniums. Here, she had a garden filled with beautiful spring plants — even if she didn't know what most of them were. She couldn't wait to see what it looked like in summer.

The air was clean, the sun warm, and everyone she'd met so far — apart from Callum on the first day — friendly and welcoming. And she'd actually enjoyed herself at work, which was something she'd never even dared hope for.

She put the glass down and let her hands rest against the stone, which was far warmer than she'd expected – no doubt heated by the sun that day. She let her eyes drift closed for a few moments and just enjoyed the peace, wishing that feeling of contentment could last. When she stood and brushed off her skirt, she didn't notice the hair band fall backwards off the seat and disappear.

* * *

'Come on, Sarah!' Callum tried to keep the frustration out of his voice, but he could practically feel the minutes ticking by. 'You're going to be late for school. Can I come in and help?'

'No!' Sarah shouted back at him. 'I don't need a boy's help to get dressed!'

'I'm not a boy. I'm your dad.' Callum pressed his head against the bathroom door.

'Still a boy. Go away!'

'Sarah, we are going to be *late*! Please hurry up. What are you even doing in there?'

'Making myself pretty. You don't make my hair pretty enough, so I'm doing it.'

What? Her answer completely threw him. She wasn't even seven yet. He'd expected a few more years to prepare before he had to handle this.

'It's just school, Sarah, and I need to stop by the surgery for the healthy-eating leaflets your teacher wanted.'

'But I want to look pretty!' He could hear her little foot stamp against the tiles, and knew the stubborn tilt her chin would be taking, and that her lips would be pursing into a cross pout.

'Can you be pretty more quickly?'

'You can't rush beauty. I'm worth the time.' The prim response surprised him, and he wondered where on earth she'd heard that.

'Who told you that?'

'Beth. Her babysitter tells her that.'

'Right. I'll have to have a word with her.'

'No, you won't!' The door flung open and he was confronted by a small, angry not-even-pre-teen who glared up at him from beneath bright, badly applied eyeshadow in hideously garish colours.

He gasped. He had to get this right, but first . . .

'Where did you get that make-up from?'

'My dressing-up box.' Her chin stuck out stubbornly.

'You have make-up in your dressing-up box?'

'With the fairy princess dress Grandma gave me at Christmas.'

'Oh.'

'Do you think I look pretty?'

'Um.' Callum had no idea what to say without upsetting her, but as he hesitated he could see her sparkly bottom lip start to wobble threateningly. 'Maybe . . . glitter is better saved for . . . special occasions?'

'But I like glitter!' The foot stomped again and Callum had to fight the urge to roll his eyes. What on earth was he supposed to do in situations like this? Sexist as it sounded — even in his own head — he didn't know how to deal with girly stuff like this. And he didn't really know who to turn to. His mum was up to her elbows in desert sand somewhere, off saving the world, his sister Kim was hundreds of miles away working, and as for his ex . . . well, the less thought space he gave her, the better!

There was only one thing for it. And he hated himself for stooping to such a low level, and so early in the morning. 'How about this? If you let me help you wash your face, and we're out of the house in the next ten minutes, I'll take you to Badger's Paws after school, and you can pick out anything you want for tea. What do you think?'

'*Annnnything?*'

'Any single cake,' he amended hastily.

'And a sausage roll?'

He had to smother a grin. She'd inherited his mother's skills for bargaining. 'OK, and a sausage roll. But only if you have vegetables with it.'

'Mushrooms are vegetables, right?'

'Yes.'

'And beans?'

'Yes.' Sort of.

'OK. Sausage roll, baked beans, mushrooms and Brockle cake. Deal?'

'Deal.' Callum strode into the bathroom, and picked up the washcloth. 'Now let's get you cleaned up and ready for school.'

'OK, Daddy.' The smile that lit up her face filled him with warmth and he gave her a brief, fierce hug.

'I love you, Sarah-bear.'

'Love you too, Daddy.' She pushed him away. 'But we need to hurry up and not be late.'

This time he couldn't help but let his eyes roll back in frustration.

'Hey Millie!' Liv waved to the auburn-haired midwife. 'How are you? Isn't it gorgeous weather today?'

'Good thanks, and yes it's lovely. And it's supposed to last, too. Perfect weather for a few drinks in a nice pub garden after work, end of this week? We had fun at lunch the other day, could make a night of it.' She left the invitation hanging in the air and watched Liv expectantly.

'Maybe not *that* warm,' Liv argued.

'Stick a jumper on, you soft southerner.'

Liv couldn't help but join in her laughter. 'OK. That sounds great, thank you.'

'Brilliant.' Millie headed down the corridor, her pony-tail swishing back and forth as she moved.

Liv almost collided with Callum as he strode out of the office, his daughter bouncing along behind him.

'Sorry.' He held up his hands, then glanced down. 'Sarah, don't you have something to say to Dr Emery?'

'I'm very sorry for hitting you with my bike.' She peeked up at Liv through her long, dark eyelashes. 'Is your leg OK now?'

'Yes, thank you.' Liv lifted up the hem of her skirt to show Sarah her rapidly healing knee.

'Good girl.' Callum briefly rested his hand on her shoulder. 'Wait here while I grab the leaflets for your school.'

'Do you like being a doctor, Dr Emery?'

'You don't have to call me Dr Emery. Liv is fine. And yes, I do like being a doctor.'

'OK. That's good. And it's good your knee is getting better. Do you like living in Broclington? I like living here.'

Surprised by the sudden change in topic, Liv answered without thinking. 'You know what? I think I do.' As soon as the words were out of her mouth, she realised how much truth was in them.

'And do you like the fairies' house?'

'It is a pretty cottage, but I don't really think there are fairies living in it.' Liv didn't want to upset the little girl, but didn't want to lie to her either.

'It's called *Aosán Taigh*? That means it's the fairies' house. Have you tried it yet?'

'Tried what?' She was struggling to keep up with the conversation.

'The wishing well.'

'I don't think there is one.'

'There definitely is,' the little girl insisted. 'I know all the village fairy stories.'

'I think I would have noticed if there was a wishing well in the house. I know I've not been there very long, but wells tend to be quite big.'

'It's not in the house.' Sarah laughed. 'It's in the garden. But it's really, really old. Like even older than my grandma. It doesn't look like a normal well, but it's still got fairy magic. It made my friend's cat better when she got sick, and if you make the right wish on the right day and the fairies like your gift, then they make it come true. You do believe in fairies, don't you?'

'Erm . . .' Liv was saved from struggling to answer the question as Callum reappeared and held out his hand.

'Come on, Sarah. I need to get you to school.'

'OK, Dad.' She grinned up at Liv. 'It was nice meeting you and not hitting you with my bike.'

Liv waved as Sarah skipped out of the surgery, closely followed by her dad. 'It was nice meeting you too.' She smiled as she headed to her office to start up her computer, and review the first few patient files of the day.

* * *

A few days later, Liv glanced up from her notes and smiled as Callum's footsteps paused just outside her door. She'd only been with the surgery for a week, but she was already feeling happier and more settled than she had done in years. And she already recognised Callum's footsteps, and looked forward to the moments he would pop into her office.

There was something about him that brought a smile to her face, no matter what else was going on around her.

'Hey . . .' Callum leaned in the door and held up a couple of steaming mugs. 'Got some time before you head off for afternoon rounds?'

'Sure.'

'Great.' He smiled at her and Liv's pulse instantly stepped up a notch, despite her ordering it not to. 'I just wanted to check in and see how things have gone this week.'

'Good.' Liv smiled, thinking back over the last few days. 'Faster than I would have expected.'

'Faster isn't an adjective I was expecting.' Callum reached across the desk to hand her a mug of coffee. When his fingertips brushed against hers, heat zinged up Liv's arm. She stared at her fingers for a few seconds, before forcing herself to look up and meet his eyes. She watched him briefly while arguing with herself, before reaching the decision she could probably trust him. She knew she wanted to.

'Can I be totally honest?'

'Of course.'

'I've been out of work for a while.' She held up her broken arm by way of evidence, but didn't tell him about the other injuries. She really liked him, but didn't need his sympathy. She didn't even like to think about what had happened, and what it might mean.

She blinked when she realised Callum was watching her, still waiting for an answer.

'I was worried it might take me a while to settle in, but it's all been a lot easier, and faster, than I'd imagined. I feel like I'm really starting to find my feet here.'

'You certainly seem to be. You've definitely hit the ground running.'

'True.' Liv laughed as Callum made himself comfortable in the chair opposite.

'Now that you've been honest, can I?'

'It's only fair.' She leaned forward, enjoying the feeling of co-conspiracy.

'I have to admit, I was a bit worried when I saw your CV. I wondered if, after all the drama of working in a major A&E, a village practice like ours might be a bit . . . mundane.'

Liv laughed again. 'Keeping up the honesty theme, I was a bit worried too, but I'm loving it now I'm here.' She didn't mention how much calmer and safer she felt in the village — she hoped her anxieties were well and truly behind her, left miles away along with the people who had hurt her.

'What was it that made you move?'

'A few things.' Liv pursed her lips as she worked out the best way to answer. 'You're right, things were a lot more fast-paced in my previous role, but I rarely got the chance to follow up on patients once they were discharged, or referred and moved on to whatever ward or team were taking on their continuing care.'

'You definitely get follow-up opportunities here.' Callum gave her a wry grin.

'You're telling me. I had an older patient at the start of this week. Age-related COPD. He was really struggling.'

'Josh Taylor? He's had breathing issues for years.'

Liv nodded, not in the least surprised that Callum knew his patients so well. He seemed to know everyone locally. 'I reviewed his 'scripts, and showed him how to use the inhalers more effectively. He came back in this morning. He's doing so much better. Apparently he's back walking his dog, meeting up with friends, and planning on taking his wife dancing next week. The improvement was amazing, and really nice to see.' She tapped a tin sitting on the desk. 'He even brought a cake that his wife baked me.'

'I hope you're planning on sharing.' Callum shot her a cheeky grin. 'Betty Taylor's cakes are a bit legendary round here. She's taken home ribbons from the summer fayre every year I can remember. But cakes aside, it's good isn't it? Being able to build up relationships with patients.'

'It's a little overwhelming,' Liv admitted.

'I get that. It can be hard not to get involved in a community this small, especially when the people we're treating are the same ones we see every day.'

Liv nodded in understanding. 'I imagine that can be really hard at times.'

'Yeah.' Callum's eyes darkened with sadness. 'Bad news and sadness is part of the job. But I wouldn't change it for the world.'

Liv glanced at the cake tin again, before letting her eyes wander back to Callum. A smile played around her lips as she realised she might be starting to feel the same. There was a lot in the village that made her feel happier than she had in a long time.

* * *

Callum ran his hands through his hair as he hung up the phone. Yet another night where he'd had to ask Mrs Turner to stay late, and give his daughter the dinner he should be sharing with her. It had taken him until past closing time to complete his case notes for the day, and he still had to handle all the administrative tasks, vital to running the surgery. Not a good omen for the weekend.

He leaned back in the chair, staring at the ceiling as he stretched and twisted to try and relieve the stiffness in his back. He groaned as a particularly stubborn crick in his neck popped loudly.

'That sounded painful,' Liv sympathised from his open door.

'Just a bit stiff after a long day. A lot of long days.' Callum still stared at the ceiling, reluctant to resume his original position at his desk and the seemingly endless list of admin tasks. He didn't know how his mother made it seem so easy.

'Is it anything I can help with? I don't mind pitching in with paperwork.'

'You know, I might just take you up on that.' He gave into gravity and let the chair swing back down as he span to look at Liv. All thoughts of administration and funding issues vanished as his brain temporarily short-circuited. Instead of the prim skirts and smart jackets Liv usually wore, she was dressed in close-fitting jeans that cupped every curve and a green jumper that brought out flecks of the same colour in her hazel eyes. The jumper looked so soft that Callum found himself wanting to stroke it, and let his fingers wander to where it dipped enticingly below her neckline and feel the creamy softness of her skin.

'Well?' Her glossy red lips formed the word, and Callum wondered if they'd taste as good as they looked. Like sweet cherries.

He started guiltily, realising that while he'd been staring, Liv had asked him something. 'Sorry, what was that?'

'I asked if you thought I looked OK.' Liv adjusted the jumper and Callum had to force himself to focus as her tugging pulled the torturous jumper a little tighter. 'Millie's invited me out tonight. Dinner at a pub and a few drinks. To celebrate the end of my first week. She said casual, but I wasn't really sure if this would be too casual. What do you think?'

Beautiful. Delicious. Desirable. 'Fine.' He choked the word out.

'Just fine?' Liv fiddled with a necklace that sparkled at her throat, catching Callum's eyes. He tried, and failed, not to glance lower, down the creamy expanse of her neck and back to where the soft jumper curved low enough to give a tantalising glimpse of something black and lacy. 'I was hoping for something a bit better than fine.' She lifted her uninjured hand behind her head where she started doing something to her hair. The movement made the soft jumper ride higher, drawing Callum's attention lower. It could have been a trick of the light, but for a moment he thought the skin that appeared at the jumper's edge had the puckered and shiny look of new scarring, but he was distracted when Liv's blonde hair cascaded down and haloed around her shoulders.

'There, any better?' She ran her fingers through her hair, making it shimmer as it moved.

'Perfect.' The word escaped before Callum realised he'd even thought it.

'From "fine" to "perfect" in ten seconds.' Liv blushed prettily as she twirled a golden strand around her finger. 'Shame I can't wear my hair down when I'm working.'

Their eyes locked, and for a long moment Callum could have sworn he felt the same heat in her gaze that pounded through his veins. He shoved his chair back, wanting to walk towards her, to take hold of her, feel the softness of that jumper and . . .

'You coming, Liv?' Millie's voice echoed in the corridor.

'Yeah. Be right there.' Liv slowly, and Callum hoped reluctantly, looked away. 'I've got to go.'

He nodded. 'Have fun.' He collapsed into his chair the second she closed the door. It was going to be an interesting few months.

* * *

A couple of weeks later, Liv bumped her car door closed with her hip, and zapped the locks shut over her shoulder as she sauntered back into the surgery. Her afternoon rounds had gone really well. She'd checked in with a few of the clinic's patients who couldn't easily make it out of their homes, and accompanied Millie on two mother-and-baby visits. Even taking extra time to reassure a panicking parent that their toddling daughter would recover perfectly well from her bout of croup, Liv had still finished earlier than planned.

She felt like everything was falling into place — better than she could have hoped. She jumped out of bed each morning, excited to get to work and start making her patients better. She surprised herself by thinking of the villagers as *her* patients — but she was already feeling like Broclington was somewhere she could belong.

36

The only challenge was Callum. As much as she tried to ignore her growing attraction to him and remain the consummate professional, her body kept betraying her. It was as though all her senses had become highly tuned to his presence. Whether it was his musky scent, the sound of his footsteps in the corridor, or the way his eyes would catch hers — her body would snap into high alert and become intently focussed on him. When he innocently brushed past her in the corridor or kitchen — or leaned closer when discussing a case or showing her how to work the computer system — she seemed to burn with heat.

Her reaction was exciting and terrifying. She wasn't interested in a relationship. Not when she was still trying to come to terms with the way her ex had treated her. He'd abandoned her when she was hurting and afraid. The man who had made so many promises had vanished like smoke in a storm.

But that still didn't stop her heart from soaring when the computer glitched, or she found an issue to discuss with Callum — whether strictly necessary or not. And if she was completely honest, there were more than a few times when she called him to fix "problems" that she could probably have figured out for herself, though she rationalised it by telling herself she was just being a good team player and ensuring she worked to the surgery's existing systems and protocols. And if she told herself that often enough, she might even start to believe it.

Shaking her head resolutely, she logged onto the computer and started updating records and reading up on the patients already booked in for tomorrow. She became so engrossed in her work that she jumped when a knock sounded at her open door.

'Sorry . . .' Millie grinned as she peered in. 'Got a bit of an issue I'm hoping you can help with.'

'Of course. Come on in.'

'I've just had a call from Sarah's school. She's throwing up and has a fever. Callum's had meetings at the hospital, and I can't get hold of him.'

'Oh no, poor Sarah.'

'I'd usually call her uncle, but he's in America still, and I've got a clinic starting in half an hour, and you're the only member of staff booked for admin this afternoon.'

'And you want me to take the clinic for you?'

'Actually, I've got one very nervous, young, first-time mum in the group.' Millie twisted her fingers together. 'She's only attending because I promised I'd look after her personally. I used to babysit for her — so we go back a long way.'

'So you want me to pick Sarah up?' Liv saved her patient records.

'Would you mind?' Millie asked worriedly. 'I wouldn't ask if there was anyone else.'

'Of course not.' Liv grabbed her bag and gave Millie's arm a quick squeeze. 'I couldn't possibly leave her feeling so wretched when I can help so easily. Though . . .' She hesitated at the door. 'You could maybe grab me a few disposable bowls and paper towels as she's being sick? And call the school back to let them know I'm on the way.'

* * *

Sarah was pale and miserable looking, hunched over a bin when Liv arrived at the school. She briefly showed her ID badge to the school nurse before sitting by the little girl.

'Hey there, little fairy. I hear you're not feeling so great.'

The little girl's face fell, and Liv felt rotten. 'Hi, Dr Emery.'

'I'm sorry your dad's not here, but he's working at the hospital today. Millie thought it might be OK if I gave you a lift. What do you think?'

Sarah nodded miserably, and retched into the bin. Without thinking, Liv gently wrapped her arm around the little girl's shoulders.

'Sorry, Dr Emery.' Sarah shook her head slightly and rested it on Liv's shoulder.

'Don't be silly. This isn't your fault. And I told you before, you can call me Liv.' Liv's heart ached for the little girl, and herself. She rested her hand on Sarah's head, who was warm, but not worryingly so. 'Do you want to come back to the surgery with me?'

'Can you take me home?'

'I'm sorry, I can't. I don't have a key.'

'I know where Daddy hides the spare.'

'I don't know if we should, sweetie. Your dad might be a little while still. And it doesn't seem right, me letting myself into his house.'

'It's my house too. Please?' Sarah sniffed. 'I really need my princess duvet and Dr Cuddlington Bear. Please, Livvy.'

'Dr Cuddlington, huh?' Liv was helpless against the pitiful look on Sarah's face. 'Tell you what. Let's get you into my car, and we'll call your dad on the way. We'll figure this out, I promise. Now, where's your coat?'

'In a bag. I got sick on it.'

'Not to worry.' Liv shrugged off her own jacket. 'You can wear mine. I think you'll look very pretty in it. And purple is a very popular colour for fairies.' She wrapped her coat around Sarah and lifted her onto her hip. She had to force back tears when Sarah snuggled into her shoulder. She cursed the bastard who had stabbed her, and maybe stolen her chance of ever holding her own child like this.

After a few moments, she took a deep breath and accepted the bag of soiled clothes from the nurse. 'Thanks.' She gave Sarah a smile. 'Let's get you home. I think it's about time I met my colleague Dr Cuddlington, don't you?'

Sarah nodded against her neck, and Liv held her a little more tightly.

* * *

Callum cursed himself again as he pulled into his driveway. He never turned his phone off, especially since his parents had gone on sabbatical again and his brother was still in America, and he'd become more aware than ever of his single-parent status. But he'd forgotten there was no signal in parts of the hospital, and the meeting with the clinical commissioning board had run late. He'd fought hard against the cuts they wanted to make to the surgery, but they were adamant: they needed to make savings across the whole county and couldn't see a place for a village surgery in their future vision.

The thought of losing the surgery turned his stomach, but at least he'd bought some time to try and come up with an alternative proposal. Whatever that was going to look like.

When he'd finally come out, his phone had gone mad beeping and flashing with missed calls and messages. His heart had pounded as he listened to his voicemails and guilt flooded him. His baby girl needed him, and he hadn't even been there to answer the phone, and was still miles away. And as much as anyone else told him she was OK, he couldn't relax until he'd seen and assessed Sarah for himself.

When Liv's voice echoed over the speaker, reassuring him Sarah was fine and it seemed to be just a mild stomach bug, relief hit him so hard it made him momentarily freeze as he thanked God his baby girl was all right. It took him a few more miles to realise that, for the first time he could remember, someone else's reassurances about his daughter's well-being actually *had* reassured him. For some reason, knowing Sarah was with Liv made him feel calm. Even his brother Jake couldn't calm him so quickly when it came to his daughter.

But rather than think about it, he shook away the feeling and the questions it raised, and concentrated on getting home as quickly as he could.

When he got there, he forced himself to take a few breaths and enter quietly, and he was glad he had. He froze at the door to his living room, floored by the scene in front of him. Liv was snuggled up on the sofa with his daughter, looking for all the world like she belonged there. Sarah was tucked under her arm, asleep as she hugged her favourite bear tightly to her chest. Liv smiled down at Sarah warmly, her full attention focussed on the little girl who looked so peaceful in her arms.

As if sensing his presence, Liv looked up and for a moment Callum was bathed in the warmth of her beautiful smile.

'Hey,' she whispered, 'she's asleep.' Her eyes flicked to Sarah.

'Amazing.' Callum tiptoed across the room. 'She usually struggles to settle when she's been sick.' He knelt by the sofa to check on his daughter, and looked up at Liv. 'Thank you so much for this.'

'It's fine.' Liv shook her head slightly, careful not to move too much and wake Sarah. 'I hope you don't mind me being here, but she begged to come home, and Millie said it was for the best.' The concern etched across her face touched him deeply: she'd gone out of her way to help his daughter, and now she was worrying about having been rude.

'You've done me a huge favour. Believe me when I say I'm grateful.' He squeezed Liv's good forearm, offering reassurance. 'How long has she been asleep?'

'She's been out for a while. I told her when she wakes up, you might let her try some dry crackers or toast. She's not been sick again since we got back and was starting to feel hungry. I hope that's OK. She's kept down some Pedialyte solution too.'

Callum smiled as he realised Liv had said exactly what he would have said. 'Liv, it's perfect. I'd have done the same myself.'

Sarah began to stir, and he smiled down at her. 'Hey, princess, how are you doing?'

'Tired. I got sick at school.'

'I know, sweetheart. I'm sorry I wasn't able to come and get you.'

'S'OK.' Sarah gave him a sleepy smile. 'Livvy came and got me.'

'I know. Have you said thank you?'

'Thank you, Livvy.'

'You're welcome, sweetie.' Liv smoothed Sarah's hair away from her face. 'I'm just glad you're starting to feel better.'

'Me too. Being sick is no fun.'

'No, it isn't,' Liv agreed quietly, an odd look on her face.

'I'm tired, Daddy,' Sarah grumbled.

'Right.' Callum scooped his daughter up into his arms, trying not to think about Liv's strange look. 'You've been poorly. I think it's time you went to bed. And Dr Cuddlington agrees with me. You can try some food when you're a bit more awake.'

'K.'

Callum smiled at Liv, suddenly feeling shy. 'I really can't thank you enough for this.'

Liv shrugged and flushed in a way that made her hazel eyes seem to sparkle. 'Like I said, it's no big deal.'

'Well, it is to me.' He jiggled Sarah slightly. 'To us.'

'Well then, you're both welcome.' She leaned closer, and her delicately honeyed scent filled Callum's senses, giving him thoughts that were entirely inappropriate when he was holding his sick daughter.

'Feel better soon, Sarah. This world needs more fairies like you spreading magic.' She planted a quick kiss on her cheek.

'You're not going?' Sarah complained, twisting in Callum's arms. 'I want to know how the story about Dr Cuddlington and the fairies and pixies ends. Can you put me to bed and finish the story?'

Liv's questioning eyes met Callum's and he shrugged. He hadn't planned on having her in his home, but now she was there he didn't want her to leave either. He was grateful Sarah seemed to feel the same — although for entirely different reasons. He held his breath and hoped Liv didn't have any reason to rush off, but didn't want to presume anything either. 'Liv probably needs to head home, Sarah-bear. She probably has things to do.'

'Please, Livvy . . . just five more minutes,' Sarah begged. 'I won't sleep if the fairies and Dr Cuddlington don't find the missing pixies!'

'Well, I suppose I can stay for a bit and tell you the end of the story. If that's all right with your daddy.'

'Only if you're sure you have time,' Callum replied quietly.

'I think I can spare a few more minutes.' Her grin did something to his stomach. 'But Sarah, you should probably still go to bed.' She picked the teddy bear up from the sofa. 'I mean, I couldn't possibly argue with two of my learned colleagues, could I?'

'Definitely not,' Callum agreed as he led the way upstairs, praying he hadn't left dirty underwear or anything equally embarrassing lying around.

* * *

Callum had just flicked the kettle on and was tidying up the kitchen when he heard Liv's soft footsteps on the stairs a few minutes later.

'She went out like a light. Must have been exhausted, poor thing.' Liv leaned against the kitchen doorframe.

'I imagine you're tired too. Having to race from work to look after someone else's sick child.' Callum watched Liv while he bustled around the kitchen. She was smiling softly, looking incredibly beautiful, but at the same time there was a sad, dreamy look in her eyes. Reminding himself of his resolution, he retrieved a couple of mugs. 'Coffee?' There was nothing unprofessional about coffee — they regularly shared it in the surgery.

'Please.' Liv nodded gratefully.

'Grab a stool. I can probably rustle up some food as well, if you're hungry?' Food wasn't anything to read into, he told himself. Just the normal, everyday reaction of someone thanking a friend who had done them a favour.

Liv shook her head. 'Coffee's fine, thanks.'

'It's the very least I can do when you bailed me out and looked after Sarah so well. I've never seen her take to anyone as quickly as she has you. She's never been the best at sleeping, even as a baby she fussed, but she became so much worse after her mother left. She has to have a certain duvet, her toys need to be in a special order, the curtains open an exact way.' He shook his head. 'Seeing her happily sleeping with you was a real surprise.'

Liv shrugged. 'She's probably just exhausted from being ill.'

43

Callum pursed his lips, knowing it was far more than that. Sarah had felt safe and happy around Liv. Just like he did. Seeing Liv perched at the breakfast bar, her hair piled up messily on the top of her head, and so at home in his house made something in his gut twist. It wasn't just that he was attracted to her. He wanted her *here*, filling his kitchen with warmth. Whatever magic she'd cast over Sarah to make her feel safe and secure enough to sleep without all her comfort measures, she was rapidly casting a similar spell over him.

But rather than making Callum feel happy, the thought scared him. He couldn't let anyone into his life like that. When Trixie had walked out on him and Sarah, it had taken him months to find his equilibrium again — though sometimes he doubted he truly had. He'd had to fight every day to get out of bed, put on a brave face, and comfort the little girl crying for her mother.

He didn't think he was strong enough to survive that again, and he definitely wasn't willing to put Sarah at risk of being hurt.

He handed the coffee to Liv, and had to steel himself not to jump when her fingers curled around the cup and brushed against his. As had happened every other time that week, electricity shot through Callum's hand. When he glanced up, Liv was staring at him, and the air between them crackled.

Liv gulped, and raised her cup to her lips. Callum watched, transfixed as she blew on the coffee to cool it, then licked her lips, and took a sip.

'So, how did your meetings go?'

Callum sighed and put his own coffee down, his stomach souring as reality crashed back in. 'About as well as I'd expected, and much worse than I'd hoped.' He kicked the stool out and sat down. 'Can I tell you something without it getting back to the rest of the team?'

'Of course.'

'The clinical commissioning group need to save money. A hell of a lot of it. Our surgery is one of the ones at risk. By county standards we don't have high volumes of patients, and the commissioning group think they would be better spending the money trying to shore up A&E and reduce waiting times for beds.'

'The targets are quite strict.' Liv tapped the edge of her coffee cup as she thought. 'So, where do you stand?'

'I'm arguing that the surgery is vital to the community. That being so far from the hospital would make removing it dangerous. They've given me some time to come up with an alternative proposal, but I don't know if it's going to help. I can't really imagine what will.' He rubbed his forehead tiredly. 'It's just so bloody unfair. My family have run this surgery for three generations. My grandmother was born in this village, and my grandfather set the surgery up. He started seeing patients in his front room. My parents worked so hard to grow the surgery, and now it's all going to end.' He thumped the breakfast bar angrily.

'Maybe not.' Liv reached out and squeezed his hand reassuringly. 'They've given you a chance to submit ideas. I don't think they would have bothered to do that if they'd made their minds up. All you need to do is come up with something that makes the surgery more valuable to them open, than closed.'

'So the holy grail. No pressure.'

'Since when has anything worthwhile ever been easy?'

For a moment, Callum thought she was talking about the attraction between them, then had to force himself to shake the thought away and focus. 'How can we, as a village surgery, be valuable to a major hospital though?'

'Well, without knowing the exact patient profile, it's hard to comment. But I'd guess, like most hospitals, that A&E is regularly inundated with the types of complaints that could be handled locally — especially if there was a surgical suite or urgent care facility here.'

'That's certainly true.'

'So give them that. As a starting point.' Liv shrugged as if the answer was obvious.

'Wow. You don't aim small, do you?' Callum was impressed.

'Honestly, I'm not sure small will be enough in this situation. In regards to reducing waiting times, I'd imagine in a community like this, there's quite a lot of older people who are staying in hospital longer than they really need to, because there aren't the resources in the community to care for them. So, if you could offer something along the lines of community re-enablement and care, then that could be a big point scorer.'

'You know, you could have something there.' Callum was incredibly impressed with Liv's response. 'I'll look into it. Evelyn, one of our nurses, used to specialise in community re-enablement before she came here.'

'You said she was in America? Is she due back from holiday soon?'

'It's not exactly a holiday,' Callum explained. 'Her daughter has been ill. The best treatment for the type of cancer she has is in Boston. We've been able to manage a lot of her care here, but they have to be in Boston a couple of times a year.'

'Oh no.'

'It's OK. Summer — that's Evelyn's daughter — has responded so, so well to treatment. It's all really positive.'

'That's good to hear.'

'Yeah, it really is.' Callum smiled broadly. 'Summer and Evelyn are family.'

'Really?'

Callum nodded. 'As good as. They're living with my brother, Jake.'

Liv nodded in understanding. 'Which is why he's in America, and couldn't pick Sarah up today. Millie mentioned it.'

Callum nodded. 'I really am going to owe you big time after today.'

'I keep telling you, it's not a big deal.'

'Well, it is to me. And if you ever need anything, just know that all you need do is ask, OK?' Callum was rapidly realising that, despite his fears, Liv was someone he wanted to keep in his life, even it was just as a friend.

'Well . . . you could give me an afternoon off this week. I need to make an appointment at the hospital and get this—' she tapped her cast — 'taken off.'

'Unless you were expecting further x-rays, I can do that in the surgery for you. We've got a plaster saw.'

'That would be brilliant. I wasn't looking forward to trekking across country and hanging around for a couple of hours to get this sorted.' Liv downed the rest of her coffee. 'I should get going.'

'I'll see you out.' His hand automatically dropped to her lower back to show her to the door, and he could have sworn he felt her tremble slightly, even as heat rushed up his arm and sent his pulse racing. He held Liv's coat out to her, and helped her to put it on. As he eased it up her arms, he paused, his hands resting on her shoulders, holding her scant inches away from him. He inhaled deeply, and the sweet warmth of her honeyed hair filled his world and clouded his mind.

She twisted in his arms, turning to face him. This close, he could see flecks of gold in her eyes that almost disappeared as her pupils widened as her eyes met his. She was so close, he could feel her breath against his skin. And it was coming faster than usual.

She licked her bottom lip, and Callum's heartbeat thundered so loudly in his ears that he was sure Liv would hear it too. Despite all his best intentions, and the promises he'd made to himself, he couldn't help but stretch his thumb up to touch her cheek. It was as soft and warm as he could possibly have imagined.

Liv turned her head slightly, still not breaking eye contact, so his thumb brushed against her full lips. She peered up at him through her long lashes, her eyes burning with desire as her hot breath against his hand scorched all thoughts from his mind.

He held his own breath as he closed the inches between them, and feathered the lightest of kisses against her lips. When she didn't pull back, he deepened the kiss, running the tip of his tongue along the burning seam of her mouth.

She moaned, a breathy sound that made him ache, and welcomed him deeper in. As he devoured her mouth, drowning in the taste and scent of her, Liv's arms slid around his waist, pulling him against her. He cradled her head in his hands, tilting her face for better access as he kissed her like his life depended on it.

'Callum . . . I . . .' Her voice was breathy and needy against his lips, but whatever thought she was about to share was interrupted by a soft thud, and a small voice from upstairs.

'Daddy?' The voice snapped him back to reality.

'Crap.' Callum rested his forehead against Liv's, still cradling her face gently in his hands.

'Daddy, I'm hungry.'

Callum stepped away reluctantly. 'I need to . . .'

'Go.' Liv nodded. 'I need to go too. This . . . whatever this was . . . shouldn't . . . I can't . . .' She ducked away from Callum, and fumbled with the door.

He stood in his hallway, torn between wanting to grab hold of Liv, and keep her there with him, and running upstairs to look after Sarah.

Liv made the decision for him, slamming the door against the hall wall as she raced through it. For a moment, Callum watched her, part of him desperate to chase after her and pull her back into his arms.

'Daddy, please?'

Callum closed the door sadly. 'I'm coming, Sarah.'

CHAPTER THREE

Liv hesitated at the surgery door the next morning, trying to avoid going in and starting her day for as long as possible. She couldn't believe she'd been so stupid as to kiss Callum. And wow, that man could kiss. Even after a restless night, she still tingled whenever she thought of his lips on hers.

And that was the problem. She didn't want to think about him like that. She wasn't ready to let anyone get that close to her.

Yes, he was kind, and seemed loyal and committed to his daughter and his family and their business, but that didn't mean he wouldn't hurt her. And Liv didn't want to open herself up to risk that much hurt again. And there was Sarah to consider as well. There was something about the little girl that turned Liv to mush. Maybe it was just that she could emphasise with Sarah — she knew how it felt to be missing a parent — but she thought it was a lot more than that.

Having Sarah come to her for comfort — being needed by her, even just for a few hours — had forced Liv to face up to the worries she'd been avoiding ever since the attack. The internal scarring and partial hysterectomy meant she was never likely to have a baby. The tossing and turning had gone on into the early hours when she'd finally given in and wandered out to the garden. There she'd sat on her stone garden seat and watched the sun come up while pondering what to do about Callum, and how she could still be around him.

When she eventually forced herself to leave the cool, steady calm of the cottage she felt scruffy and unprepared for the day, and in desperate need of a few more hours of sleep. She tried to focus on the peace and the calm of the day, and enjoying her walk to the surgery, but by the time she arrived she felt as stressed and rumpled as if she'd fought her way through the worst London rush hour.

She smoothed down her jacket and strode through reception and down the corridor to her office door, which she darted through, grateful to have avoided bumping into Callum. She almost slammed the door shut in her eagerness to be alone for a few minutes longer, then cursed herself for her stupidity. The kiss had just been a brief moment of silliness caused by tiredness and . . . other things. Callum had been beating himself up for failing to achieve the superhuman task of being everywhere all at once. And Liv had been feeling raw and emotional after spending time with Sarah and being forced to contemplate possibilities she had been avoiding.

It had just been two people, feeling a bit emotional, seeking to comfort each other. It had only been a kiss.

And, at some level, she might even believe that.

Refusing to think about it any further, she settled behind her desk, opened her first case file of the day and focussed on that instead. She still surprised herself by genuinely enjoying the work. She'd always worked in hospitals, and had worried that without the high energy, drama and pressure to make life and death decisions within a few heartbeats, she'd find something missing and end up feeling underwhelmed. But Callum had been right when he said it was hard not to get involved in the lives of patients and follow up with them. She was rapidly coming to feel like she'd been adopted by the community. And it had been so long since she'd really felt like she belonged anywhere.

* * *

Liv peered at the clock in the corner of her screen a few hours later. Just over ten minutes late finishing morning surgery. Not too bad at all. She grimaced as the back of her hand itched inside of her cast, but resisted the urge to do what she'd always advised patients against and itch with a pen. If nothing else, it would be embarrassing explaining to Callum why it was there if she got it stuck.

She paused and peered in the mirror above the sink, reapplying her lipstick, and trying to convince herself that it had nothing to do with the fact that she was about to be in close proximity to Callum.

She shook her head at her own foolishness, and walked down the corridor to Callum's door, but before she got there, her nerve gave out and she span on her heel and raced back to her own room. After a couple of seconds of mentally berating herself, she tried again — but only made it halfway before turning around again. She barely made it back down the short corridor between their offices before changing her mind and heading back. She was being ridiculous. It was just a kiss which meant nothing, and they were both professionals. It wasn't an issue.

'Are you all right, Liv?' Millie's voice called out from her own office. 'Are you looking for something?'

A spine, maybe? Liv forced herself to smile at Millie through the open door. 'I'm fine, thanks. Just seeing if Callum was free to cut this thing off.' She held her arm up. 'He offered to do it here and save me a trip to the hospital, but I didn't want to interrupt if he's consulting.'

Millie nodded in understanding. 'I bet you'll be glad to get back to normal. And be able to scratch again.'

'Absolutely.' Liv walked the few steps to Callum's door, forcing herself to act more calmly, and hoping that her racing heart would listen and calm itself as well.

* * *

In his office, Callum plugged the plaster saw in and checked that it was revving up and working. He wandered around the room, straightening files and tidying his desk before cursing his own foolishness. Liv, no — Dr Emery, he corrected himself — was coming in for her cast to be removed. A medical procedure. Not a social visit. But he still glanced at the clock on his desk.

When the soft knock sounded, he took a moment to sit behind his desk and look busy. 'Come in.'

Even though his eyes were glued to a file he wasn't reading, he knew it was Liv before she spoke. There was something about her presence that made his skin tingle in the nicest way. He hit a couple of pointless keys on his keyboard, before looking up and flashing her a smile.

'Hey, come to get that thing off?'

'If you've got time. I could still go to the hospital.'

'Even if I didn't have time, I'd make it for you.' Callum inwardly winced at his own words. 'I mean . . . you helped out with Sarah. In comparison this isn't even a favour, merely a professional courtesy.' He gestured to the seat to the right of his.

'Well, it's one I appreciate.' Liv smiled and smoothed her skirt as she sat, sending Callum's mind into overdrive as he tried, unsuccessfully, not to remember her comment about stockings the first day they'd met. He absolutely was not going to wonder about whether she was wearing stockings today.

He forced his mind back to the job. 'So, how long have you been wearing the cast?'

'This one?' Liv cradled her arm against her. 'About eight weeks.'

'This isn't the first cast?' Callum was instantly concerned. Multiple casts usually meant a serious injury.

'No. It's the fourth.' Liv pursed her lips briefly before continuing. 'Stabilisation cast post-surgery while waiting for the swelling to go down. Then a few weeks with transfixing pins.'

'And then what?' Callum tried to focus on the medicine, and not the fact Liv had been so badly hurt that she needed fairly major surgery to pin her bones back together again.

'Complications. Healing wasn't as good as we'd hoped initially. So they had to go back in.' She rubbed at the cast. 'Went better the second time, though. This cast has been on since around then.'

'Wow. So the joint needed pinning, follow-up surgical intervention, and an extended period in a cast. You must have done some real damage. How many bones did you break?'

'Two.' Liv didn't offer any more detail.

'Are you going to tell me which, and how?' When she didn't answer, Callum leaned forward and gently added, 'Liv, if I'm going to remove the cast, I have to satisfy myself it's safe to do so. You know that.'

She sighed heavily. 'Ulna and Radius. Torsion fractures.'

Callum's concern instantly ratcheted up into full-blown worry, though he did his best to maintain his professional mask. There were lots of ways to fracture a wrist, but the type of injury and severity she was describing weren't common. It usually meant either a very serious set of injuries, or it was indicative of far darker, nastier issues: it took a great deal of force to twist a bone hard enough to break it. 'You spiral fractured both of the long bones in your forearm?'

'That's what I said.' Liv was defensive.

Callum decided to drop the subject. 'And your surgeons were happy with the healing progress?'

'Yes. Last consultation was the day before I came up here. He cleared me to drive so long as it wasn't too painful, and said the cast could come off in about four weeks, so long as there weren't any complications.'

'How long ago was the initial injury?'

'Nearly four months.'

'And how's it feeling today?'

Liv grinned. 'Like it's time to take off the cast.'

'All right then.' Callum took her wrist gently, and carefully placed it on the disposable pad already covering the edge of his desk. 'If you get any pain from the vibration, let me know and I'll stop immediately.'

'I will,' Liv agreed. 'But it's going to be fine.'

Callum wrapped his left hand around Liv's, securing her wrist against the desk. Even though he knew it was medically necessary, and part of the procedure, he couldn't help the thrill that raced up his arm at the warmth of her fingers against his.

He ran the vibrating saw up each side of Liv's wrist, cutting through the plaster in easy, confident movements. When he was done, he set the saw aside and reached for the spreaders that would ease the cast gently apart.

Slowly and carefully he slid the shears into the gaps he had created and sliced through the protective padding. Gently he pulled apart the strappings and wrappings, baring her skin inch by slow inch. Slipping his fingers into the new space, he tore apart the padding, brushing his fingers against her creamy, velvety skin. He tried to convince himself that the goose pimples racing along the path his fingers took were nothing more than the normal reaction of over-sensitive skin being exposed to cool air for the first time in months. But try as he might, he couldn't stop himself from memorising the warmth and feel of their journey over her forearm, or the feeling of her rapid pulse beneath his fingertips.

He looked up and caught Liv watching him, her eyes sparkling and lips slightly parted. She flushed briefly and pulled her hand away from his, now free of the cast. She massaged her wrist and forearm, flexing and twisting her hand.

'How does it feel?' Callum busied himself clearing up.

'So much better.' Liv sighed happily as she scratched the dry skin. 'Scars are healing well too. But I'll get some vitamin E cream on them.'

Callum pulled her hand back towards him, gently turning it under the light. 'Very neat work. Especially considering the second surgery you needed.'

'Yeah, the surgeons looked after me really well. Everyone did.'

'Well, I assume they were your colleagues.'

'Yes, gold star treatment all the way.'

He ran his thumb over the inside of her wrist and up her arm, palpating gently as he worked his way towards her elbow, looking for any points of tenderness, or unusual lumps or bumps.

Liv gasped, a delicious sound that shot straight down Callum's spine.

'Sorry. Tickled a bit.'

'Everything seems to be fine.'

'Told you it would be.'

After a few long moments that he would have been happy to stretch out for hours, Liv shifted reluctantly in her seat, and pulled her arm away from him. Desperate to end the uneasiness that had thickened the air, he fought to bring back some air of professionalism and find something they could talk about. 'I've been thinking about your suggestions for trying to save the surgery.'

'Really?' She leaned forward, eager. 'What do you think?'

'I think you're right. I think we need to expand the surgery to offer more services, and increase how we support our residents in the community. It's high risk, but I don't see any other option that's realistic.'

'That's really exciting.' Liv gave him a reassuring smile. 'And you know I'll help however I can.'

'I'm counting on it.' He smiled back at her, meeting her eyes.

Eventually, Liv looked away. 'Callum, about last night—'

'Oh crap, I'm so sorry about that,' he interrupted before she could get any further and say something he didn't want to hear. 'It shouldn't have happened. It was unprofessional and yet again I find myself begging your forgiveness and asking you to excuse the inexcusable when it comes to my behaviour. But is there any chance you'll forgive me — again — and we can go back to being colleagues?'

Liv studied her newly bare arm, running her fingers over the scars.

'Or even friends?' The words were out before Callum had thought them through, but any concerns he may have had evaporated when Liv's gorgeous smile lit up her face.

'Friends? I think I'd like that.'

'Me too.' Callum felt himself grinning back like a fool, but he just didn't care. Being around Liv nurtured something in him that he thought had been long ago stamped out. He trusted her. More than he did anyone outside his family. And more than that, she made him happy — and making her smile like that made him feel ten feet tall. For that, he'd work out how to be her friend. Just her friend.

* * *

The rest of the week flew by in a blur of consultations, appointments and referrals, and despite her best effort, her mind kept wandering. And it was always the same distraction that stole her attention: Callum. She was inexplicably thrilled that he loved her ideas for trying to save the surgery. Of course professional pride was part of it, but it felt like so much more than that.

She desperately wanted the proposals to be a success and for the surgery to survive. Of course, she recognised the surgery's importance to the village, but it had rapidly become important to her too. Even though her time there was temporary, she wanted to help ensure it would survive. She owed Tom that much. But if she was totally honest with herself, her desire to help was less to do with her old mentor, or the villagers she'd come to care for: she was doing it for Callum. She wanted to help him secure the surgery's future for another three generations, and she wanted to see his eyes light up with excitement because of something she'd said or done.

She'd been so relieved when he'd asked if they could still be friends, because even after a short time she didn't want to lose him from her life. She'd been terrified the kiss would make things impossibly awkward, but they'd found a way to handle it. A mature, sensible way that didn't disappoint her in the slightest. Not even a little bit.

'Hey,' Liv said, looking up when Millie knocked at her door, grateful to be pulled away from her own thoughts. 'Oh dear, you look a bit rough. Come on in, sit down and tell me what's wrong.'

Millie winced as she lowered herself into the chair. 'I'm hoping it's nothing.' Her voice was rougher than usual, 'But I wanted to be sure. Sore throat that's come on quickly, mild fever and aches, and swelling and tenderness in cervical and occipital lymph nodes.'

'Oh dear.' Liv frowned, already understanding Millie's concerns. If she had a streptococcal infection, she couldn't safely be around her more vulnerable patients. 'Does it hurt to swallow?'

Millie nodded. 'Like razor blades. Just what I didn't need for half term.'

'It can't be helped. Let's have a look.' Liv snapped on gloves and reached for a tongue depressor and her torch. 'Red spots on your palate and swollen tonsils. I can run some cultures, but I'm pretty sure you've got strep throat. But even if it's not, I'm recommending you're probably not well enough to be working.'

'I'm fine for admin,' Millie tried to argue, but her voice broke into a coughing fit that she smothered with tissues.

'Yes. You sound it.' Liv pulled a wry face. 'Look, we both know you're not feeling well, and that you're probably going to feel worse before better. You can take my professional advice, or I can sign you off and make you go home and rest.'

Millie sagged in her seat. 'You're right. Thank you.'

'Not that you need to thank me for doing my job, but you're welcome. I'll run your swabs on a rapid test. While we're waiting for the results, I'm going to make you a cup of tea, tell Callum what's going on, and you can write down anything I need to know about your case list that isn't in your files.' Liv tore open a swab. 'Now open up.'

* * *

By the end of that week, Callum was about ready to collapse. With late spring and early summer colds running riot through the village and surrounding area, Millie at home recovering from her own illness, and Evelyn still not back from Massachusetts, the surgery had been overrun by coughs, burning throats, mild fevers and sniffles as well as all the usual appointments, ailments, injuries and referrals that were the daily business of any GP. He'd given good news and bad that week, reassured, sympathised and mourned alongside his patients, as well as covering the pregnancy and baby appointments that Millie usually handled, while still juggling his life with Sarah.

He'd just finished loading up the autoclave with equipment from his last minor procedure — removing a micro toy car from the nose of a very relieved toddler who had been told in no uncertain terms to not try and "smell" his big brother's toys like that again — when someone knocked at the door.

He groaned inwardly. Though the surgery was technically closed, in reality when you were one of only a handful of medical professionals locally, there was no such thing as "closed". He'd been hoping for some peace and quiet to get on with the proposal for the local commissioning group.

'Come in.'

He instantly brightened when Liv peered around the door. 'Well, that was a week and a half, wasn't it? I don't know about you, but I could really use a drink. Do you reckon your babysitter can hang on a bit longer tonight?'

'You want to have a drink with me?'

Liv laughed, and the sound lightened Callum's mood, instantly revitalising him.

'I don't see anyone else here, and my usual end of week drinking partner is still laid up with strep.' Liv hovered by the door. 'It's only a thought — no pressure either way.' She unclipped her hair while she was talking, letting it spill down her shoulders, and Callum found himself wondering, yet again, how it would feel to tangle his fingers through that hair — preferably while he tilted her lips up to his again. The last time she'd tasted of the coffee they'd just shared. He wondered what she'd taste of if he kissed her again.

'Well? What do you think? Fancy a friendly drink?' Liv interrupted his train of thought, bringing it to a screeching halt as he mentally chided himself for such inappropriate thoughts. Friendly was the operative word. He'd promised they were going to be *friends*, just friends, and he needed to stand by that.

'Sarah's at a sleepover tonight. I was going to try and take advantage of the peace and quiet and get that proposal finished off . . .'

Liv shrugged. 'Say no more.'

The door swung closed behind her, and Callum was immediately filled with regret. He'd meant to say he was happy to change his plans to spend the evening with her instead of working, but somehow he'd not quite managed to get the words out. It used to be his younger brother who tripped over his tongue as soon as a pretty girl smiled at him, but now Jake had found someone he cared about enough to turn his life upside down, Callum felt like the stumbling tongue had caught up with him instead.

He stared at the door, and briefly thought about chasing Liv down the corridor, but resolutely glued his feet to the floor. He *needed* to get the proposal finished, and he wasn't sure that spending more time with Liv was a good idea, even though it was incredibly enticing.

But that was the problem. To him, Liv was as enticing as a frosty cold beer on a hot day. Being almost constantly on call as a doctor and father, he couldn't remember the last time he'd indulged in a few pints. Or the attention and company of a beautiful woman either. But that was more dangerous than drinking on duty. And just as irresponsible and unthinkable to him. Sarah, and the surgery, were his only priorities. Liv leaving in a few months was a good thing.

* * *

Back in the safety of her own office, Liv leaned against the door, her stomach sinking in disappointment. After screwing up the courage to ask Callum to join her in the pub, she felt a bit deflated. His refusal shouldn't have meant anything to her, but it did. A friend being too busy to make it to the pub had never made her feel so . . . let down, which made her question her "friendly" resolutions.

Irritated at herself, she rubbed her fingers against her scalp as if hoping she could scrub away the unwanted emotions. Her eye was caught by the boutique bag tucked under her desk. When she'd gone for a walk at lunch, she hadn't been able to resist the dress in the small shop's window. The bright blue had immediately caught her eye as she sauntered through the village. She worked hard, and it wasn't often that she treated herself. Even though it was more than she'd usually spend on a dress, it was so pretty and light that she'd decided to splash out and add a bit more colour to her wardrobe and life. It was unlike anything else she owned, and she knew Mike would have hated it — which somehow made her like it all the more. Technically it was a summer dress, but the weather was warm enough that she could get away with it.

Wanting to dispel the feelings dragging her down, she slid her suit jacket from her shoulders. A few seconds later she smoothed the dress down and smiled as she made a decision.

Callum hadn't *actually* said no to the idea of a drink, just that he'd planned to work on the proposal to save the surgery. At least half of the ideas had been Liv's, and she wanted to see them through. Besides, they'd agreed to be friends, and friends helped each other out.

Feeling happier, she grabbed her laptop from the desk and sauntered out the door, the dress swishing around her thighs.

* * *

Just as Callum was finally getting into the proposal to try and keep the surgery open, the door burst open and Liv strolled in. He had no idea where the short, blue summer dress that flowed around her legs to stop just above her knees had come from, but he was incredibly glad she'd changed. He'd always thought Liv looked good in her smart skirt suits and pretty tops, but this dress clung to her curves and made her eyes sparkle.

'Figured two heads are better than one.' Liv held up the laptop Callum hadn't even noticed. 'I told you I've been involved in proposals like this before. Plus, I really want to see this through to the finish. Could you use a hand?'

All of Callum's resolutions vanished into thin air. 'Sounds good to me.' He hooked his foot around the chair usually reserved for patients and pulled it closer to his desk, and slid a stack of files along, making space for her.

'Thanks.' Liv settled next to him and flipped her laptop open.

'And maybe, after we've done a couple of hours work here, I could buy you that drink in one of our fine pubs?' Callum wanted to swallow the words almost as soon as they'd escaped.

Liv nodded happily. 'That sounds good.' She typed in her password and gave him a cheeky grin. 'Come on then, Dr Mac, show me what you've got.' She leaned closer to peer at his screen over his shoulder.

Callum took a deep breath as he felt Liv's arm brush against his, sending shivers down his spine. Honey filled his nostrils and momentarily froze his brain. After a few seconds he remembered himself, typed in the password to cancel his screensaver, and forced himself to focus.

* * *

'Here's to a job well done.' Liv held her glass up. 'Cheers!'

Callum clinked his glass against hers. 'Cheers to you, Liv. I couldn't have put together such a strong proposal without your help.'

'I'm sure you could have.' Liv felt herself flush, embarrassed by the praise, but secretly pleased that Callum found her so indispensable. Though she quickly quashed that thought. Her role here was temporary. She'd known that when she agreed to provide cover, but it was still nice to feel needed and valued. Really, *really* nice.

'Well, I'd have thrown something together. But it would have taken me a lot longer, and probably wouldn't have been as good as what you came up with. Your idea of extending the surgery and increasing the procedures we can provide was far bolder than anything I would have imagined.'

'I hope it's not too much of a stretch.' Liv bit her bottom lip, suddenly wondering what on earth she was doing. Did she really have any right to be pushing Callum to follow such a risky idea? The surgery was so important to him and his family — they'd created it from nothing, and now she was encouraging him to take massive risks. It wasn't *her* home or business being put at risk.

'I think it's perfect.' Callum interrupted her thoughts. 'I'll email the proposal to my parents — they'll need to sign off the final submission — and Evelyn who will probably have some more to add on the community re-enablement as that's her background but—' he took a swig of his beer — 'I've already run the ideas past them, and they liked them. To be honest, I think we were all a bit relieved with your ideas.'

'Relieved how?'

'We've been trying to figure out a way to survive these cuts for months. Then you come in with all these brilliant suggestions that might just be the IV infusion we need.'

'Do you really think so?' Liv was thrilled to have played such an important role in resuscitating the surgery.

'I know so.' Callum reached for her hand, and Liv had to stifle a gasp at the sensations that such a simple gesture caused. She watched their entwined fingers as Callum stroked his thumb across her knuckles, sending goose pimples racing up her arm. She tried not to think about the sensations those fingers could produce on more *sensitive* parts of her body.

She forced her mind away from those dangerous thoughts. Pleasure and sexual tension alone — however strong — weren't enough. She'd already learnt that the hard way, and knew following that road would only lead to more pain. She'd had enough hurt recently to last her the rest of her lifetime.

Reluctantly, she slowly pulled away her hand. 'I'm glad you think it's got potential.'

'You—' Callum gave her a warm smile — 'are a breath of fresh air. You've brought a new perspective to the surgery, and the patients are loving it. Do you have any idea how many compliments I've had about you?'

Liv shook her head, feeling embarrassment creep up her throat and warm her cheeks. 'I'm sure you're exaggerating.'

'I'm really not.' Callum traced a pattern in the condensation on his bottle. 'The staff adore you as well.'

Liv's flush rose higher as she wondered if Callum was including himself in that adoration. She'd like to think so. 'I'm glad. Community practice is so different to working in a hospital, especially A&E.'

'But you fit in perfectly . . . like the last piece of a jigsaw puzzle.'

Liv laughed, nearly choking on her drink. 'Wow, that was incredibly cheesy.'

'Yeah.' Callum laughed at himself. 'I have to admit, that one sounded better in my head. Well, it's a good thing we're just colleagues, and I'm not trying to impress you. Like if we were on a date or something.'

'Hmm. I guess so,' Liv replied quietly, silently disagreeing. After allowing herself a few seconds of wallowing, she downed the last inch or so of her drink.

'Can I get you another?'

Liv shook her head. 'You bought the first round, so it must be my turn. Same again?' She waited for his nod before heading towards the bar.

* * *

Callum watched Liv as she walked away, her skirt flipping around her legs and emphasising the sway of her hips. He

63

took a deep breath and let it out slowly, almost regretfully. If he were any other single guy, he would have taken one of the dozen or so cues Liv had given him over the past weeks and gathered her up against him and kissed her thoroughly. Again. Or pushed her against the nearest wall, or desk. He'd even had inappropriate thoughts about the examination table in his surgery.

But he wasn't any other single guy. He was a father, and protecting Sarah from any more harm was far more important to him than sating his own libido. Even if his fingers tingled with the desire to stroke Liv's bare legs, and push that flirty little skirt out of his way.

He watched as Liv leaned over the bar to speak with the barman, and gulped hard as the damn skirt rode even higher, revealing acres of toned, creamy skin. His attention was so focussed on Liv that he was barely aware of the argument breaking out near her as a couple of young men, who had clearly had too much to drink, started to squabble.

It was only when the squabble turned into an argument, and Liv got involved that Callum stood. Liv said something that he couldn't make out, and rested a placating hand on the large guy's arm.

Callum watched in horror as the guy spun around angrily, throwing Liv's hand away and knocking her off balance. Though Callum all but sprinted across the small bar, the distance between them seemed phenomenal as she wobbled, lost her footing, and toppled backwards. She smacked her head against a nearby table before crumpling to the floor where she lay, scarily small and still.

CHAPTER FOUR

The panic Liv had been fighting for months bubbled up in her throat, choking her and stealing her voice. Her head ached and as the room spun around her, the memories she'd worked so hard to bury took hold and pulled her back to A&E and that awful night.

She curled into a small ball trying to protect herself from being hurt more as she fought against the remembered pain. Her wrist throbbed and her lower abdomen ached in sympathetic remembrance as she tried to hold still, not wanting to attract further attention and injury.

'Don't touch her. Give me some space to work, please.' The familiar voice sounded far away, and Liv couldn't quite place it. Gentle hands reached for her, but she shied away, still terrified.

'Liv, you need to hold still.' The voice was authoritative and calm, and Liv froze, confused. Shouldn't they be rushing her into a trauma bay?

Cool fingers traced over her head and down her neck, sending goose bumps racing over her skin. Warm muskiness filled her nose and she sighed in relief. *Callum.* He wouldn't let any harm come to her.

'Liv, can you tell me where it hurts?'

Reality crashed back in and the nightmare memories faded under Callum's soothing touch.

'My head, a bit.' Liv went to move but Callum's hands gently surrounded her face and held her still.

'Na uh. Not until I've done a cervical spine assessment. It looked to me like you cracked your head pretty hard as you went down.'

'It's just a bump,' Liv tried to argue. 'I'm fine.'

'And it will only take me a few moments to double-check that.'

'Gee, it's almost like you fancy yourself a doctor or something.'

Callum smiled down at her. 'Sense of humour intact. That's one thing checked off the list.'

'You're seriously going to do a full spinal assessment while I'm lying on a pub floor?' Liv glared at him, embarrassed by the fuss being made. She hated being the centre of attention, and having what felt like half the village staring at her was making her skin crawl.

'Just focus on me.' Callum leaned forward. Still cradling her face, he forced her to meet his eyes and she instantly felt better. Surrounded by Callum's scent, his warm hands protecting her from moving and risking hurting herself, Liv felt safe and cared for. 'The sooner you stop complaining and let me start, the sooner I'll be finished.'

'All right.' Liv took a deep breath, already mentally running through the procedure, but her mind went blank as Callum's fingers traced gently down her neck, pressing against each vertebrae. The sensation sent pleasant tingles racing throughout her body.

'Is there any pain? Any tingling or numbness?' Callum's eyes were filled with concern that seemed more than "just professional".

'Nope.' At least nothing she wanted to share with him.

His hands slipped across her shoulders, scorching her skin through her thin dress.

'Still OK?'

'Fine.'

He stroked down her arms to hold her hands in his. 'Squeeze.'

Liv obeyed, proving there was no weakness in either hand. She had to suppress a gasp as Callum ran his hands down the side of her legs and rested gently on her ankles. She knew it was just part of the procedure, but she could have sworn his hands lingered slightly, and the heat from his palms distracted as he asked her to move her feet, proving there was no nerve damage lower down.

He came back into her field of vision, and rested his hands back on her shoulders. 'Can you move your head from side to side?' Carefully, Liv did as he asked. 'Up and down? No pain?'

'No pain,' she confirmed.

'Do you want to try sitting up? Carefully.' He held Liv's hand in his to pull her upright, and wrapped his other arm around her shoulders, supporting her. 'Feeling all right, still?'

'Yes.' Liv nodded. 'I want to get up.'

'OK.' Callum kept a firm hold of her as he helped her to her feet, and tightened his grip as she stumbled against him. 'What's wrong?'

'A little dizzy.' Liv rested her head against his shoulder while she waited for the room to stop spinning. But as Callum held her against his muscular chest, her head resting in the crook of his neck and breathing him in, she wasn't sure she ever wanted to move. She felt safe, and warm and protected for the first time in months. For a moment, she let herself wonder how it would feel if she gave in to temptation and nuzzled against him.

The desire became overwhelming as he slid his fingers through her hair and caressed the back of her head.

Liv couldn't help the quiet moan that escaped her lips.

'You've got quite a bump here.'

Liv felt her cheeks redden with embarrassment, horrified at the mistake she had nearly made. He really was just being professional. She was nothing more than the patient of the moment to him.

'With a bump that size, the dizziness and disorientation, you know you probably have a mild concussion, right?'

'I'm not concussed.' Liv tried to push Callum away and shake her head, but immediately regretted the action as dizziness swamped her again and she staggered.

'Right.' Callum caught her again and guided her into a chair. 'You're dizzy, disorientated and have one hell of a lump on your noggin. I think we should pop you up to the hospital to check everything's OK.'

'I don't need to go to hospital.'

'Liv, if one of your patients . . .'

'Callum, please. I do *not* want to go to hospital.' The thought of being a patient again made her stomach roll. 'Will you just take me home. Please?'

He nodded reluctantly. 'Only if you're sure.'

'I am. Please, just take me back to my cottage.'

'All right. I'll call a cab. But if you get any dizzier, or develop any other symptoms, you're going to the hospital.'

'OK.'

'And I'm staying with you.'

'Callum, I don't need you to do that . . .'

'No arguments, Liv. You know a patient with suspected concussion needs observation. It's this or the hospital. Your choice.'

'Home. I want to go home.' She'd have agreed to almost anything to avoid another trip to the hospital. She'd figure out a way to get rid of Callum later, and she could let herself curl up and have the good cry she really needed.

* * *

Callum watched Liv as she stared out of the cab window, his concern growing. 'Still with me?'

'Yeah.'

'Sure?'

Liv took a deep breath and turned to him, her smile brittle and eyes overly bright.

'I'm fine.'

By the time they reached her cottage, she was shaking, and even in the poorly lit street, Callum could see a grey tinge to her tightly-pursed lips. He paid the cab driver and followed Liv up the path to the chocolate box cottage. She still hadn't managed to unlock the door, so he gently took the keys from her trembling fingers and did the necessary.

Liv sighed gratefully and rushed into the hallway where she grabbed hold of the banister, her knuckles whitening with pressure.

Callum watched her warily. She wasn't fully coherent or present, but he couldn't tell if it was a sign of the concussion he'd warned her about, or the stress she was clearly experiencing. People reacted differently to injury and stressful events, but even as Callum tried to remember that, he was worried about Liv's response. In all the time he'd spent with her over the last few weeks, she'd proven to be calm and level-headed, and he didn't think she was someone usually likely to panic.

'Do you need a hand?' He grimaced at her sharp gasp and the sudden tension in her shoulders. He longed to reach out and touch her, to soothe her pain away, but knew she wouldn't accept it.

'No.' Her voice was thick with emotion, and she still wouldn't look at him. 'Just want to clean myself up a bit.' Still avoiding his gaze, she started up the stairs.

'You'll leave the door unlocked?'

'For God's sake, Callum, I'm not concussed!'

'Then it won't matter, because you'll come straight back down. But if you had a dizzy spell and fell, then I really don't want to have to break down your door, OK?'

'OK.'

Callum knew she was far from OK, but decided to let it slide. For now. 'Can I do anything to make myself useful? Get you a drink or something to eat?'

'Tea would be good. Everything's in the cupboard above the kettle.' Liv turned to give him a watery smile. 'Thanks.'

'None needed. You go do whatever you need to . . . with the door unlocked . . . and I'll put the kettle on.' He watched as she slowly, gingerly, made her way upstairs. Her left arm was crossed tightly across her abdomen, and Callum couldn't help wondering — again — how that wrist had been so badly broken a few months previously.

Still pondering how he could help Liv when she was so resistant, he opened the first door off the hallway. It was a cosy living room, with the traditional wide stone fireplace he'd expect in cottages like this. He closed the door and opened the next in the corridor to reveal a typical cottage kitchen, with wooden countertops and cream cabinets surrounding a well-scrubbed table.

Within moments, the kettle was making promising noises, and Callum had found everything he needed and was leaning awkwardly against the countertop, trying not to nosey around Liv's kitchen too much. From the stacks of books and paperwork spread across the table and teapot out on the side, he guessed she spent a lot of time here. He smiled at the image of Liv sitting at the table, hair loose as she pored over a book.

The shattering crash from upstairs had him in the hall in seconds, and he raced up the stairs, heart pounding. 'Liv, what happened. Are you OK?'

'I'm fine.' Her strangled response did nothing to reassure Callum, but it did tell him which of the three doors she was behind.

'I'm coming in.' He didn't bother to ask, because no wasn't an option he was willing to accept. He pushed the door open carefully, and his stomach clenched painfully at the sight of Liv sat on the floor, tucked partly beneath the sink, tears streaming down her cheeks and her hand wrapped in a white towel that was slowly reddening with blood.

'I'm sorry.' She choked the words out before covering her face with her hands, and drawing her knees tightly against her chest as if trying to make herself as small as possible.

'For what?' Callum was genuinely confused. He couldn't see anything Liv needed to apologise for.

'Everything is such a mess. And it's all my fault. I thought I could do this, but I can't. I'm so sorry.' She rocked back and forth, sobbing.

Callum grabbed a towel from the rack and used it to carefully brush up the shattered remains of a vase and some bedraggled flowers from the floor, before sitting beside Liv. Wriggling in the awkward space, he did his best to wrap a comforting arm around her shoulder. She tensed, and he held his breath, but after a few seconds she relaxed and rested her head against his shoulder.

Gently, Callum took hold of her bleeding hand and gingerly unwrapped the towel. He hissed in sympathy at the large gash running the length of her thumb. 'I need to sort this out. It's pretty deep.'

Liv looked at the wound dully. 'I suppose.'

Her lack of interest really worried him. The wound was bleeding profusely, and must have hurt. But Liv seemed almost oblivious. Not knowing what to do immediately about her mental state, he decided to focus on the easier problem of her bleeding hand.

'Come on.' Callum struggled to his feet before bending down to Liv and half-lifting her from the floor. He balanced her on the edge of the bath before looking around. 'First-aid kit?'

Liv sighed hugely. 'Bottom drawer.' She sniffed loudly, but tears still streamed unheeded down her face.

Callum pulled Liv's hand gently over the sink and retrieved the kit. He rummaged through the box for gloves, gauzes, saline and Dermabond. He hadn't examined the wound closely, but from the amount of blood he was expecting to have to glue — if not suture — it shut.

He pulled the gloves on and reached out for Liv's hand. 'Sorry, this is probably going to sting a bit.'

She murmured in response, her eyes staring at something only she could see. She didn't flinch as he irrigated the wound, which worried him all the more. Callum had seen similar reactions before — but usually only in people who

71

had experienced some level of bereavement or trauma, and seeing Liv zone out like this really worried him. Her reaction seemed so far out of proportion with the events of the evening, that he couldn't help wondering what she'd been through that was hurting her so badly even now.

He glued Liv's torn skin back together as gently as he could, aware that it would hurt her, but she still didn't flinch. Biting back a sigh, Callum tidied up quickly, rolled off the gloves and washed his hands. He watched her, still worried about her reaction.

'Liv?'

She didn't look at him, her face hidden by a curtain of silken blonde that Callum longed to brush back.

'Liv, tell me what to do. Please.'

'I just need some time.'

'All right,' he agreed reluctantly. 'I'll finish making the drinks. Leave the glass, and I'll clear it up later. But you'll come down in a few minutes?'

She shrugged one shoulder.

'Liv, you've had a head injury today and are clearly upset. I'm not leaving you alone for long.' Callum summoned all his patience. What he really wanted to do was wrap his arms tightly around her, and not let go until she was happy again. But he knew that wasn't the right thing to do. This time he couldn't resist the urge, and justified it by telling himself that he needed to know she was listening. So he reached out, and tucked her hair behind her ear, and gently lifted her chin to look at him.

She flinched, but didn't pull away. Callum took it as a good sign.

'I'm right here, Liv. I want to help you. Will you let me?'

Her cheek whispered against his palm, and golden strands tickled the back of his hand as she nodded. Even when she was so upset, Callum couldn't help but notice how soft her skin was, and how silky her hair.

After long moments, she pulled away, and wiped at her tears. 'This isn't just about what happened tonight.'

'I figured.'

'I just need a few minutes. I'll be down soon. I promise.'
'OK.'

* * *

Liv stayed in the bathroom for as long as she dared, not wanting Callum to have to come back upstairs, but she really didn't want to go down and face him. She removed what was left of her make-up and pressed a cool flannel against her swollen eyes. After a few moments she forced herself to meet her own eyes in the mirror. Sadness met her gaze, and she grimaced at her reflection: she'd hoped that the harrowed, broken version of herself currently staring back at her had been left behind, along with so many other things.

She didn't want to think about what had made her look like this, and she really didn't want to tell Callum everything. She couldn't bear it if he changed the way he looked at her, and the sympathy all her well-meaning friends in London had tried to hide, was reflected in his eyes.

But if anything was clear from tonight, it was that her approach of trying to bury everything in the past — or a few hours down the motorway — wasn't doing her any good. And Callum's offer of help had seemed genuine . . .

Before she gave herself the chance to change her mind, Liv dumped her now bloodied dress in the bath, ran some cold water over it, pulled on comfy yoga pants and a soft hoody, and headed downstairs. The sitting-room door was open, and the stove in the fireplace was flickering promisingly under Callum's ministrations. He looked up when Liv stepped into the room, perched herself on the sofa and reached for one of the steaming cups.

'I know it's not exactly cold, but I thought a fire might be nice. You don't mind, do you?' Callum dusted off his hands and gave her a warm smile that helped thaw the cold that had seeped into her bones, and reassured her that she was making the right decision in trusting him. 'How's your hand?'

'Fine.' She wrapped her uninjured hand tightly around the cup of tea, letting the slight pain from its heat ground her. 'So, I guess you're wanting to know what tonight was all about.'

'Only if you want to tell me.' Callum picked up his own cup, and leaned against the hearth.

Liv inhaled the floral steam: chamomile instead of caffeine. She wouldn't argue that some calming herbal tea was a good idea now. The fragrance soothed and fortified her.

'I told you upstairs — I want to help you, Liv. You just have to let me in.'

She nodded, knowing she had to do this, but knowing it would be incredibly difficult, and would probably change how he looked at her in the future. But she couldn't carry on as she had been, tamping down the anxiety and waiting for it to explode again.

Callum settled on the opposite end of the sofa to her, leaving her plenty of space but at the same time letting her know he was there for her.

'I don't know where to start,' Liv admitted quietly as she returned her cup to the coffee table.

Callum took a sip of his drink, and appeared to watch the flames crackling in the stove. 'My dad told me some. That there was an incident at the hospital where you worked. Is that how your wrist was broken?'

'Yeah.' Liv nodded, absent-mindedly rubbing the achy joint. She must have jarred it in the pub when she'd fallen. 'You know all the posters we display, about pledges against violence and aggression, and how the hospitals and surgeries won't stand for it, and will always prosecute perpetrators to the fullest extent of the law?' She waited for his nod. 'And we all talk about dealing with violent patients in team meetings, and go on de-escalation training?'

'Yeah. You never really think it will apply to you.'

'No, you don't. Not until it does.' Liv took a deep breath, steeling herself to continue. 'It was a normal, busy weekend shift, so when the paramedics brought in an apparently drunk man with some glass in his hand, it didn't ring any alarm bells.'

'But it should have?' Callum prompted gently.

'Yeah.' Liv nodded sadly. 'While he smelled of alcohol, it turns out he was in the middle of a psychotic break. He'd seemed calm, and compliant enough when the paramedics brought him in, but as soon as he saw the syringe, he freaked out. I tried to calm him down, but when I went for the buzzer, he grabbed me. I managed to get away, but . . .'

'The torsion fractures in your wrist?'

Liv nodded, struggling to breathe past the panic rising up in her throat as she relived those horrible moments. She swallowed hard, before reaching for her cup, and realising her hand shook.

Callum must have spotted it too, because he took her hand in his and squeezed it gently. He held on, gently rubbing the back of her hand and flooding her with warmth. Liv relaxed, and enjoyed the sensation for a few moments before forcing herself to look up and meet his gaze, a gaze filled with such kindness and concern that she had to close her eyes to find the strength to try and pull her hand away.

But Callum held her fingers firmly, forcing her to look at him again. 'If discussing this can help, then please talk to me, Liv.'

She nodded, knowing that she needed to talk. She'd thought about taking her hospital up on their offer of seeing a professional counsellor, but as much as she knew they worked and had referred people to them in the past, she couldn't see herself being able to open up to a stranger about something so incredibly personal. But Callum was different — she liked him, knew she could trust him. He was her friend — at least he would be for the next few weeks or months until Tom returned from his latest sabbatical.

She pulled her hand from Callum's, immediately missing his warmth, so picked up her cup and wrapped her fingers around that instead. She didn't think she'd be able to get through this conversation with the distraction of his hand in hers. And if he reacted badly and pulled away from her when she told him everything, she wasn't sure she could bare it.

'Sorry.' She gave Callum a weak smile. 'This is really hard for me.'

'Take your time. I've nowhere to be.'

Liv hesitated again.

'He broke your wrist. Badly. But there's more to the story than that, isn't there?'

'Yes.' Liv nodded sadly and tried to answer as if she was relaying the details of a patient in a case conference. If she spoke dispassionately and as though talking about an event that happened to someone else, then maybe it would be easier. *Maybe*. 'I managed to get away, but he followed me out of the room. That was when I saw he'd grabbed the scalpel out of my kit. He was in a paranoid dissociative state.' Her professional approach failed her as her memories transported her back to those horrible few moments. 'You know what A&E can be like at weekends.'

'Busy.'

Liv nodded. 'We were really full. There were so many people there. Sick, hurting and scared. We'd called security, but their office wasn't in A&E. It took them time to get to us. There were children there, Callum. I couldn't let him hurt them.' Her voice cracked. 'I couldn't let him hurt anyone. I was the nearest person to him, and I don't think anyone else had realised what was going on. It was all so fast. I tried to get the blade away from him, to protect my patients. I couldn't let them get hurt.' Tears streamed freely down Liv's face, and she stared up at the ceiling, trying to compose herself.

Callum replaced her cup with a tissue, but didn't interrupt her.

Liv wiped away the worst of her tears, and squashed the tissues in her fist, wishing she could crush all the pain, and damage, as easily as damp tissue. She forced herself to continue. 'So I put myself between him and my patients. I didn't have any choice. I couldn't let him hurt anyone else. He . . .' She took a few deep breaths as she paused to remind herself that she was safe in her living room with Callum by her side, and that the man who'd hurt her was just a sick patient, not a bogeyman who would reappear by some nightmare magic if she spoke his name. 'He stabbed me with my own scalpel. More than once. The first few hits were minor flesh wounds — painful but not life threatening. But the last one . . .'

'It was worse?' Callum's face was impassive, his voice flat with enforced calm.

Liv nodded as she shifted in her seat to lift the hem of her hoody and tug down the waistband of her trousers to reveal the puckered skin beneath. Callum sucked in a gasp through his teeth, the breath whistling in sympathy.

'As you can see, he caught me in the lower abdomen. The scalpel went in deep, and the bleeding and damage was profuse. The surgeons did their best — of course they did — they were working on one of their own, but they had to remove the ovary on that side, and the scarring internally is worse than externally. They saved my life, and I'm incredibly grateful for that, but they couldn't save the future I'd planned.'

'It compromised your fertility.'

Liv nodded, although it wasn't really a question. 'Hormonal shock. I've not had a menstrual cycle since.' She held up her hand when Callum went to interrupt. 'I know, I've still got one ovary left, and it's only been a few months, but the scarring is extensive, and like I said, my cycles seem to have stopped completely. Even if I were in a position to want to conceive anymore, I probably couldn't, and my chances of carrying a baby to term are low because of uterine scarring.' Her voice broke as the truth poured out of her, and the tears rampaged down her cheeks again. 'He took it all. My life, my home, my relationship, my future family. My sense of safety and sanity. He stole it all.'

* * *

Callum stared at Liv in horrified wonder — injured and scared for her own safety, she had still put the wellbeing of total strangers above her own, and had paid a terrible price. Yet still, every day she came into the surgery with a smile, cared for his patients and his community as if they were her own, and was one of the most kind and positive people he knew. She looked after Sarah without appearing to hold back, despite how difficult it must have been to care for someone else's child so soon after learning she might never be able to have any of her own.

Though Sarah's entry to the world had hardly been ideal, Callum couldn't imagine a life without being a father, and his heart broke for Liv.

'I wish you wouldn't look at me like that,' she mumbled from behind a curtain of hair.

'Like what?'

'Like I'm broken.'

Callum reached out to her in desperation to make her understand, brushed her hair from her face and tilted her chin to make her look at him. 'Look again, Liv. I'm not thinking that at all. I'm thinking you're one of the most amazing people I know.'

She snorted in response, shaking her head and breaking his hold and gaze. 'I'm nothing special.'

'The fact you don't see how special you are, makes you even more special, Liv.' He told her honestly, amazed that she thought any different.

'I'm not special at all.' She shoved away his concern and his touch as she leapt to her feet. 'I'm a screwed-up, damaged, unlovable mess. You're an idiot if you can't see that, and if you're not an idiot, then you're a liar!'

Callum gasped in shock, completely taken aback by her anger.

'Liv, I don't understand.'

'What is there to understand?' Liv whirled on him angrily. 'I'm ruined, Callum! Broken and unworthy of love. I suspected it my whole life, and now I know it's true.' She hung her head and wrapped her arms tightly around her own waist, as if trying to comfort herself as sobs wracked her body.

He didn't even think before he seized hold of her shoulders. 'Why would you say that, Liv?'

'Because it's true.' She sniffed. 'Everyone leaves me.'

He pulled her into a rough hug. 'I'm not going anywhere.'

'No, but I am. Your parents will come back, they won't need me anymore, and I'll just be cast to the wind. Again.' She shook her head, overwhelmed by tears.

Callum's heart ached for Liv, and he wished he could take away the pain he still didn't fully understand. He knew she was suffering, but the wounds that hurt her so badly seemed far deeper and darker than anything he could have imagined. He wondered why his father hadn't warned him about Liv's pain, but then it occurred he might not even know. Not knowing what else to do, he held Liv against his chest, letting her tears soak into his shirt and stroked her back in calm, soothing motions similar to those that eased Sarah's tears. He only hoped Liv was able to take some comfort from his presence.

After what seemed like agonisingly long minutes, her tears eased and she eventually looked up at him.

'Sorry,' she murmured, the word barely audible under the weight of more tears.

Callum looked down at her and swallowed hard — she was beautiful. Even with her eyes red and swollen, and her face blotchy, he had to resist the urge to lean down and kiss away the salty tears that glistened on her cheeks and lips. For a moment, he let himself believe that might take away her pain for a while, but she was clearly vulnerable and in need of a friend far more than anything else. There's no way he'd compromise that.

So, instead, he reached for the blanket on the armchair and wrapped it around her shoulders, tucking it around her so she would feel safe and warm. 'You've nothing to apologise for, Liv.'

'I feel like I do. You didn't need any of this.' She took a deep breath, stepped away, and gave him an overly bright smile when she looked back up. 'Thank you for seeing me home, Callum. I really am feeling much better. I promise you I'll be fine. You should get off home.'

He drummed the fingers of his right hand against his belt as he considered what to do next. It was clear Liv was giving him permission to leave — dismissing him even — but it was equally clear to him that she was still incredibly upset, and he was willing to bet she'd be in tears again before he made it down the path of the cottage garden. And there was no way he was going to abandon her to that.

He gave her what he hoped was his most winning grin, and flopped down on her sofa. 'I told you already, after that knock to your head it was a hospital check-up or obs by yours truly. If you think I'm reneging on that, especially now you're upset, you've got another think coming.'

'You are so frustrating.'

'And you are *sooooo* stuck with me for tonight.' He kicked his feet up on the footstool, making himself comfortable and sending her the clear message he wasn't going anywhere. 'So you might as well sit down, get comfy, and we'll find a movie to watch or something.'

He watched as Liv gaped at him in shock — exactly as he'd planned — and emotions played across her face as she tried to decide how to react. He really, really hoped she was going to give in and open up to him rather than get angry.

'Or,' he added quietly, 'you could sit down, and tell me what's made you believe such horrible things about yourself.' He knew it was a risk, and he could end up being turfed out on his behind, but he couldn't think of any other way to help her.

He let out a breath he hadn't realised he'd been holding as Liv's shoulders slumped, and she sat back on the sofa, the blanket still held tightly around her shoulders as she stared into the flames. And began to talk.

Her voice was flat and quiet, and Callum hardly dared breathe for fear of disturbing whatever mood it was that made Liv feel able to open up. He hated that she looked so worn and tired, without the bright smile and happy glow he was so used to lighting up his day. But whatever it was that had hurt her so, he wanted to take it away, and the first step to treatment was always accurate diagnosis, so he'd listen to whatever she was willing to share — no matter how much worse it got.

* * *

Liv stared at the glowing light of the stove, and wished the heat was reaching her. It usually did but tonight, even with the blanket pulled tightly around her, she felt numb. 'I never knew my father. And even though I know very little about him, and obviously never met him, I still missed him. When all the other girls were going to Daddy and Daughter dances, I was by myself. Every other kid made Father's Day cards in June, and I had no one. I missed the idea of what having a dad should have been like. Mum brought me up by herself, because apparently her parents weren't too pleased to find out she was pregnant with me and without a husband to support her. They actually told her to get rid of me. That they weren't willing to interrupt their lives to help her. And when she refused, they told her to have me adopted. Or else.'

She risked a glance at Callum.

'It was their loss,' he told her earnestly. 'You're amazing. And your mum must be pretty amazing too, to bring up someone like you.'

Liv smiled sadly. 'She was. She brought me up by herself — just her and me against the world. And it worked so well. I couldn't have asked for a better family. She was my parent, best friend and biggest cheerleader. We didn't need anyone else. Right up until she got sick when I was thirteen.'

Callum didn't say anything, but his presence gave her the strength to carry on, forcing herself to remember the worst weeks of her life.

'She fought hard — and we tried so many different treatments. But the cancer was in her pancreas and spreading before it was even found, and you know how that goes. She died a few days before my fifteenth birthday. Overnight I lost my family, my home and everything I'd known. My grand-parents were apparently contacted, but didn't want to step up, so there's another rejection right there. At a point where I could have really, really used some family. But then again, I'm not sure I would have wanted to see them.' Tears threat-ened to choke her again, even after all these years. 'They let her die alone, Callum. Their own daughter. Even at the very end, they couldn't be bothered to leave their retirement home in the sun to be by her side. What type of person does that?'

'I don't know, Liv.' Callum stretched his hand out towards her, and she gratefully slid her good hand from under the blanket to wrap her fingers around his. His warmth seeped into her, driving back some of the cold that had filled her, giving her more strength to continue.

'So I ended up in foster care. The people were nice enough, but they didn't have any idea how to help a trau-matised teen who'd just watched her mum die. And if I'm honest, I wasn't exactly nice or easy-going back then.' She shook her head, ashamed of her previous behaviour.

Callum squeezed her fingers reassuringly. 'You were hurting, and had every right to be angry at the world.'

'I shouldn't have taken it out on them.'

'I'm sure you're remembering it worse than it was.'

Liv pulled a face, unconvinced. 'I don't know. I was pretty bad. But it didn't last long. None of the placements did. I lost count of how many there were before social services decided I was probably old enough for a supported living flat. Something clicked in me that first night in the flat. Yet again I'd been packed up with little warning, half my things bundled into black bags, as someone else gave up on me — decided I wasn't worth the effort — and shoved me out the door. But lying in that bed, knowing there was a specialist support worker in the next room waiting for me to screw up again — being paid to make sure I didn't hurt myself or get into trouble — something changed. It was my last chance. Everyone was expecting me to fail, and if I did, my life would basically be over. And I realised how heartbroken Mum would be if I'd given up so easily. She gave up everything to have me, and bring me up. I couldn't disappoint her. I know it sounds silly, but I realised I was the only real thing left of her — the only person who really knew and loved her. And if I let myself fade away to nothing, then it would be like she never existed. I felt like I owed her so much better. Like I said, silly.'

'It's not silly at all.' For a moment, Liv thought he looked pained, but he gave her a reassuring smile, and she put it down to the firelight. 'So that's when things changed for you?'

Liv nodded, glad to be moving on to happier times. At least temporarily. 'The organisation providing the flat helped me get back into school. Before Mum got sick, I'd always enjoyed school, and been quite good at it. My support workers helped me get on to some catch-up courses, then into a half decent college. I kept my head down and worked hard. Because I'd been in care there was some help — not much — but enough to help me do well in my UCATS and got a place in a good uni.'

'Imperial and then your residency at Queen Elizabeth's?' He named the hospital his dad had worked at.

'Yes, which is obviously where I met your dad. But only for the first couple of years. Then I moved back to London, and Hammersmith and Queen Charlotte's.'

'So obstetrics was one of your specialisms?' Callum instantly recognised the hospital name.

'And gynae.' Liv nodded. 'But my passion was for A&E — I loved the bustle and challenge of constantly changing cases.' She swallowed hard, her enthusiasm waning. 'And that's where I met Mike.'

'Mike?'

'My fiancé.' She looked down, and rubbed the spot where her ring had been, all signs of it faded beyond visibility now. 'My ex-fiancé.'

If Callum had any strong feelings on this, he hid them well.

'Mike was a trauma surgeon. He was young, attractive, really popular and funny. All us juniors, and the nurses loved him. They either wanted to be his best mate, or his date. So when he was interested in me, I couldn't believe my luck. He was more worldly than me, focussed, driven. I loved him like crazy.'

'Should I ask what happened?' Callum's question was tentative.

'It's OK.' Liv nodded. 'You have to understand, the person he was in private was different to the person he was in public.'

'Did he hurt you?' Callum's anger startled her.

'No. Not at all. At least not in the way you mean.' She sighed. 'He was precise, pedantic, good traits for surgery, but sometimes less so for someone to live with. Everything had its place, and it would be in that place. The coffee machine clicked on at the same time every morning — even when we were off shift — and dinner was at the same time every night — precisely one hour after he'd finished his shift. His whole apartment was modern and clean and perfectly styled. Everything was perfect, like living in a glossy magazine feature. And if something got scratched, or marked with even the slightest chip, it would be thrown away.'

She paused to wipe more tears from her eyes. 'And what happened to me, it was a lot, lot more than a scratch.' She rubbed at her ring finger again. 'He asked for his ring back.'

'What a bastard!'

Liv shrugged. It had hurt at the time, but she'd endured worse. 'It was his grandmother's. He'd promised her he'd give it to the woman he was going to marry, and that wasn't me anymore. I couldn't give him his perfect two point four children in his perfect two point four years, because I wasn't perfect anymore. I'm scarred and battered and broken, and a screwed-up mess. Everyone who's ever gotten to know me sees it sooner or later, and they leave me.' She stopped fighting the tears, and let them come as she stared into the flames — anything was better than meeting Callum's gaze and seeing disgust, or maybe worse, sympathy in his eyes.

* * *

Callum stared at Liv in outright admiration. She was such a kind, generous and warm person; he'd never have guessed she had been so badly hurt and let down over the years. He was shocked that anyone could treat another person so badly, let alone one as kind and open as Liv. And he was truly amazed that she could take such hurt, and still be the wonderful person who was so quickly becoming a central feature in his life.

Liv finally looked up, and even blotchy with tears and crying she was still beautiful to him. Callum had to remind himself — yet again — that she would be leaving all too soon.

'You're being unfair on yourself, Liv.'

'Am I really? Everyone I ever cared about has left me, or hurt me, or both.'

'Yes.' He told her honestly. 'I think you're being incredibly harsh on yourself. You've been through hell and back, and you have been treated horribly by some of the people who should have loved you the best and had your back every single second of your life.'

'You think I don't know this?' Liv wiped her eyes on the edge of the blanket. 'I don't need you to tell me what I've been told my whole life.'

'You going to let me finish?' He gave her a crooked smile, half-frustrated, and half-praying that he had the right words to say.

She nodded slowly, but looked at him with scepticism written across her face. She didn't believe he had anything worth listening to, but was too polite to tell him to shut up.

'Liv, you're missing the point of what I'm trying to say. You are amazing.'

'I'm really not.' She shook her head sadly.

85

'Yes, you are. You're kind, intelligent and beautiful — inside and out — and despite everything you've been through, you're one of the most giving, caring people I know. In spite of all the pain you've been through, you are someone truly special, Liv.'

Liv hung her head, shielding herself from Callum's intense gaze.

'Please don't do that, Liv.' Callum leaned forward and tucked the loose strands of hair behind her ear. 'Please don't hide from me, and put yourself down. Because you are truly special.'

When she didn't respond, he continued. 'If someone you cared about, like Millie or Sarah, told you they were broken, and that no one would ever love them. What would you say?'

'I'd tell her she was talking nonsense, that she's wonderful, and that the people who didn't see how amazing she was were the ones being stupid, and they didn't deserve to have anyone as wonderful as her in their lives.'

'And what if it was someone else telling them that?'

She looked up at that, her eyes flashing with anger. 'I'd call them a liar. And I'd probably get in trouble with the General Medical Council because I'd skin them alive!'

Callum shared her laughter for a moment before becoming more serious. 'So why do you tell yourself these lies, Liv? Why do you let the voices of "idiots you'd skin alive" have so much power over you now?'

She shrugged half-heartedly.

'Why do you refuse to see how amazing you are?'

'I don't feel amazing,' she admitted quietly, before turning to face him. 'I feel tired, and worn down, and like every bad thing everyone has said is true.'

'Do you trust me, Liv?'

She looked up, clearly surprised at the question. 'How do you mean?'

'As a colleague, and expert . . . maybe a friend too. Do you trust me?'

'I guess so.' Liv nodded.

'Then will you please trust me — at least for now — when I tell you how truly and spectacularly awesome you are?' He tucked a hand around Liv's cheek and wiped away a tear. 'Until you're able to start healing, and know that the voices are just lies, will you please believe me. Until you can start seeing the true version of yourself — the one that I see.'

'I can't promise anything.'

'You can promise to try.'

Liv sighed and pulled Callum's hand into hers, and leaned back against the cushions. Callum copied her, and smiled as she shifted slightly to rest against his shoulder, her fingers still loosely entwined in his.

'All right. I promise I'll try.' She yawned hugely, and shifted against Callum's shoulder.

He tugged the blanket more tightly around her and, with nonchalance so forced he was surprised he didn't pull a muscle, he reached for the TV remote. 'So, as you're still officially not discharged from observation, fancy a movie?'

'Sure.' She shifted in her seat to get more comfortable, her arm resting scant inches from his. 'Guest's choice.'

CHAPTER FIVE

Light filtered into Liv's dreams, nudging her back into consciousness. It stabbed at the back of her eyes, sending flickers of pain running through her head. Rather than risk opening her eyelids, she turned away and tucked her face into the warmth beside her. Strength wrapped around her back and pulled her closer to the warmth that soothed her aches and pushed away the unwanted light.

She shifted to get more comfortable, rolling slightly on her side and tucking her hand beneath her ear and cheek. Her fingers tangled in cloth and brushed against hot skin, and in her sleep-addled state she snuggled closer, enjoying the feel of a heart beating beneath her palm.

A deep vibration echoed through his chest as he repositioned and started to snore. As the vibrations tickled Liv's palm, awareness crept in and she froze against Callum, suddenly fully conscious and having no idea how she was supposed to act, or if she was even supposed to. For a few moments, she contemplated feigning sleep just to stay where she was for a little longer.

'I guess, as you're awake, we should move.' Despite his words, Callum didn't make any effort to shift her away from him, and his arm stayed still and warm around her waist.

'Probably.' Liv stayed where she was for a few heartbeats longer, then forced herself slowly upright. She grimaced as her head gave a warning thump that matched the throbbing ache in her hand. Her eyes felt gritty and raw, and her throat ached from all the tears she'd shed the night before.

'Should I ask how you're feeling?'

'Maybe after a coffee and some painkillers.' Liv rubbed her hands over her eyes and groaned. 'I feel like I'm owed a really good night out. That's what it usually takes to feel this bad the morning after.' She tried to crack a joke.

'I've got time to make coffee before I need to collect Sarah from her sleepover,' Callum offered easily.

'You don't need to.'

'I know that.' He grinned easily. 'But I could do with a caffeine hit, and maybe something to eat before facing a gaggle of over-excited six-year-old girls.'

'So now you're inviting yourself to breakfast too?'

Callum shrugged. 'You supply it, I'll cook it.'

'Sounds like more than a fair deal.' This time, Liv's smile felt genuine.

* * *

Callum rinsed the last of the breakfast plates before handing it to Liv to dry. Despite her complaints, he'd not only cooked but cleaned as well. And, unlike at home, he'd enjoyed the time in Liv's kitchen, cooking for her while she sipped her coffee at the table, and bumping elbows and laughing with her as they cleaned up. The simple, easy domesticity and back-and-forth between them felt so natural that it took almost no effort. Though it was something he'd never experienced with another woman — especially not his ex who hadn't liked to get her hands dirty and avoided chores as much as possible — it felt oddly familiar.

He'd already made it halfway to the house of the family brave enough to host a sleepover with half a dozen little girls before it hit him. The feeling with Liv was familiar because he'd seen the same interactions hundreds, if not thousands, of times before: it was how his parents were around each other. The realisation slammed into him with such force that, for a moment, it eclipsed everything else. He'd known he was attracted to Liv, but now he was thinking there was a lot more than physical attraction pulling him towards her. The thought that maybe, just maybe, there was the potential for something more, teased the edges of his mind.

The impatient honk of a car behind him made him jump, and look up. The traffic lights were burning bright green, and he shoved the car into first gear, and waved an apology to the driver behind. He shook his head as he pulled away; he was being silly, focussing so much on a few minutes in the kitchen when he had more important things to think about. Like Sarah.

She threw herself at him as the door opened. 'Hi Sarey-fairy, did you have a good time?'

'It was awesome sauce! We had pizza and chips and chocolate, and we all sang to *Frozen*, and then we made fairy cakes. With magical sprinkles that make your tongue fizz and pop!'

'They sound great.' Callum ruffled her hair. 'Did you make one for me?'

'I made lots!'

'I look forward to them.' He accepted Sarah's backpack and bag of cakes from her friend's tired-looking mum with a brief thanks, and scooped Sarah up.

'Ewww. You smell bad.'

'I know, I need a shower.'

'Why didn't you shower at home?'

'I . . . um . . . had a patient who needed me to keep an eye on them. I've not been home yet.'

'Who?'

Crap! He concentrated on helping Sarah into her booster seat, hoping she'd forget. Some hope.

'Who was poorly, Daddy? Was it one of my friends?'

'Liv,' he admitted reluctantly. 'Did you stay up very late?'

'Yup!' She grinned happily. 'Why is Liv poorly? Is she OK? I like Liv. I don't want her to be poorly.'

'She's not poorly, poorly.' Callum climbed into the driver's seat. 'She just banged her head.'

'Oh no.' She fell quiet for a few seconds. '*Daddeeeey*?'

Callum winced, recognising the tone that he was almost always powerless to resist. 'Yes, munchkin.'

'I think we should go see Livvy.'

'We're going home. She's probably busy. Or having a rest.'

'But what if she's not?'

'She probably is. And you did say I smelled and needed a shower.'

'*Pleeeease Daddeeeey*. I want to go see Livvy and give her a magic cake. I have to. I really like her and I don't want her to be sad and alone if she feels poorly. She looked after me when I was poorly, and I want to give her a magic cake. Please, please, please, please, please!'

'OK, OK.' Callum rubbed his eyes tiredly. 'But if she doesn't answer, we'll leave the cake by the front door and not disturb her, OK?'

'OK. But she's going to be awake.'

'You sound very sure.' Callum watched her in the rearview mirror.

'I am.' Sarah smiled cheerfully.

* * *

Liv looked up from the weeding she was trying to do when a car pulled up, and two doors slammed. 'Hey.' She grinned at Callum. 'Did you forget something?'

'Hi Livvy!' Sarah boosted herself up on the wall so she could wave. 'Is your head feeling better?'

'Yes, thank you. Did you have fun at your sleepover?'

'Yes, thank you.' Liv had to smile at how well the little girl mimicked her tone. 'I bringed you a magic cake.'

'Did you really?'

'Uh huh.'

'You better come in then.' Liv gestured to the gate. Almost before she'd finished speaking, Sarah had raced through — her patience worn out — and flung herself at Liv.

'Daddy said you weren't feeling well. So I bringed you cake. I made it yesterday.' She looked up at Liv, her arms still wrapped around her waist. The look of adoration in the little girl's eyes was so open and unabashed that Liv felt her throat thicken with emotion. What had she done to deserve such sweetness? She felt completely unworthy.

'That's really kind. Thank you.'

'You're welcome! You looked after me when I got sick at school. And cake makes most things better. Except sick tummies. But Daddy said you had a banged head, and that's not the same as tummy sick, so you can have cake, right?'

'Right. Thank you so much for bringing me some. Do you and your dad want to have a drink, and share the cake with me?' Her eyes flicked up to meet Callum's. She didn't want to put him in an awkward situation, but did want him to say yes — and it was only polite to invite them in. 'Unless you need to race home?'

'Say yes, Daddy. Please.' Sarah didn't wait for his response, instead threading her fingers through Liv's and pulling her towards the house, chatting nineteen to the dozen.

'I guess we're coming in for tea.' Callum shot Liv a smile that filled her with warmth.

'Can I see the fairy well?' Sarah tugged at her hand.

'I told you, Sarah, I don't think there is one.'

'There really is.' She paused at the door and peered in the bucket where Liv had been dropping weeds she'd pulled up. 'Don't you like purple bells?'

'What?'

Sarah picked up one of the "weeds" and showed it to Liv. 'Grandma calls them bell flowers. They have a proper name but I can't remember it.'

'Campanula,' Callum murmured quietly, making Liv glance at him in surprise.

'Yup.' Sarah nodded. 'You shouldn't pull them up. They don't look good now, but they sleep in winter then grow again and flower in summer. They're only just waking up now, that's why they're not pretty yet. That's what Grandma says.'

'Oops.' Liv laughed. 'Maybe you can help show me what are weeds and what aren't. I'm not very good at gardening, but I want to keep it pretty.'

'OK. My grandma taught me lots.' She paused and looked up at Liv with an expression that, on anyone else, Liv would have called sly. 'Daddy knows lots about plants too.'

'Really?' Liv ushered them into the kitchen.

'A bit,' Callum admitted with a shrug. 'Mum loves her garden, and I got some lessons growing up.'

'I don't think I'd pictured you as the gardener type.'

'It's cool. And did you know lots of medicines come from plants?' Sarah asked. 'That's why you shouldn't eat things in the garden. Plus you might accidentally eat a fairy's flower and that wouldn't be a good idea. You don't want to upset fairies.'

'No, I suppose you don't,' Liv mused as she filled the kettle. 'Would you like some juice, Sarah?'

'Yes please. Can I go see the fairy well?'

Liv shook her head. 'I'm really sorry, Sarah. But there isn't one.'

'Yes, there is!'

'Sarah, don't be argumentative, please.' Callum shot her an apologetic glance. 'It's Liv's cottage, and if she says there isn't a well, then there isn't a well. You're probably thinking of a different cottage.'

'I'm not!' Sarah's bottom lip stuck out and trembled slightly, and Liv instantly felt bad.

'If it's OK with your dad — and only if he says it is — maybe you can go out in the garden while I make our drinks. Then you can see that there's no well, and maybe we can figure out which cottage does have it.'

'Can I, Daddy?'

Liv winced as Callum rolled his eyes.

'Sure.' He watched as she bounded out the door. 'Sorry. We've disturbed you.'

'It's really fine.' Liv smiled, surprising herself at how "fine" it really was. 'Besides, it sounds like you rescued the owners' flowers.'

'Always glad to be of service.' He grinned as he took the steaming cup from her hands. 'I think we should maybe wait until Sarah's back before we open the cakes. Though I've no idea what they'll be like!'

'Of course we should. And I'm sure they'll be fine. To be honest, even if they're not, I'll still say they are. Before I came to Broclington, I couldn't have told you the last time someone made me a cake. Now it's becoming a weekly occurrence!'

'It's like that round here. Everyone looks out for everyone else, and they try to do nice little things for each other — like bake cakes and bring food when someone's feeling a bit down.'

'It's very different.'

'Different good?'

'Very good.' Even as she said it, Liv was aware she was only just starting to understand how true that was. Back in London, she hadn't even known the names of all her neighbours, let alone everyone in the building. Everyone was so busy, so involved in their own fast-paced lives, that they didn't have time for much else. People had their own groups of friends, their own hangouts. Instead of talking to someone in the elevator, or on the train, people tapped furiously at their phones, answering emails, and messaging, messaging, messaging non-stop — trying to make every second of the day count. She'd been as bad, visiting her online communities and chatting to friends she'd never met.

She shook her head at the ridiculousness of it all. She'd been so caught up in the never-ending pace of it all, that she hadn't realised how much she was missing. In Broclington, people made time, and cakes, for each other. They smiled, and talked to each other, and they talked to *her*, making her feel welcome. She was already feeling more at home than she could remember feeling in years.

And it was as refreshing to her heart and soul as the sweet, fresh air was to her nose.

'Hello.' Callum waved his hand across her face. 'You still here?'

'Yeah, sorry.'

'You looked a million miles away.'

'No.' She laughed softly. 'Not quite that far.'

'Um, how big is your garden?' Callum glanced towards the door.

'Not that big. But it's enclosed and safe.'

'I don't doubt it. But I should probably still see what she's up to.'

* * *

Callum stared at the mess and ran his fingers through his hair. Vines, ivy and bindweed littered the ground, and the lawn and pathway were sprinkled with clumps of dirt and leaves that had been torn up by small fingers. 'Sarah, what have you done?' His jaw clenched, and he had to fight to stop his teeth from grinding. 'You know better than to damage plants.'

'But Daddy . . .'

'But nothing. This is Liv's garden, not yours. How would you like it if Liv came into your bedroom and broke your toys?'

'Callum, it's OK, they're just plants. They'll grow again.'

'That's very kind of you, Liv, but it's not acceptable to damage other people's things.' He glared at his daughter. 'Look at the damage you've done to Liv's nice garden. What were you thinking? Actually no, I don't care. There's no excuse for this. Apologise to Dr Emery, and then we're going home where you will be getting no TV or computer or tablet privileges. Do you understand?'

'Yes.' Sarah stared at the ground as her foot scuffed back and forth against the path.

'Don't you have something to say to Liv?'

'I'm very sorry for damaging your plants. Even if they are just weeds.' After a few more scuffs of her foot, she looked up at Liv, her eyes sparkling with defiance and mischief. 'But I found the fairy well.'

'You did?' Liv was shocked.

'Yup.' Sarah grabbed her hand and pulled her past the large tree, towards the curved stone seat where she so often sat to have her breakfast.

* * *

Liv gasped as she rounded the tree. The rest of the garden was far messier than what she'd already seen, with bare earth and stripped, bare stems where there had once been bright green leaves and flowers. But now, the curve of what she'd thought had just been an old stone seat seemed to continue, sweeping towards the edge of the property in a rustic circle, exposed from its green veil. It was muddy and still partly buried, but now Liv could clearly see its true shape.

'You know, your dad's right. I should be angry at you for all the mess, but now I'm more worried that you could have been hurt.'

'How? It's only plants.'

'You could have . . .' Liv had to swallow hard to finish the sentence. 'You could have slipped and fallen.'

Sarah laughed. 'I wouldn't have fallen in. I was careful. Everyone knows fairy circles are dangerous.'

'You're still in a lot of trouble, young lady.' Callum's voice was stern, but Liv was barely listening.

Instead, she knelt and grabbed a loose branch to try and brush away some of the soil that still covered the ancient stones. Now that the top level of plants and debris had been removed — and deposited all over the garden, thanks to Sarah — Liv could see that the carvings she'd idly traced during many a morning coffee out here were part of detailed swirls that danced and dipped in and out of the remaining greenery and weeds. When she peered inside of the circular bench, or well as she'd now have to think of it, she could see that the greenery — while thick and lush — was growing across darkness that hinted at a depth she hadn't noticed before.

'I was right, wasn't I?' Sarah knelt beside her, and pulled away a few more leaves. 'Isn't it pretty?'

'It really is. I'm going to have to call my landlord and see if I can get permission to uncover it all properly. It must be hundreds of years old, and it would be really cool to reveal it all.' She glanced up when Callum cleared his throat. 'But what you did wasn't good. You could have been hurt, and you shouldn't go changing other people's things without asking them first.'

'Even when it's a lost fairy well?'

'Even if there's a lost fairy well.' She glanced up at Callum again. 'You know, if my landlord is happy for me to uncover the well properly, there's going to be a lot of work to do.'

Callum nodded. 'There's a lot to do just clearing up this mess.'

'Maybe the person who made the mess, should help clear it up,' Liv offered.

Callum grinned at her over Sarah's head, his eyes sparkling. 'Maybe they should.'

'Me? Really?' Sarah looked between them both, her eyes wide.

'Yes. And you have to rake up every single leaf. Do you understand?'

'Yes, Daddy.' Sarah was clearly trying not to grin.

'Right. We'd better get you home and cleaned up.'

'OK.' Sarah hung back next to Liv while Callum shook his head at the mess once more, and headed up the garden path. 'Can I tell you something now?' Sarah said.

'Sure.'

'It's a secret. You have to promise not to tell.'

'OK.' Liv smiled.

'I like gardening with Grandma. I think I will like gardening with you.'

'Maybe it's not a very good punishment if you enjoy it,' Liv mused aloud.

'That's why it's a secret, silly.' Sarah laughed, and Liv found herself joining in.

'I think I'm going to like gardening with you too. But you're right, let's not tell your dad that!'

'Deal!' She wove her fingers through Liv's, and smiled up at her as they walked up the path.

'What's that?' Callum asked as they giggled their way into the kitchen.

'Nothing, Daddy.'

He glanced at Liv, who shrugged. It was a harmless enough secret between her and Sarah, and she suspected Callum knew the truth anyway. And the look on the little girl's face warmed her heart.

'OK then. We should get going. Rest up, and feel better soon.'

'I will, I promise.'

'And if you're feeling better, maybe this little monster of mine can come round after lunch tomorrow, and spend her Sunday afternoon helping clear up the mess she's made in your garden. And next weekend too, if it's still needed. I can bring my laptop and work on finishing off the proposal while she tidies up.'

'Only if you're sure.'

'I am.' Sarah answered for both of them, and Liv had to smother a smile.

'Well, I'm sure I'll be feeling much better by then.'

'See you tomorrow, Livvy. Enjoy your cake!'

'I will do. And thank you again for bringing them by, and finding the well.' She waved and smiled to herself as she shut the door behind them, and headed back into the kitchen. She opened the cardboard cupcake box and smiled again. Inside, the pink cakes were messy and slightly skew-whiff, but covered in sparkles and made with such love that just looking at them made her feel a little better. They truly did have some sort of magic.

CHAPTER SIX

Noise infiltrated Callum's dreams, dragging him awake. He rolled over and hit the snooze button, figuring he might get just a few more minutes of peace before . . . *Thump*! The whole bed shook as Sarah launched herself at him.

'Morning Daddy.' She bounced up and down.

'Morning Sarey-fairy.' He grabbed her and tickled her, laughing as she squealed. 'What's this, you're already dressed. How come you're up so early?'

'Too excited to sleep. It's my last day gardening with Livvy and I'm so excited to see Uncle Jake and Summer next week! Do you think Tilly will be at their welcome home party too?'

'I don't know.'

'I hope she is. I like Tilly. Do you think I can have a dog like Tilly one day?' She snuggled against him, tucking her hands against her cheek and making his heart melt.

'Maybe when you're a bit older.' He didn't fancy restarting this argument. 'This is nice. You used to do this all the time when you were little.'

'I know.' She yanked the pillow out from under his head and thumped him with it. 'Get up!'

'It's still early, Sarah.' He groaned.

'But quicker you get up the quicker I can see Livvy.' She grabbed the duvet and yanked it back.

'All right, all right.' He rubbed the sleep out of his eyes. 'I'm getting up.' He knew he needed to get moving. The time Sarah had been spending gardening with Liv had meant he'd been able to work on finishing the proposal to keep the surgery open — one more read-through and he'd be ready to submit.

The truth was, the proposal had been ready for a while, but the thought of actually sending it to the clinical commissioning group was something he was still struggling to get his head around. But he pushed the worries back, along with what was left of his bed clothes, and stumbled to the bathroom. He'd ask Liv if she minded watching Sarah for a few hours, and try to read it one last time before sending it off.

* * *

Liv gasped in surprise when the cool water hit her warm neck and trickled down her back. She spun around to find Sarah looking sheepish, the dripping hose half hidden behind her back.

'I'm sorry.' Sarah shrugged, nibbling on her lower lip as she watched Liv carefully. 'It just went off.'

'Oh it did, did it?' She advanced on the little girl.

'Umm.'

'Umm, indeed.' She pounced, grabbing Sarah and tickling her as she tried to get the hose away, getting soaked in the process and laughing out loud. When she dropped the hose, Sarah seized it and gleefully chased Liv around the garden, spraying her with water and giggles.

Liv's hair and clothes were plastered against her skin, cooling in the heat and washing away the dust and sweat from the garden. She laughed as Sarah sent the water gushing into the air, flinging a shimmering rainbow over the ancient well as the light played with the glistening droplets. For a few long moments the droplets seemed to hang in the air, making the rainbow appear almost tangible enough to touch.

She squealed and danced away again when Sarah flicked the water towards her — and collided with a solid, warm chest that smelt of musk and sweat.

'Hi.' She looked up, laughter still teasing her lips into a joyful smile.

'Er, hi.' For some reason, Callum was struggling to meet her gaze and looked decidedly uncomfortable.

Liv followed his gaze and felt the heat race across her chest and up her throat when she realised the formerly pale blue T-shirt had become almost transparent under Sarah's attack, and moulded itself to her breasts. She bit her lip as she looked up and met his gaze, which heated her cheeks even further. Mischief flared and despite her best resolutions, and despite knowing better, she couldn't help a cheeky grin.

'See something you like?' She kept her voice low and was rewarded when his eyes flicked lower again. This was *interesting*. His gaze locked with hers again, and warmth flushed through her stomach and lower body. Despite the cold, wet clothes clinging to her, her skin tingled and flared with heat, and she was scared, excited and relieved to see the same heat burning in his eyes.

'Liv . . .' His voice was husky in his throat, his hands scorching through her thin T-shirt as he reached up and caught her shoulders. He gasped, the sound deep, as water hit him and Sarah's giggle filled the garden. But for a few moments, Liv struggled to focus on anything but the look on his face. She regretted teasing him as her mind wandered to places that she wasn't ready to go: what other actions would draw similar noises from him?

The water hit her again, dragging her from her thoughts and firmly back to her sunny garden. She looked down at her wet clothes and up at Callum's damp hair, forcing herself not to focus on *his* own wet T-shirt that clung to his broad chest.

'I guess I should go get some towels, or something.'

'Probably a good idea.' He shook his wet hair out of his eyes, sprinkling her with shimmering droplets. 'And I feel like I should apologise for my daughter. Again. She was supposed to be helping, and now you're soaking wet instead.'

'It's fine. We've had fun. She's a really great kid. I'll go grab some towels and something dry.'

* * *

Callum struggled to tear his eyes away from Liv as she walked up the garden path, her hips swaying back and forth in the worn denim shorts that fit far too well for his comfort.

'Daddy, are you listening?' Sarah's fingers wove through his, giving him a shot of guilt. He'd come outside to tell his daughter it was time to go, and instead she'd caught him ogling Liv like some horny kid. 'Come see the fairy's magic well!'

'OK.' He threw a final glance after Liv before letting Sarah tug him further down the garden. 'Wow, you've done really well.'

'I know! Isn't it great?'

'It really is.' He wasn't exaggerating. The whole, sweeping circle had been cleared of ivy, bindweed, vines, nettles and what looked like a few hundred yards of brambles. The stones had been brushed and washed clean of the dirt and debris of hundreds of years, leaving them to sparkle and shimmer as the sun bounced off the granite. The strange carvings seemed to twist and move with newly uncovered shadows. He traced one of the swirling patterns, leaving his finger tingling from the rough stone. 'You've really done all this in a couple of weekends?'

'Yes! And we put magic lights in the tree.' He followed Sarah's finger as she pointed them out. 'Livvy says the sun charges them in the day and they turn on when it gets dark. Isn't that cool?'

'Very cool.'

'Do you think the fairies will like them?'

'If I was a fairy, I'd like them.' Liv put down the tray she was carrying and offered Callum a towel that she had draped over her shoulder. Her hair was still damp and tousled, and she wasn't wearing a scrap of make-up — he was damned if that didn't make her even more attractive. When she knelt to wrap the second fluffy towel around Sarah, he buried his own face in the soft cotton and inhaled the honeyed scent that he remembered so well from the night Liv had slept wrapped in his arms on the couch just a few dozen steps from where they stood now.

He rubbed his hair brusquely, forcing the memories of Liv in his arms firmly out of his mind. When he was done, Liv smiled at him and offered a glass of lemonade that was already frosting in the warmth of the sun. 'Thanks.'

'So, you've seen our work, how's yours?' Liv asked.

'Yeah, have you saved the surgery now?' Sarah looked up at him with such trust that he felt like he'd been punched in the gut.

'The proposal is as good as I think it can be.' He fiddled with the edge of the towel. 'If I'm totally honest, I'm worried. The clinical commissioning group need to save money, and we're submitting an idea that will cost them even more.'

'Initially.' Liv nodded. 'But longer term it will save them a small fortune, free up hospital beds, and extend services.'

'It's the "initially" bit that I'm worried about.'

'But you said yourself that it was the only idea they've shown any interest in.'

'I know. I don't have any choice but to submit it, and hope. But it's a lot of money. A huge amount.'

'You can have my money box. I've got lots of pennies.' Sarah's offer filled him with equal amounts of guilt and pride. Pride because somehow, he had raised this incredible, caring, sweet little person — and guilt that he couldn't protect her from such worries.

'That's a really nice offer.' He wrapped his arm around her, squeezing her tightly. 'But I think we might need a little bit more than your money box.'

'OK.' She wriggled against him and pulled something out of her pocket and seized his hand. 'Here you go.'

103

Callum peered down at the couple of coins and shiny button resting in his palm, and then looked back up at his daughter's proud face. 'You know, you really are one of the best little girls ever.'

'I couldn't agree more.' Liv held up her glass. 'You helped me find a magical fairy well. Cheers!'

'Cheers!' The glasses chinked together.

Sarah perched on the edge of the well and swung her feet back and forth.

'Be careful!' Callum and Liv shared an amused glance as they spoke simultaneously.

'I'm fine,' Sarah argued as Callum sat next to her, his spare arm firmly behind her back to make sure she couldn't slip backwards. 'It's a fairy well.'

'Fairy well or not, gravity still applies,' Callum chided. 'You could still slip and fall.'

'Nuh uh.' Sarah wriggled to lean over her dad's arm and peer into the darkness.

'Sarah, you need to be more careful.' He grabbed the waistband of her shorts. 'If you slipped and fell in, you could be badly hurt.'

'I *am* being careful!' she argued. 'But I needed to look.'

'What is it you're looking for?' Liv peered over the edge of the well with them.

'Magic.'

Callum tried not to roll his eyes at Sarah's answer. As much as he wanted to fill her world with everything good, and encourage her imagination, he struggled when it came to the fairies and unicorns that seemed to fill her life.

'Can you see any?' Liv asked earnestly.

Maybe it was a girl thing, and that was why he couldn't understand.

'No. But fairies hide lots. Daddy, can I have my button back?'

'Here you go, Sarey-fairy.' He watched as she held the button in her fist, squeezing so tightly that her small knuckles turned white as she whispered something, eyes shut and face scrunched-up in concentration. After a few seconds she grinned at him and threw the button into the well. They watched as it bounced off the ancient stones, plinking as it hit and flashing in the sunlight.

She grinned up at them both. 'Your turn.'

'Our turn to what?'

She rolled her eyes. 'To give the fairies a gift and make your wishes. For the people with the money to like your ideas and give you the money you need for the surgery.'

'*Riiiight.*' Callum nodded, humouring her. It was what good parents were supposed to do, he was sure of that.

'Can't hurt.' Liv shrugged. 'What type of gift would a fairy like?'

'They like shiny things.' Sarah nodded knowingly.

'Like coins?'

'If they're shiny.'

'OK.' She held her hand out to Callum.

'Two of the shiniest coins, coming right up.' He tried not to notice when Liv's fingers brushed the sensitive skin of his palm as she picked out a bright silver five-pence piece.

'It's your turn.' They both watched him expectantly.

'OK.' He tried not to roll his eyes at the ridiculousness of it all as if a wish would be able to magic up money from the cash-strapped CCG.

'Go on, Daddy. Throw in your wish and gift.'

What the hell? He tossed the coin in and turned away. At least it would keep Sarah happy.

* * *

'It's your turn, Liv!' Sarah watched her expectantly, and suddenly the coin in her hand felt a lot heavier than it had any right to. Liv curled her fingers around it tightly, and felt its smooth edges dig into her palm. Somehow, the childish game had taken on much more significance and she found herself struggling to let go of the coin — of the wish — that she held in her fist. Just like it had so many times in her past, in emergency situations, the world slowed around her and sounds became muted as complete focus took over.

But instead of a patient and a medical problem, the realisation that snapped her thoughts into clear focus was the understanding that suddenly — for the first time that she could remember — she had something she really, *really* wanted to wish for. It was Broclington. It was her patients, and feeling like she was part of a community. It was the new friends she'd made. And it was Sarah and Callum — whatever they were, and whatever they'd become to her. The happiness she felt around her, as tangible as if she'd wrapped herself in a cosy blanket, was what she wanted to wish for. It was what she wanted to keep.

She squeezed the coin — her wish — even more tightly in her hand, hoping that somehow the magic Sarah so fervently believed in could be real, before releasing it into the well. She watched as it flashed and twinkled, bouncing off the ancient stones. For the moment before it disappeared, it seemed to hang in the air, before vanishing with the faintest of splashes.

'What did you wish for?' Callum watched her with interest.

'No!' Sarah squealed. 'It's fairy magic. If you tell your wish too soon, it won't come true. You can only tell when it comes true. And only then if you really want to!'

'Apparently it's a secret.' Liv shrugged, relieved that she didn't have to share her innermost thoughts, or make up a trite lie.

'We should get going, munchkin.' Callum held out his hand to Sarah.

'Do we have to?'

'Yes, we have to.' He mimicked her tone almost exactly, and Liv found herself having to smother a laugh. 'I have things to do, Liv has things to do, and I'm pretty sure you have homework.'

'Only reading and drawing.'

'It's still homework.' He glanced at Liv. 'And homework is important, right?'

'Right.' She nodded firmly. 'If me and your dad hadn't done our homework when we were younger, we wouldn't have been allowed to become doctors.'

'All right then.' Sarah sighed dramatically, and Liv could see Callum struggling not to laugh.

'Say thank you to Liv for having us visit today.'

'Thank you, Liv,' Sarah parroted obediently before wrapping her arms around Liv's waist. 'But I'll see you next weekend.'

'Maybe.' Liv nodded, not wanting to promise anything, or put Callum in an awkward position.

'Yes you will. At the party.'

'What party?'

'The one for Summer being better and coming home.'

'Summer? Isn't she the daughter of the other nurse? The one who's been in America?'

'Yup. Her mum works with Dad. And Uncle Jake and her mum are boyfriend and girlfriend. Summer was sick, but she's better now, 'coz Santa came to Broclington in summer to make sure she could get the special medicine and now we get two Christmases. But only in Broclington.'

'OK.' Liv wasn't sure she understood, or how she was supposed to respond.

'You are coming to the party, aren't you?'

'I don't think I'm invited.' She tried not to feel left out as she said the words. It was obviously a family event, but she still felt the pang at the reminder she was only a temporary fixture in their lives.

'Dad! Why didn't you invite Liv to the party?'

'You really don't have to.' Liv felt awkward beyond words, aware Callum had just been very effectively backed into a social corner, and that she definitely didn't want to receive a pity invite.

'I had planned to. But—' he leaned down to tweak Sarah's nose — 'I got distracted by a mucky little munchkin digging up someone's garden, and hadn't had a chance yet.'

'So ask her now!'

Callum shot her a lopsided grin that made Liv's insides squirm in the most delicious way. 'You heard her ladyship. Would you like to come to a party next weekend? It won't be a big deal: BBQ, few drinks, that type of thing.'

'And cake!'

He grinned over Summer's head, and rolled his eyes. 'And cake, of course.'

'You really don't have to. Not if it's a family thing.'

'Millie and the rest of the surgery staff and a few other people will be there too. And it would be good for you to meet Evelyn — you'll be working with her soon enough. If you don't have anything else planned?'

'No, I don't. And it sounds lovely.' Liv surprised herself by meaning the words. She hadn't especially liked parties — or the soirees that passed for them in the life she'd had with Mike — but a relaxed, sunny BBQ with the friends she'd already made at work? That sounded much more up her street.

She glanced at the old, curved stone of the well suspiciously. Surely not?

CHAPTER SEVEN

'Liv, I need you.' The words she'd thought she'd wanted to hear from Callum were tainted by the panic that filled his usually calm voice and chilled her to the bone. 'With your OB kit. The cottage opposite the police station.'

'Sergeant Brown's place?' She loaded up the bag with all the things she hoped she wouldn't need, but knew could make the difference between things going badly and really going badly.

'Yeah, his wife's expecting their second. There's an ambulance on route but . . .'

She didn't need him to finish the sentence. 'I'm closer. I'm on my way,' she promised.

'Thanks — just, Liv?'

'Yes?'

'Please hurry.'

'I will.'

She slammed the door behind her, not bothering to check that it locked and threw herself and her bag into the car. She wasn't even a mile away, but knew that every second could count, so slammed the car into gear and tore out of the small driveway. She drove as quickly as she dared, not wanting to risk an accident, but also not wanting to leave Callum to deal with whatever pregnancy emergency had called them both out on a Sunday morning.

The drive seemed to take an age, and by the time her tyres hit the kerb outside the address she'd been given, her pulse was racing with the familiar adrenaline blasting through her circulatory system. She forced herself to calm her breath instead of taking the gulping gasps she wanted and raced up the garden path. There was no paramedic parked in the street, but they would doubtless be on their way.

'They're all upstairs.' A worried-looking woman holding a toddler met her by the open door.

She was halfway up the stairs when she heard the all too familiar keening cry of a woman in active labour, followed by muted male soothing. She took a second to take a deep breath at the door. The last thing her patient needed to see was a panicked doctor.

'Hi, Liv.' Callum's relief at seeing her was painted across his face, and she hoped her newest patient couldn't read it as easily as she could. 'This is Marie. And you know Harry already. Marie, this is Dr Olivia — Liv — Emery. This is their second baby. Marie's thirty-seven and a half weeks, ten centimetres dilation and baby is showing a bit of distress on the monitor . . . I could really use your expertise.'

'Hi, Marie.' Liv shot her what she hoped was a reassuring smile as she snapped on her gloves. 'I'm Liv Emery. I don't know if Callum's told you, but I've got a background in obstetrics and emergency medicine. I'm going to help you. I'll just take a quick look, all right?'

Marie nodded, her face pale against the pillows. 'It feels different from last time. Something isn't right.'

Liv saw the problem immediately: a partially prolapsed cord. 'How far apart are contractions?'

Marie's groan and arched back answered her question before Callum could, and she saw the cord bulge as the rapid bleep of the baby's heart changed in a worrying direction. 'All right, Marie. I need you to just breathe through this one contraction and not push. I know it's going against what your body wants to do, but please try so, so hard not to push right now. Dad, you can help her through this. You've been to the classes and remember the breathing, right?' She turned to Callum. 'Please tell me the ambulance will be here soon.'

He shook his head, a tiny motion that replaced the warmth in Liv's body with ice. What she needed was a full obstetrics surgical suite, an experienced anaesthesiologist and theatre nurses, and preferably a neo-natal ICU nearby. What she had was a baby in distress, a terrified mother and father, and Callum.

'OK, Marie. Just concentrate on your breathing. I'm just going to try and relieve the pressure a bit.' She slid her fingers into place, holding the baby's head in a better position. 'Just concentrate on your breathing, and we'll talk in a minute. Just breathe. There's a good girl. You're doing so, so well.' She coaxed her through the rest of the contraction.

'All right, you've done really well.' Liv rubbed her leg soothingly.

'OK.' Marie nodded eagerly.

'Besides, you've got two doctors and the local police sergeant as your husband. You wouldn't get this much attention even if you were in the hospital.' She shot a wink to the sergeant. 'Now, I need you to stay calm, and we're all going to work together to get baby here as soon as possible. You've got something called a cord prolapse. That means the umbilical cord is trying to come out first, and baby is pressing on it when you have a contraction.'

'Oh my God, is that bad? That sounds bad!' Her husband started to panic.

'Harry, she knows what she's doing.' Marie's faith in her touched her deeply, and made her more determined than ever to make sure this was a good outcome for them all. 'You heard what she said, she's a specialist. Right, Dr Callum?'

'One of the best I know.' He nodded, and Liv's heart warmed a bit. She knew what she was doing, and Callum knew that she did too. His confidence in her bolstered her own.

'But it's bad?' Harry persisted.

'If we don't get baby out fast, it could be. But we're not talking about that, because we're all going to work together to bring baby into the world. OK?' She pulled the emergency delivery kit out of her bag and spread it out beneath Marie's akimbo legs. 'Harry, do you want to come here and loop your arm around Marie's leg? We need to keep her knees up to help keep her pelvis in the best position. And it will give her something to brace against. Now, Marie, with your next contraction I'm going to try and help you. I need you to just keep breathing, and when I tell you — and not before — I want you to push harder than you've ever pushed before, OK?'

'How can I help?' Callum was by her elbow, gloved up and reassuring.

'Take her other leg. Keep an eye on the monitor, and Marie, and be ready to catch.' She tore open the packet that had kept the forceps sterile. 'I'm really sorry, Marie, but this next bit is going to be uncomfortable.' She angled the forceps and slid them into place, using years of experience to make sure that the positioning was the best she could get it, and the cord was as protected as possible.

'It's coming. *Ohhhh*, I really need to push . . .'

'Just breathe, Marie.' Liv checked the positioning of the forceps and cord before putting her weight behind the shiny silver instruments she hoped would help her guide the baby safely into the world. 'OK. Now, Marie. *Push*!' She leaned back, concentrating on keeping the tension perfect. She carefully applied more and more pressure, pulling harder and harder.

'Come on, Marie. Really bear down and push. As hard as you can.' Callum's voice was demanding and urgent.

Finally, finally, after what felt like an age, Liv felt the baby start to move and carefully eased him towards daylight, maintaining the tension until she could see a head full of thick dark hair, visible even beneath the blood and mucus of birth. 'OK, Marie, I've got the head. Stop pushing and just breathe again. Just take a moment to relax, and then you're going to give me one more really big push, and then you'll be able to say hello to your newest family member.'

'Did you hear that?' Harry looked at his wife with utter amazement. 'We've nearly got a new baby. You're doing so, so well.'

'You really are,' Liv agreed as she slid her hands in position to deliver the shoulders. 'Callum, can you be ready with the cord clips and scissors?'

'Ready.'

'All right, Marie, one more big push and you can meet your baby. Push hard now, really, really *hard*!' She supported the baby's head while helping the first shoulder to be delivered. 'Nearly there, keep going, Marie!' A few moments later the other shoulder was out and Liv was able to gently guide the baby into the world. He was a little floppy and lacked the healthy pink she'd really want to see. She could feel the weight of Callum's gaze as she snapped the clamps quickly into position, and snipped the cord.

'Is it a boy or girl?' Harry leaned forward eagerly. 'We wanted to wait to find out.'

'A boy. You have a son.' Liv tapped the bottom of his feet, willing him to take a breath.

'Why isn't he crying? Is he all right?' Marie struggled to sit up.

'Just give me a moment.' Liv held her hand out for the suction bulb Callum was holding ready. She used it to suction the mucus and other delivery muck from the baby's nose and mouth before giving his chest a brisk rub. 'Come on, little guy.'

'Oh my God, he's not breathing. Oh please, God, no!' Marie started to shake and cry.

Liv did her best to focus, and gave the baby a few firm taps to the back and closed her eyes in relief when she felt him gasp. When he let out his first mewling whimper, she let out a breath that she hadn't even realised she'd been holding.

She smiled as she listened to his chest, gently pressing the stethoscope to his rapidly moving ribs. Tenderly, she wrapped him in a blanket and held him up for his parents to see. 'You have a boy. A beautiful, healthy little boy. Here you go, Dad. You and Mum can give him a nice cuddle for a few minutes. If we need to, we can give him some oxygen, but he looks like he's pinking up nicely.'

'You've done a brilliant job, Marie,' Callum praised her. 'You too, Liv.'

'Nah—' she flushed — 'Marie did all the hard work, I just offered some guidance.' She knew it had been more than that, but didn't want to make a big deal of things. 'Can I use your bathroom please, Harry?'

He nodded, not taking his eyes off his son. 'Second door on the left.'

'Great. We're just going to clean up and give you three a few moments of privacy, but we'll be within calling distance. Marie, I'll be back in a minute. But call me if you feel like the afterbirth is going to come more quickly.'

'OK.' She looked up and caught Liv's gaze. 'Thank you. So, so much. Thank you.'

'You're more than welcome.' Liv's voice caught in her throat as she headed to the bathroom.

* * *

Callum found her sitting on the edge of the bath a few moments later, staring at her hands still encased in their bloody gloves. He shook the yellow hazmat bag open and placed it on the side. 'Thought you'd be needing this.'

'Thanks.' Liv's voice was shaky.

'You were amazing,' he told her honestly. 'You just saved his life.'

'Yeah, I think I just did, didn't I?' She stripped off the gloves and dumped them in the bag before soaping up her hands.

'No question about it.' He handed her a towel.

'Thanks.' She dried her hands, avoiding his gaze.

'Out with it.'

114

'What?'

'There's clearly something bothering you, Liv. You can trust me. What is it?'

She rounded on him, hands on hips. 'What the hell happened, Callum? Why is Marie here at home when she should have been in a hospital? Where is the ambulance and paramedics? Do you know how dangerous this was? How often an umbilical cord prolapse requires an emergency C-section? What if I hadn't been able to relieve the pressure on the cord? What if forceps hadn't been enough? Callum, *what if I hadn't been here?*'

'But you are here, Liv, and you were able to help. More than that, you saved a life. You were amazing.'

'But I shouldn't have had to be!' she hissed angrily. 'Marie should never have been put in this position. *We* shouldn't have been put in this position.' She sank back down onto the edge of the bath. 'What happened?'

'Apparently, Marie went to the hospital yesterday, but wasn't dilated and the pains were intermittent enough to be put down to Braxton Hicks. Her first baby was late, and the labour was lengthy. She was two and a half weeks from her due date, so the hospital sent her home. Her waters broke an hour or so ago, and an ambulance was dispatched but apparently there was an accident that meant the call was re-prioritised.'

'Wow. So much for eight minutes.'

'Eight minutes? I don't think ambulances have ever been that quick round here.'

'No, I guess not.' Liv sighed and seemed to crumple where she sat. Before he'd even thought about it, his arms were around her and he'd pulled her against his chest where he held her.

Eventually she pushed away from him. 'Sorry, I just . . . felt a bit overwhelmed.'

'You really don't need to explain. I understand.'

'I know you do.'

'This situation should never have happened, but you being here meant it was OK. You're bloody brilliant, Liv.'

She shot him a grateful, slightly embarrassed smile. 'I should go and check on our patients.'

'We should.' He stepped aside and gave her a grin. 'After you, Dr Emery.'

'Well, thank you very much, Dr Macpearson.'

She knocked on the bedroom doorframe. 'So, how are you three doing?'

'We're really good.' Marie smiled at her tiredly. 'I think he's getting his colour nicely now, don't you?'

'Let's have a look.' Liv gently pulled away the blanket and smiled. 'I agree, he is looking good. Almost as if nothing unusual had happened at all.'

'We will need to bathe him and clean him up.' Callum rested a finger against the baby's tiny hand and smiled when he squeezed it tightly. He bounced the hand up and down gently and smiled when the baby hung on. 'Look, he's a strong little chap.'

'You think he's going to be OK?'

'Well, Liv is the expert, but I think he's looking good.'

'I wholeheartedly agree.' Liv smiled up at him. 'But we'll let the paramedics take a look. They might want to take you both to the hospital, just to check you over, make sure you get the attention you deserve, and that you're both fit and well. And, I'm afraid you might need a couple of stitches. I'm really sorry about that.'

'It doesn't matter.' Marie stroked her baby's cheek gently. 'He's here, and he's safe, and we have you both to thank for it. There aren't enough words to say it, but thank you.'

'You're more than welcome,' Liv replied honestly. 'I'm really glad I was able to help.'

'So are we.' Harry sat behind his wife, his arm cradling her and his new son. 'That's why we're planning to call him Oliver Callum.'

'Wow, are you sure?' Callum glanced at Liv, whose eyes had grown glossy and bright.

'We can't think of anything better than to name him after the doctors who saved his life.' Marie smiled warmly at them both. 'If you're OK with it?'

'OK?' Liv's voice trembled. 'I'm completely honoured.' She leaned over the bed. 'Hi, Oliver Callum, welcome to the world. You sure know how to make an entrance.'

Callum watched as she cooed over the baby, and felt his stomach twist with sadness and anger; she really didn't deserve all the pain that had been dealt her. As he watched, he realised he was really, really going to miss her. They'd worked together so well that he wished he could find a way to keep her in Broclington. For far, far longer than the few weeks she had left.

* * *

Liv looked up from where she was examining the placenta. Its delivery had been far easier, and far less dramatic that Oliver Callum's entrance into the world. She smiled to herself as she folded the delivery pack around it, wrapping it up safely for disposal. Every time she looked at the newborn she'd help bring into the world, she felt a flush of warm pride.

She felt a deep sense of relief too. He was the first baby she'd delivered since the attack, and rather than the feelings of loss and envy that she'd feared, she felt nothing but joy and happiness. And she was so proud to know that even though she'd probably never have a baby of her own, this little one would carry her name for years and years to come, permanently tying her to Broclington, and Callum, even after the locum term was over and she was hundreds — or maybe even thousands — of miles away. It was a wonderfully comforting and reassuring thought.

She smiled at the young family sitting on the bed, where Oliver's big sister was saying hello to her new brother under the watchful eyes of her parents and the neighbour who'd looked after the toddler while she and Callum had worked upstairs.

'What do you think? Do you like him?' The little girl nodded silently, her thumb still tucked firmly in her mouth.

'Shelley's going to make a great big sister,' her proud dad told them all.

'I don't doubt it.' She looked up at the thump of heavy footsteps on the stairs. 'Sounds like the reinforcements are finally here.'

'Yup, cavalry has arrived.'

Liv recognised one of the paramedics. 'Took you long enough, Jerry.'

'Wasn't even supposed to be me. Your first lift got re-routed halfway here. Plus, we heard the super docs were here and figured we could take our time.' He grinned good-naturedly and dropped his heavy bag to the floor and started pulling out supplies. 'Looks like we were right. Do you want to run through the handover while my partner grabs the stairchair? I'm assuming you don't fancy a walk yet, eh, Mum?'

'Not really.' Marie winced at the thought.

'Even if she did, we wouldn't let her,' Callum replied. 'It's platinum level, five-star treatment from here on out.'

'Agreed.' Liv nodded. 'She's been a champ, and should be treated like one.'

'And you needn't worry about anything here,' their neighbour offered, again reminding Liv of how wonderfully different things were in Broclington. 'I can stay here with Shelley and take care of everything while you get looked after.'

A few minutes later, Liv was stood in the front garden waving as Marie was loaded into the ambulance, followed by her beaming husband who proudly cradled their new son.

Callum's hand landed on her shoulder, and she smiled at the familiar warmth. 'Thank you, Liv. Seriously.'

She shook her head, not knowing what to say.

His hand squeezed her shoulder before falling away, and despite the warmth of the sun, Liv found herself missing the heat of his touch. 'You were amazing. I'm fully aware of how easily this could have gone much, much worse.'

'We were lucky.'

'We were lucky you were here. And I think today has proven how important it is to get more expertise into the community, not less.'

'Can't argue with that. I hate to think what would have happened if you'd had to wait for an ambulance. It's easy to forget how isolated we are here sometimes.' She stretched and cricked her neck. 'I really need to go home and shower. I must stink.'

'I couldn't possibly comment.' Callum grinned at her. 'I'll still see you tonight at the party?'

'You know, in all the excitement I'd forgotten about that.'

CHAPTER EIGHT

Music and laughter filled the air as Liv hesitated by the gate. The address was the one Callum had given her, and although he and Sarah insisted she was welcome and almost demanded that she came, she felt nervous. She didn't know Jake or Evelyn, and felt like she was intruding, even by standing in the driveway.

But she hadn't wanted to disappoint Sarah, so had turned up, clutching a bottle of wine despite Callum telling her not to bring anything. She'd spent time and effort pampering herself — which was something she almost never did. But after the morning she'd had, and the battle to bring Oliver safely into the world, she'd treated herself to a long soak in the cottage's old-fashioned, roll-top bathtub. And as she was already in the bath, she'd decided to treat herself to a facemask and deep conditioning treatment on her hair. She'd even taken time to paint her nails and felt fresh and pretty in the summery dress that swished around her ankles and the sparkly sandals she'd found in a village store.

She ran her hands through her loose hair and gave herself a pep talk: *you can do this*. And she'd already learned, a dozen times over, that Broclington was a lot further removed from her former city life than the geographical miles involved. She smoothed her dress and straightened her shoulders before knocking on the gate.

'It's open. Come on in.'

She came face-to-face with a slim blonde woman with the brightest green eyes Liv had ever seen. She was balancing a plate piled high with burgers in one hand and a huge bowl of salad in the other. 'You must be Olivia. Just let me put these down. Come in, come in.'

Liv followed, still feeling slightly awkward.

'There.' The blonde put the salad bowl down on a table already groaning with food, and handed the pile of burgers off to a tall man with dark hair and eyes as blue as Callum's. 'It's so nice to meet you, Olivia. We've heard so much about you. I'm Evelyn, and this is Jake. And somewhere, running around here, is my daughter, Summer.' Her handshake was firm and warm.

'Well, you already know who I am,' Liv said with a smile as she remembered the wine. 'This is for you. And please call me Liv. Most people do.'

'That's so sweet. You really didn't need to. But thank you. Come with me. We'll pop this in the fridge, get you a drink, and introduce you to everyone you don't already know.'

Liv followed her, glad to be told what to do rather than standing around feeling like a spare part. 'You have a really lovely home.'

'Thank you.' Evelyn opened a cupboard. 'I'd love to take credit for it all, but most of it is Jake's handiwork. Summer and I just rolled on up and unpacked. Come and say hello to Angela. She runs the local animal rescue, and works with Jake a lot.'

'I also make a mean mojito. Can I offer you one?' The brunette called Angela gave her a friendly smile and held out a hand. 'Nice to meet you. I'm on bar duty today. There's juice and home-made lemonade if you'd prefer something soft.'

'A mojito sounds lovely—' Liv shook the offered hand — 'and it's nice to meet you too.'

'Should be champagne, from what I hear,' Millie said, walking into the kitchen and giving Liv a quick hug. 'I'm so, so sorry I wasn't there. I thought I'd had a busy shift up at the hospital, but it sounds like it was a walk in the park compared to your day!' Millie's eyes took on a serious look as the smile fell from her face. 'Thank you so much for being there, and for everything you did for Marie.'

'You'd have done the same.' Liv tried to shrug away the compliment, not wanting to draw any more attention to herself. She'd done her job, that was all.

'What have I missed?' Angela looked to Millie when Liv refused to answer.

'The successful emergency home delivery of Marie Brown's baby. Despite a cord prolapse.'

'Oh, wow. That's brilliant.' Evelyn gave her a warm smile. 'I know how easily that could have gone badly. Well done you.'

'It was a team effort,' Liv said as she felt the colour rising in her cheeks.

'Well, I'm glad to have you on our team.' Evelyn grinned. 'And I've been hearing amazing things about this new proposal for the surgery.'

'It's brilliant, isn't it?' Millie agreed. 'Callum gave me a copy after he'd submitted it.'

'Er, what did you think about it?' Liv wasn't sure she really wanted to know. She felt compelled to ask, but was incredibly worried about the answer. What if they didn't like it? Or, worse, what if they all did but the commissioners didn't? It was more than a likely possibility.

'I think—' Millie grinned at her — 'that you might well have saved all of our jobs. It's such a curve ball that they might just agree to it. Especially when they see the calcu-lations put into the final pages. I mean, we all know delay-ing people's release from hospital isn't good for them and is expensive . . . but I didn't realise it was *that* expensive, or that getting people back into their own homes is so much more cost-effective.'

'It's always been a huge problem. In every area I've worked in,' Evelyn agreed. 'And the money is just part of it. As brilliant as they are, hospitals aren't the best places for long-term recovery. With a bit of extra support, most people are much happier at home. The team I worked for before Broclington specialised in re-enablement. I'd be thrilled to see more of it here. And I loved the idea of having a minor surgical suite. It's ridiculous that we have to send lacerations and aspirations to the hospital. We could even do some biopsies here, which could speed things up and reduce the stress and worry on our patients.'

'It sounds like it would be good for everyone.' Angela nodded.

'Absolutely,' Millie agreed. 'The CCG would be crazy not to give us the money.'

Liv bit her lip, hoping that Millie's and Evelyn's trust and enthusiasm wasn't misplaced and that the proposal wasn't going to be the last nail in the coffin of the local surgery.

'Livvy!' Sarah's voice reached her a moment before the little girl slammed into her, wrapping her arms tightly around her. 'You came. You look really pretty.'

'Thank you!' Liv took in her sparkly dress and fairy wings — this time purple — and the glittery face paint. 'You look very pretty too. I like your make-up.'

'Summer did it. She got super special sparkly fairy make-up in America. You have to come and meet her.' She tugged at Liv's arm. 'Come on.'

'Well, it looks like you're going to have to excuse me.' She grinned at Millie and Evelyn. 'Apparently I have to meet the lady of the hour.'

'Just be careful,' Evelyn warned. 'She's been threatening to do make-up on everyone who walks through the gate.'

'Yup—' Angela held up her hand to show a wobbly butterfly as she handed over a frosty glass — 'you have been warned.'

* * *

Callum smiled when he found Liv again. She'd fitted in well with his friends, and the parts of his family who were local, and that meant a lot to him. Though he spoke to his parents semi-regularly through the freezing and juddering video calls that was the internet during their sabbatical, he still missed them.

And he missed the regular, first-Sunday-of-the-month roasts his mum served around the kitchen table with his brother and sister, and whatever friends, family and strays tagged along. It was always a lively, noisy affair in a room packed with love and friendship. And he missed that feeling of being surrounded by family. He was glad Jake was back from the States, and thrilled that he and Evelyn had formed their own family, but he still felt . . . lonely and a bit empty.

But Liv somehow filled some of that emptiness, and when she was around he felt anything but alone. And seeing her sat in a deckchair, with Sarah leaning up against her legs — probably covering her in glitter — as they chatted and laughed together, filled his heart with warmth. He worried about how Sarah would react when Liv moved on to her next placement. Hell, if he was honest, he worried about how *he* would react, but he tried to push the thought away and concentrate on the happy scene in front of him and hope that his plan worked out.

'Hey.' He offered them both glasses: champagne for Liv and fizzy apple in plastic for Sarah. 'Jake said we'd need these soon. I think he's planning a speech.' He rolled his eyes. 'Considering how shy and awkward he used to be, he does a lot of things like this now. I guess love changes a person.' He wondered why it hadn't been enough to change his ex, and make her want to stay — for him and for Sarah.

'I don't know,' Liv mused, 'maybe when you're with the right person, you just become a better version of yourself. Maybe the right person gives you the confidence to be everything you're really capable of.'

Crap. When he saw the sad, wistful look on her face, he remembered what she'd been through, and wished he could take back the words. He started to explain, but his words were drowned out by the ding-ding-ding of a spoon against glass as his brother stood and waved for everyone's attention.

'Well, what can I say?' Jake started.

'Something interesting . . . for the first time!'

Callum didn't see where the cheerful heckle came from, but was happy to join in the good-natured laughter at his brother's expense.

'Ignoring that, and Nick's attempts at being funny—' Jake smiled out at his small audience — 'I . . . that is we . . . want to thank you all for being here. Family and friends . . . old and new . . . we're lucky to have you as part of our lives. The love, generosity and kindness you've all shown to me, and my new family—' he rested a hand on Summer's shoulder and smiled at Evelyn — 'has been nothing less than awe-inspiring. It's been nearly two years since the first Summer's Christmas, and you've quite literally changed our lives for the better, for-ever. And we could not be more grateful. So, we're thrilled to share this news with you all.'

'I'm better!' Summer squealed happily and jumped up and down.

Evelyn nodded, a happy smile playing across her face. 'Apart from regular check-ups, she's been discharged. And it's all thanks to all of you.'

'Which is why I couldn't think of any time, or any group of people, more appropriate to share this with.' Jake turned, fell to his knee and took Evelyn's hand in his, reaching out a hand to Summer.

Callum glanced down to where Liv's fingers suddenly grasped his forearm, and grinned. His eyes briefly met hers before returning to his brother and — hopefully — soon-to-be sister-in-law.

'Evelyn, Summer, since you both came into my life, my world has become a better and brighter place. I used to think I was fairly happy with my lot looking after my vet's surgery and animals, but I don't think I really knew the meaning of happiness before I met both of you. You, both of you, have filled my world with joy and magic, and even though it's been really, really hard at times, I wouldn't change a moment of the last two years. In fact, the only thing I want to change, is your names. So, Evelyn—' he paused as he looked into her smiling face — 'will you do me the greatest honour in the world, and agree to marry me? And Summer, will you let me be your dad?'

'Yes, yes, yes, yes, yes!' The little girl threw herself at him, and Callum laughed as his brother lost his balance and toppled backwards under her assault.

Jake grabbed her and twisted her around so he could look up at Evelyn again. 'I have one yes. Is there any chance of another? Will you be my wife?'

She nodded, her voice inaudible to the crowd.

'Louder!' someone heckled.

'Yes.' Evelyn cleared her throat. 'Yes, I will.'

'Thank goodness.' Jake grinned, before letting out an ear-piercing whistle. 'Tilly! Come!'

A muffled bark sounded behind Callum before the little fox-like dog trotted gleefully to the front of the garden, clearly enjoying the attention as everyone watched her. As soon as she reached Jake's feet she collapsed, all four feet in the air while grinning wolfishly. 'This is not how we practiced this,' he complained as he wrestled her upright, only to have her immediately jump away and play bow. 'C'mon, Tilly. You're showing me up here!'

Callum fought back a laugh. 'I guess this is why they say you should never work with children or animals.'

'I don't know, I think they're adorable. I always quite liked dogs, but it wouldn't have worked in the city.' Liv leant in close, her perfume filling his senses as her silky hair brushed against his bare arm, momentarily stealing his concentration from his brother's proposal. He wondered if he would ever find someone who would want to share his and Sarah's life, and found his eyes wandering back to Liv, smiling warmly at him.

'Aha!' Jake's triumphant cry dragged Callum's attention back to where he'd finally succeeded in wrestling a bag away from the small dog. He emptied two boxes into his hand and flipped them open, holding them out to his new family. Even from where he sat, Callum could see the light bouncing off the gems and splitting into rainbows that danced across the garden.

'Just magical,' Liv breathed next to him. And he couldn't help but agree. She was enchanting.

* * *

'Callum really got chased by a chicken?' Liv fought to keep her expression neutral.

'Girl Scout's honour.' Angela held up her hand in salute. 'And not only that, but she chased him right into the duck pond.'

'That's brilliant.' Liv gave in to the laughter.

'It gets even better,' Jake joined in. 'This was when his medical degree was all shiny and new, and he went out in his shiny suit and equally shiny shoes. And he splodged back to our parents' house with pond weed in his pockets.'

'It's not true.' Callum rolled his eyes.

'So, you didn't get chased into a duck pond by a chicken?'

'Maybe I slipped when trying to avoid further upsetting an already distressed animal.'

'Yeah, you just keep telling yourself that.' Jake snorted into his drink.

'Keep winding me up, you're the one needing a best man.'

'True.' Jake grinned good-naturedly at his brother. 'But I can always ask Nick.'

'And, bro . . .' Callum flung his arm around his brother's shoulders, before tightening his grip into a headlock. 'I can always give him plenty of embarrassing photos and dirt.'

'He knows everything anyway.' Jake jabbed his brother in the ribs.

'Even about your girl posters that you stuck all over the inside of your wardrobe door?' He laughed as Jake tried to wriggle out of the headlock. 'Which, now I think on it, did feature a lot of blondes.'

'Shut up!'

Evelyn laughed as she joined the group and rolled her eyes at Liv. 'These two. They're worse than the kids, honestly.'

Liv glanced at Summer and Sarah who were excitedly examining Summer's new necklace and already planning their bridesmaid dresses, then looked back to Callum and Jake who were attempting to wrestle each other to the floor. 'I can't really argue with that.'

'Give, give. I give!' Callum held up his hands. 'Get off me!'

Once the tussle had stopped, Evelyn realised she could hear a familiar ringtone: Callum's. 'Surgery line?'

Callum nodded as he pulled the phone out of his pocket and flicked his fingers across the screen. 'Callum Macpearson.' His breath was rough between gasps and Liv couldn't help but think how similar it sounded to the moments after he'd thoroughly kissed her. Despite her best intentions, she felt heat flood her cheeks. To try and hide her reaction, she took another gulp of her drink, and then regretted it. If it was a medical emergency, she'd need her wits about her. Though neither she or Callum were on call — and she had every right to enjoy a drink or two — she was also well aware that there was no such thing as being off duty. That was as true in this village as it had been in the city. Probably more so, except for major incidents, there was always someone else on call at the hospital.

She watched Callum for signs that she might need to start grabbing her things together, and that the fun, relaxing party might be about to come to an abrupt ending.

'They are good-looking, these Macpearson boys.' Evelyn sat next to her.

'What? I wasn't . . .' Liv felt the heat in her cheeks again. She bit her bottom lip, trying to will the embarrassment away. 'We're just colleagues.'

'Oh? My mistake.' Evelyn gave her a knowing smile.

'Really,' Liv insisted, trying to convince herself as much as the woman sat beside her. 'We're just colleagues. And temporary ones at that.'

'So you said.'

'I mean, I'm only a locum here while Tom and Julie are on sabbatical. While I figure out what I want to do next in life.'

'I know.' Evelyn nodded.

'I'm just watching Callum to try and get a bit of advance warning . . . in case we're about to be called into work or something.'

'Do you think that's likely?'

Liv studied Callum's profile. His jaw was tense, his shoulders square, but she didn't see any urgency in his movements. If anything, it was the opposite. She watched as he sagged slightly. 'I'm not sure, but I don't think so.'

'I wonder who would be calling him on the surgery line at the weekend, then,' Evelyn pondered. 'Maybe it's just a patient with a query.'

'Maybe.' Liv pursed her lips, unconvinced.

* * *

Callum sighed as he ended the call and tried to unclench his jaw. Angry, disappointed tears filled his throat and he forced them down with a gulp of his beer that nearly choked him. The anger surged back, leaving him with a bitter taste in his mouth. He was angry that he'd failed, angry that he felt led on, and that he was going to let everyone down. But most of all, he was angry that he'd actually let himself believe — for a few days — that it might actually have worked. His parents were stupid to have trusted him, and he was stupid to have trusted himself, or to believe that he could have pulled this off.

'Callum?' Liv's gentle hand on his shoulder sent another wave of misery through him. He'd wanted to succeed for her, because somewhere in the parts of his mind that he didn't even want to give conscious thought to — let alone voice — he'd hoped that if everything worked out the way he'd planned, and hoped, and even bloody *wished for* in that stupid well, then Liv would have been able to stay. And maybe she could have been part of his and Sarah's life going forward.

But that had all been blown away like leaves in the wind with that single call. What was being asked of him just wasn't possible. And no amount of coins thrown into a wishing well would change that.

He screwed up his confidence and turned to face her.

'I was going to ask if you're all right, but I can see you're not. How can I help?' Her kindness somehow made it worse.

'You can't.'

'Are you sure?' she persisted. 'It can't be that bad.'

'It is,' Callum argued. 'It really, really is.'

'What's wrong?' Evelyn joined them. 'Do we need to go? I can grab my bag if you need me.'

'It's nothing like that.' Callum ran his hands through his hair. 'Just admin stuff. Nothing to worry about.'

'Why don't I feel reassured?' Evelyn pursed her lips as she watched him.

'Because he's a terrible liar.' Liv glared at him too.

'OK, it's not totally nothing, but it's not anything I want to talk about today and ruin the party. You just got *engaged*, Evelyn.'

'You're right, I did.' She studied the ring that sparkled around her finger. 'Which means I'm going to be your sister in-law soon. And family don't keep secrets from each other. Right, Liv?'

Liv shrugged. 'If it's something we can help with, please let us.' The sincerity in her hazel eyes cut into him, making him feel guilty for trying to withhold the news from them both.

'I really don't want to spoil your day.'

'Cal, I'm already worried and thinking the worst. You not telling me what's bothering you isn't going to make things any better,' Evelyn argued.

He recognised her tone of voice. He could argue with her for the rest of the day, and she'd still get her own way. He glanced at Liv, hoping that she might be on his side, but he was met with a calm concern as she gave the slightest shake of her head. She wasn't going to help him either. 'OK. But can we keep this between ourselves?'

Evelyn nodded. 'Summer, look after Sarah please. We've got some boring adult-type stuff to do.'

'No probs. We've got dresses to design.'

'Thank you, sweetheart. We won't be long.'

Callum followed her into the house, with Liv by his side. But instead of the usual comfort she offered, having her so near made things worse. Every step felt a little heavier until his legs felt like solid lead that he had to drag up the couple of steps to the back door. How was he going to tell them that they — along with the whole surgery — were about to lose their jobs? His brother had just proposed to Evelyn, and weddings weren't cheap. And he knew neither of them were well off, with Summer's treatments draining their savings, even with the help of the community's fundraising.

And Liv? She was only supposed to be temporary, but he'd hoped so, so much that she could have made her permanent home in Broclington. The withdrawn, anxious city doctor — still healing from her past — that he'd met so recently had disappeared, melting away in the warm village community that she'd so quickly become a part of, to leave a bright, caring, beautiful person who was becoming incredibly important to him and his daughter. Now that hope was dashed.

Evelyn closed the door on the small sitting room and turned to look at him. 'All right, Callum. Spit it out.'

He took a deep breath. She was right. There was no point trying to make this hurt any less than it was going to. It was like setting a dislocated joint: sometimes you just needed to accept that the only way to help someone would cause them pain before they got relief. 'It was the local lead from the clinical commissioning group.' He could feel their eager eyes on him, and hated himself for the pain he knew the next words would cause. 'It's not the answer we wanted.'

'They turned us down?' Evelyn's voice was a whisper of disbelief.

Callum nodded slowly.

'Oh no! This is all my fault.' Liv's face was ashen, her eyes filled with tears. 'I'm so, so sorry.'

'You're not to blame.' Callum reached out to her, but she yanked her arm away from his touch.

'I bloody well am! I suggested going too far. What the hell was I thinking? I'm not from around here. I clearly had no idea what they wanted and now . . .' She took a ragged breath which tore at Callum's heart. 'Now you're going to lose the surgery.'

'Liv . . .' She didn't flinch when he wrapped his arms around her shoulders, so he took it as permission to pull her in tighter. 'Your idea was good, they really liked it.'

'Just not enough to invest or commit their money to.'

'There's just not enough money to go round.'

'How do you know they liked it?' Evelyn asked.

'The feedback was really good, and the offer they made—'

'What offer? You didn't mention any offer.'

'That's because it's a pointless one. It would never work.' Callum wished he hadn't let the words slip out. There was no way they would be able to meet the terms of the offer, and he didn't want to dash their hopes further. It was too unkind. They'd all worked so hard, and invested so much — in his family's case, for decades — to take any more pain.

'*What* wouldn't work?' Evelyn watched him with narrowed eyes.

Liv pushed away from him and matched Evelyn's stare. 'What do you mean? There's something you're not telling us. What is it?'

'It's nothing.'

'Sounds like something,' Liv argued, the colour returning to her cheeks.

'They did make an offer—'

'What! Why didn't you tell us?' Evelyn demanded.

'Because it's a pointless one.'

'They wouldn't have made it, if that was true.'

'Maybe you should tell us what the offer is and let us decide for ourselves.' Liv's eyes were filled with so much hope that he found himself forced to look away. It was preferable to seeing the light fade from her eyes and sadness take over again.

* * *

Callum refused to meet her gaze as he spoke. 'They like the proposal and offered to put up just over one point five million.'

'That's fantastic!' Evelyn exclaimed.

'There's more, though, isn't there?' Liv could hear the hesitation in his voice. He was holding something back.

'The condition is that it's a match-funding deal. We have to put up the rest of the money: three hundred and ninety thousand give or take.'

'So we pay twenty-five per cent of what . . . the first year?' Liv waited for his nod. 'And they fund with another seventy-five per cent? Sounds like a good deal.'

'It might be. If we had the best part of four hundred thousand pounds hanging around in a bank account.'

Liv studied her nails and tried not to let her disappointment show. 'I see the problem.'

'I have to admit, I don't.' Evelyn shrugged. 'It's only money.'

'Only money?' Callum tried not to roll his eyes, and almost succeeded. 'It's a helluva lot of money. And unless you've won the lottery recently, it's more than we have any chance of getting.'

'We could try to find a sponsor, I suppose,' Evelyn mused.

'Who's going to sponsor a little village surgery? No one's that interested in us. That's half the problem,' Callum argued.

'The Broclington community probably would be,' Evelyn pointed out.

'The community here is lovely,' Liv argued. 'But it's hardly the most affluent of places.'

'Individually, you're right. But as a community, Broclington is capable of amazing things . . .' Callum's eyes now lit up, but Liv couldn't understand why.

'It really is.' Evelyn sniffed. 'I can't ever repay the community for what they've done. But helping to save the surgery . . . that might be a good way to start.'

'It would be,' Callum agreed. 'So many people rely on the surgery. But do you think we could really pull it off? There's not much time.'

'True, but the arrangements for the actual event are already well started, it's just the cause we're awaiting an announcement on. But do you think the committee would support this?'

Liv was getting more and more lost by the minute. 'Support what? Pull what off?'

Callum took a swig of his beer and gestured to Evelyn. 'It's your story more than mine.'

Evelyn took a deep breath. 'Have you heard of our Summer's Christmas?'

'The village fundraising thing where you had tinsel and trees in summer? Sarah has told me about it — and Tom sent a couple of photos in one of his emails. He said he was roasting in the beard and hat last year.'

'It was a little more than "just a little village thing". In fact it was pretty big,' Callum explained.

'How big?'

'Maybe big enough,' Evelyn replied. 'The first year was successful enough to get Summer to America for treatment when her cancer came back a couple of years ago. There wasn't any hope of finding enough money in the family to pay for the treatment — and that's where Broclington's community came in. The traditional summer ball became a Mistletoe Ball, and the summer fete became Christmas themed, and a few very opportune press interviews and over three hundred thousand pounds later, Summer was in hospital getting the treatment that's saved her life. That's how Summer's Christmas was born.'

'Wow.'

'Wow is right.' Evelyn smiled. 'When I said I couldn't begin to repay the community for what they have done, I really meant it. They honestly saved my daughter's life. We held the same event again last year, and it was almost as big and successful as the first time. We raised enough money to help extend the local hospice. And I happen to know the committee were holding off on making the final decision on their charity this year until Summer, Jake and I were back from the States.'

'So, this really could work?' Liv asked, and was surprised when she felt Callum's fingers twist around hers and squeeze them tight.

'Yes, this really could work. There will be a lot of work we have to do — like setting up a charity for the surgery to make sure everything is legal and above board, but I don't think that is too difficult, and we'll need to get a proposal to the committee, and put out press releases . . .' Evelyn ticked off points on her fingers. 'In fact, I'm going to go and find my soon-to-be-husband and start getting things moving.'

Callum turned to Liv as the door swung shut behind Evelyn. The look in his eyes made her heart race to the point of palpitations.

His free hand reached up to stroke her cheek, his hand sliding gently down to cup her chin as his thumb brushed against her skin. 'The commissioners loved your proposal. We're going to get the money . . .'

'If we manage to raise the match-funding amount.'

'Evelyn is pretty convinced we will. But we wouldn't even be getting a chance to do this if it wasn't for all of your ideas, and passion.' His voice dropped on the last word, sending chills down her spine.

'We should get back to the party.' Part of her regretted the words even as she said them, the part that really wanted to stay in the quiet room where there was nothing to distract them from each other. Where she could lean into his arms and let him do everything that his eyes hinted at. And the other part of her? It wanted to run away and hide from any more pain or risk.

'Yes, I suppose we should.' He placed a soft, lingering kiss on her cheek that stirred the butterflies in her stomach into a full-blown whirlwind. 'But I couldn't have done this without you Liv. I hope you know that.'

'It was a team effort. We work well together.'

'We really do. But Liv, I feel like I owe you. Big time.' His fingers slid from hers as he opened the door, and as his touch lingered, Liv couldn't help thinking that really, she owed him far more than he could even begin to realise. He'd given her hope, a place that she felt safe — and for someone who hadn't really had a home for her whole adult life, that was something incredibly precious. And worth fighting for.

CHAPTER NINE

The next Friday, Callum stepped outside of the village hall and looked around the car park before doing a little dance.

'You look funny, Dad.'

'I know, and I don't even care. Do you know what happened in there?'

'Yup. The fairy magic worked.' She smiled up at him happily.

'That's not exactly it, Sarah.'

'Yes it is,' she argued. 'The committee said yes, and Santa will come and you'll get lots of money to make the surgery better. Just like I wished in the fairy fountain.'

'You wished for this?'

'Of course. It's important. And if you give the fairies a nice gift and ask very nicely, they help with important things. But you have to be very careful.'

'So you don't fall in the well?'

'No, silly. Because fairies are tricky. You shouldn't upset them.'

'You probably shouldn't upset anyone,' Callum mused.

'No. But 'specially not fairies.' She hesitated when he headed towards the gate. 'Daddy, are you in a good mood?'

'A very, very good mood.'

'So now is a good time to ask you something?'

He froze and looked at her suspiciously. 'Like what?'

'Like can I please sleep over with Summer soon? She's going to be my cousin properly soon and we have lots of bridesmaid things we need to talk about and plan — she said it's really hard but really fun being a bridesmaid, and it's really very important.'

'Very important, huh? Did you ask the fairies about it too?'

'Of course not!' Sarah seemed offended, and for the life of him Callum couldn't work out why. Honestly, he sometimes felt like he and his daughter were from different planets, not just different generations. Though as soon as he'd thought it, he laughed. Trying to speak to her about glitter and fairies and princesses was as alien to him as "icky squelchy slugs" were to her.

'So, you don't ask fairies for things like sleepovers?'

'Nope. That would be wasting a wish. I just asked Evelyn.'

'You did? I hope you were polite.' Callum wasn't sure how he felt about his daughter taking on the organisation of her own social life — which was clearly far more complex and demanding than his own.

'Of course she was.' Evelyn came up behind them. 'She's always lovely and polite. And for the record, I agree. Assuming it's all right with you, I'd love to get to know my new niece better. And it's good for Summer to have more friends who aren't . . . well . . . from the hospitals. And, of course, Jake would be there too.'

'And I love Uncle Jake! And I really, really missed him when he was in America. I know he had to be there to look after Summer and Evelyn . . . but I missed him. Please, Daddy?'

'Please, Dr Macpearson?' Summer added her voice to the plea. One look at the two girls, their arms wrapped tightly around each other, and Callum was helpless to say no. And they did have a point: now they were going to be cousins

— officially — it was only right that they spend more time together. And it was obvious to him — if no one else — that Sarah would benefit from having more feminine influences in her life. He'd done his best, and his mother and sister had helped as much as possible, but he often felt at a complete loss when it came to all things sparkly and girly. Lately, whenever he thought he'd finally gotten it right, he'd be treated to an eye roll so pity-filled that no six-year-old should have been able to manage it.

'OK. When were you thinking?'

'Tonight!'

'I think tonight might be a bit soon . . .' He didn't want to abuse Evelyn's hospitality. 'Evelyn and Jake have likely got plans tonight.'

'Actually, we don't.' Evelyn shrugged. 'Jake's already gone to get pizza to celebrate. He always orders too much, so there will be plenty to eat. You and Sarah are more than welcome to join us.' She shot him a knowing smile. 'Or, Sarah can come with us, and you can drop a bag round later. If, say, you were planning to head out and share tonight's news with a certain doctor who I noticed was missing tonight?'

'Yes, she took the community rounds this evening. Late call out to the care home. It didn't sound too serious, but she didn't want to leave it until next week. And I think she might have been a bit glad of the excuse.'

'Well, it is all a bit nerve-wracking.'

'You're really sure a sleepover tonight is OK?'

'I wouldn't offer if it wasn't. Just drop Sarah's bag in later. And go enjoy an adult evening with Liv.'

'I don't know what you mean.'

'I think you do.' Evelyn winked over the heads of their two giggling girls. 'I've seen the way you look at each other.'

'And how's that?'

'Like you're completely and one hundred per cent aware of each other. I noticed it at the party. When you weren't checking on Sarah, you were checking on Liv. Even when you were playing with the kids or talking with others, you'd still look for her and when you found her your eyes would lock. Just for a moment or two.'

'What's your point?'

'That I recognise that look.'

'Really? Where from?'

'Your brother.' She rested her hand on his and drew him a little way away from their girls. 'I don't want to speak out of turn, but . . .'

'But you're going to anyway.' He grinned. 'You're as good as family, Evie. Just say it.'

'I've never seen you so happy, and relaxed, as when you're around Liv. She brings something out in you that other people don't. And she chases away the sadness that I so often see in your eyes. You're less guarded when you're around her.'

Callum shook his head, struggling to understand her point.

'She's good for you, Callum. Jake and I can both see it, even if you can't. Don't let her get away.'

'She's only here on a locum contract.'

'Initially. But with the surgery expansion, we're going to need more staff. She could be perfect.'

'But she's only here temporarily,' Callum argued, not wanting to admit that he'd already imagined Liv as a permanent part of their team — and his and Sarah's life.

'Then that's all the more reason to stop wasting what time you do have. Let me and Jake take Sarah tonight, and you go and spend some time with Liv. If there's nothing there, then there's nothing there. But I think you owe it to yourself and her to try and find out. Without interruptions. Besides, the girls will have a great time together. I can't promise they'll sleep all that much, but they'll have fun.'

'OK. Thank you.' He went over and knelt down next to Sarah. 'You really want to sleep over tonight? Without me?'

'Yes, please!' She threw her arms around him tightly.

He picked her up and buried his face in her hair and inhaled the smell of her bubblegum shampoo as he hugged her hard. As much as he was glad that she was finding her independence, he sometimes wished he could keep her young — and safe — forever.

She whispered in his ear, 'When you bring my PJs, can you bring Dr Cuddlington? It's not for me. But he gets scared in the dark sometimes, and I wouldn't want him to be scared.'

'No, we wouldn't want that.' Callum tried not to grin in relief. For now at least, she was still his little girl. 'Have fun with Summer, be good for Jake and Evelyn, and I'll see you later. And if I hear you've misbehaved in any way, what will happen?'

'You'll build a tower in the garden and lock me in it like Rapunzel?'

'Well, I was just going to take you home and confiscate your tablet, but a tower could look good at the bottom of the garden.' She giggled as he carefully dropped her back to her feet. 'Be good, munchkin.'

'Yes, Daddy.'

* * *

Liv had just pulled on a pair of comfy shorts and switched her smart blouse for a stretchy vest top when the knock at the door sounded. She sighed as she tugged her hair out of its bun and massaged her aching scalp. It had been a long day and she wasn't really in the mood for entertaining anyone. Whoever it was, she'd get rid of them so she could curl up on the couch with her book and maybe throw a pizza in the Aga. She really, really hoped it wasn't a patient who needed urgent help. She hadn't exactly publicised her address, but it was a small village and most people knew someone who knew where everyone else lived. Especially when you were one of the few medics around.

She yanked a cardigan on over her too-skimpy-for-public-viewing top and stuffed her feet back into her fuzzy slippers to open the door.

'You. Are. Amazing.' Before she had a chance to speak, Callum caught her face between his hands and stepped towards her, crowding her against the wall in the most delicious way. His lips were against hers before she could catch her breath and he kissed her so gently and softly that she struggled to hold back a whimper. After a long moment in which she could hear her heart racing, he pulled away, leaving her craving his touch and taste.

'Umm . . .' Her senses were so clouded with his presence and his kiss that she couldn't form a coherent thought, let alone a sentence.

'Sorry.' He held his hands up, looking so sheepish that she couldn't help but smile. 'I just couldn't resist. Sorry. I'm just so excited. The committee approved the surgery as the charity for this year's Summer's Christmas. We're going to save the surgery.' His eyes were alight with joy. 'And it's all because of the proposal we put together.'

The words filtered through the haze he had created. 'That's fantastic.'

'*You* are fantastic.' He leaned in to kiss her again, but she ducked to the side.

'Callum . . .' Her voice was strangled by emotion, but she forced herself to speak. 'I don't think we should be doing this.'

'Doing what?'

She forced air into her lungs on a shaky breath. 'This. You kissing me.'

'Oh, Liv.' He stroked her cheek gently. 'If you'd let me, I'd do a helluva lot more than just kiss you.'

'Callum, I don't . . .'

'Relax. I'm not propositioning you right now, although I wouldn't say no if you wanted me to.' He gave her a grin that turned her knees — and her resolve — to jelly. 'Let me take you out to dinner tonight, to say thank you properly.'

'I don't know if that's a good idea.' The way he was looking at her, she knew it wasn't the smart, safe thing to do — but at the same time she really wanted to say yes.

'I disagree. I think it's a very, very good idea.' The heat in his eyes was as tempting as Brockle cakes fresh from the bakery's oven. 'And it's only dinner, Liv. In a public place. It's perfectly safe.'

'But I'm already planning on leaving.' She didn't know why she was still arguing.

'But you're here right now.'

'What about Sarah?'

'She's sleeping over with Summer. Apparently they have "super important bridesmaid stuff" to talk about.' His thumb traced the line between her cheek and her chin, leaving a trail of goose pimples that tickled down her spine. 'Tell me if I'm wrong, if you don't want to have dinner with me, and spend time with me, and explore this. Tell me that, and I'll back right off. But if I'm right, maybe try to stop worrying so much, Liv. Maybe, just for tonight, you should give your big, beautiful brain a rest and just do what you *want*, without second-guessing everything and worrying so much about every little thing.'

He had a point, and she found herself nodding. 'OK.'

'Brilliant.' He brushed a kiss against her cheek, just catching the corner of her lips and making her skin tingle. 'Now don't take this wrong, because I think you look breath-taking right now, but I was thinking maybe the Old Mill? It's about half an hour drive. It's beautiful, and sits on the river's edge, but it might get a little chilly.'

'I'll get changed. Make yourself at home.' Liv slipped past him and raced up the stairs, already calculating exactly how many minutes she could spend getting ready before she was officially "trying too hard" for their . . . *date*? Officially, he'd asked her out to thank her for her help — and to celebrate the next step in saving the surgery. A friendly gesture. But the way he'd kissed her, and the promise he'd made of "a helluva lot more" was so, so much more than just friendly.

* * *

Callum smiled at Liv as she polished off the last potato on her plate and folded her napkin and placed it on the table.

'That was absolutely delicious. And the company hasn't been too bad, either.'

'Well, I do try my best.' He lifted the bottle of champagne from its frosty ice bucket and offered to top up her glass.

'It's been a wonderful evening.' She gave him a smile so happy and open that he couldn't resist the urge to reach out and take her hand.

'The evening isn't over yet, unless you're in a rush to head home?'

'No, no rush.'

'Good. They do this amazing chocolate fondue dessert and serve it over the firepits on the deck. Sarah loves it, but I have the feeling that sharing it with you could be a whole different experience.' He didn't miss Liv's slight shiver.

'It depends.' She toyed with her champagne glass. 'If there are firepits, are there marshmallows?'

'Handmade, gourmet, with different flavours depending on the chef's fancy.'

'Well, if you put it like that, how can I say no?'

'I'm hoping you can't.' He waved to their waitress and waited until she came over.

'Are you ready to see the dessert menu?'

'We'd like to do the firepit fondue, if you've room, please?'

She nodded. 'We've a few spaces left. Can I interest you in some of our home-made, fresh marshmallows? The specials today are kiwi and passion fruit.'

'Definitely,' Liv answered for them both.

'Great. If you'd like to make your way outside whenever you're ready, I'll bring your dessert to you.'

'After you.' Callum held the door open for Liv, and guided her to one of the rattan benches that sat on the deck overlooking the water. The bench itself was laden with cushions and blankets, and positioned in front of a round fire basket that rested on raised legs and was carved with a pattern of swirling branches and leaves that sent the firelight flickering across the water and the deck.

'It's so beautiful here.'

'You're right. The view is stunning.'

Her hair shimmered in the firelight, and her eyes shone as she turned the prettiest shade of pink at his compliment.

'You know, I've eaten in some of the hippest, most fashionable and *expensive* restaurants in London,' Liv mused.

'It's the best we have here.' The Old Mill was one of the best restaurants locally, but Callum was more than aware that even the nicest of country pubs wasn't going to compare to the shiny, chic eateries she was used to. It was just another reminder of how out of his league she really was. And that she was probably looking forward to heading back — or at least somewhere similar — as soon as her locum contract was over.

'But I was going to say, I've never been anywhere like this. It's so lovely.' She stood at the balustrade and stared out over the water. 'It's like something out of a fairy tale. The way the light bounces off the water . . . you could almost believe in magic.'

'Sarah always says it's fairies dancing. It's one of her favourite places.'

'Do you come here a lot with her?'

'They do family events every so often. We dress up and have a Daddy Daughter date. It probably sounds dumb.'

'No. It sounds lovely.' She shivered.

'Here . . .' Callum grabbed the blanket off the seat and draped it around her shoulders.

'Thank you.' She nuzzled her cheek against his hand and leaned back against him. 'For tonight, for making me feel so welcome in Broclington, and with your family. It's meant so much.'

'It seems wrong that you're the one thanking me when I owe you so much,' he argued.

She turned and stretched up on her tiptoes to place a soft kiss on his lips that made him want to grab her, drag her up against him, and do things that would probably get him barred from the Mill. He wanted to taste her mouth, feel her move against him, and explore every inch of her body from the creamy skin of her neck to the long, slender legs that appeared from beneath her short skirt, and back up again.

But it was more than that: he wanted to make her laugh, to comfort her when she was sad, and to just be with her when she was doing nothing at all. And he wanted to teach her about the different plants in his garden, and watch her play with Sarah, which surprised him. He'd spent so much time protecting his daughter from any new person who could harm her, that he was surprised to find himself excited for when they spent time together.

Liv pulled away, and he instantly missed the warmth of her touch. 'Wow, is that our dessert?' She stared at the pile of pastel marshmallows and mini cauldron of chocolate that had been hung over the firepit in amazement. 'No wonder Sarah likes it here.'

Callum speared one of the powdery cubes and swirled it in the heated chocolate. 'Here, you have to try this.'

The moan that escaped her lips as she bit into the sweet, fruity concoction shot straight from his ears to his stomach, and lower, causing muscles to tighten in excitement. The smile she gave him as she licked a smudge of powdered sugar from her thumb, her eyes never leaving his, made him think he would never, ever be able to look at a marshmallow the same again.

'Delicious.' She gave him a shy smile. 'You've been here before. Do you know if they can put this into a to-go box?'

'I don't know, Sarah and I have never had leftovers.'

* * *

Liv took a deep breath and winced inwardly. She'd thought that Callum was interested in her, but his polite dismissal to what she'd thought was an obvious invitation made her question herself. All the self-doubts she'd been fighting against since Mike threw her out of their life together flooded back. Callum had seen her scars, and knew her history — at least most of it, so he was well-aware of how damaged she was. She had hoped he was different, and that he liked her in spite of her problems, but maybe that was just a hopeful, silly dream. Maybe she really was too damaged for anyone to ever be attracted to again.

'Liv? Are you all right? You're a million miles away.'

'Sorry, just thinking.' Her voice came out quieter than she intended.

'About what?'

'Nothing, just . . . nothing.' She forced a smile onto her face.

'Oh crap, I'm an idiot.' He dragged a hand through his hair. 'At least, I think I am. I kind of hope I am. Am I a complete idiot, Liv?'

She shrugged, not knowing how to reply.

'When you asked about a to-go box, you meant to go home. Now. Together. Didn't you?'

'Maybe.' Liv wasn't sure how he was going to respond. She took a deep breath, and forced herself to plough on. 'I've been thinking, I'm not going to be here all that much longer, and I know you're not looking for anything serious either, but . . .'

'But what, Liv?' His face was unreadable.

'But . . . we're friends right?'

'Of course.'

'When you kissed me, I felt like there was more there. And I was thinking, we're both mature adults, and . . .'

'And you thought maybe we could be the type of . . . friends . . . who enjoy a very friendly mature relationship? Is that what you're saying, Liv?'

'Maybe.'

He leaned in closer, sliding his hands up her arms and sending goose pimples racing over her skin beneath the blanket. 'Maybe yes?'

'Maybe yes.' Her breath caught in her throat as he leaned even closer, and his mouth hovered so close to hers that his breath tickled her lips.

'Maybe definitely yes?'

'Definitely yes,' she murmured.

'Good.' He was so close that she felt the smile she saw in his eyes as his lips met hers, softly at first, and then more insistently. One of his hands traced up the back of her neck as his tongue teased hers. He filled her senses: his hands burning on her skin, his mouth tasting of the smooth, rich chocolate they'd been sharing, his musky scent surrounding her as he drew her closer, kissing her until he had driven all other thoughts from her mind.

She couldn't help but press up against him, crushing her breasts against his chest as she wrapped her arms around his neck, tugging the blanket around them both as she pulled him closer.

When he eventually paused, Liv struggled to catch her breath, and couldn't manage to marshal her thoughts into a coherent sentence. Kissing hadn't been like *that* before. She couldn't remember the last time anyone had kissed her senseless. If they hadn't been in a public place, she would probably have crawled into his lap — and the thought both thrilled and scared her.

'So, do you still want to ask about a to-go box.'

'You know what? I couldn't care less about dessert any more.' She bit her lip as she looked at him, thinking that she was after something much sweeter.

'Sweeter than handmade, chocolate-dipped marshmallow?' He chuckled.

'Shit.' She covered her face with her hands. 'I hadn't meant to say that aloud.'

'I'll take that as a compliment.' His eyes sparkled as he caught her hands in his, and leaned in to kiss her again. 'I promise I'll do my best to be . . . sweet.'

She nodded, wordlessly, not trusting herself to speak. It all felt so tentative and fragile that she didn't want to do anything to risk breaking the spell. She kept her fingers woven through his as he paid the bill, and they headed back to the village. There was a moment of awkwardness as they approached the turning to her cottage and he slowed, but Liv squeezed his knee and smiled, and he drove on past. They both wanted the same thing now, and there was little point in pretending.

She shivered with anticipation as they pulled into his driveway and he turned the engine off and turned to look at her. 'I've had a really good night with you, and if you want me to turnaround and take you home right now, I will. I won't lie and say I wouldn't be disappointed, but I would understand. And we'd still be friends tomorrow.'

Liv's heart melted a little at his vulnerability, and she hushed him with a finger over his lips. She leaned across the handbrake to replace her finger with her lips. 'I've had a really nice time with you too . . . too nice to want things to end yet. And if I'm totally honest, I think we can do a bit better than "nice" or even "really good", don't you?'

He opened the front door, then instantly winced and bent down to scoop up a couple of pairs of small, pink shoes and sweep them into a cupboard along with a purple sunhat and mini handbag. 'Sorry, it's a bit of a mess.'

Liv smiled as they headed into the living room and Callum hastily stuffed a couple of dolls and set of fairy wings into a toy box. Part of her was glad to see that he hadn't planned on bringing her back with him and hadn't tidied the house or set a seduction scene. The house was just a family home, complete with the mess of normal life, and it was raw and honest, and that was exactly what she wanted and needed.

She caught his hand as he reached for a stuffed dog sprawled across the floor. 'Callum, it's fine.'

He sighed and kicked the dog under the couch. 'Can I get you a drink? There's beer or wine in the fridge. Or I can put the kettle on.'

'Wine would be lovely.' She followed him to the kitchen and perched on one of the stools at the breakfast bar.

He poured the drinks and handed one to her. She took a sip, before setting it down and spinning on the stool to face him. 'So, where were we?'

'I think somewhere around here.' He stepped closer and caught her face in his hands. He studied her for a moment before bowing his head and worshipping her lips with his. As he deepened the kiss, she moaned against his lips and slid her arms around his waist. He pushed against her, parting her knees and leaning her back against the breakfast bar as he kissed her even more thoroughly.

She moaned and pressed against him, thrilled and heated to the core by his touch. For the first time in far too long she felt desired, excited and protected. She knew she was safe with Callum, and that knowledge meant she could relax and open herself up to him, wrapping her legs tightly around him and shamelessly taking her pleasure from him.

They made out like teenagers: hot, heavy, with abandon and hands moving everywhere as the heat built to almost unbearable levels.

Eventually, when Liv was so frustrated she felt like she was about to explode, Callum pulled back, gently lifting her upright.

'As much as I'm enjoying this, this is not how I want this to go.'

'Oh.' Liv had thought it was exactly what he'd had planned.

'You deserve much, much better than a horny grope against the kitchen counter.' He grinned and took her hand in his. 'And I have to admit, I'm getting old. I like my creature comforts. Like beds.' His grin was infectious, and Liv couldn't help but laugh.

'Bed sounds good to me.'

'I was so hoping you'd say that.' His eyes darkened with desire that made Liv shiver in the most delicious way. She was still shaking as he led her gently up the stairs and to his bedroom, where he captured her face between his hands and kissed her again, teasing her lips with his.

She laughed lightly when he pulled away for breath. 'Oh, Callum . . . what you're doing to me . . .'

'It's more than mutual, Liv. Believe me.' He reached for the light switch, but she caught his hand in hers, kissing his palm.

'Can we leave it off?'

'Whatever you want.' His voice rasped in her ear. 'Anything I have to give is yours for the asking.'

'You. I want you.'

She felt his smile against her neck. 'That's easily arranged.'

* * *

Callum stretched as Liv wriggled and tugged at the sheet, tucking it around herself before she rested her head on his shoulder, warm and solid in his arms.

'Wow.'

'Yeah.' He chuckled. 'If I'd known you were going to do that to me, I'd have sent Sarah for a sleepover weeks ago.' He swore softly under his breath. 'Sorry, that sounds really bad, doesn't it? Putting presumptions on you and making me sound like one of the worst dads in the village.'

'You're not a bad dad,' Liv reassured him as she doodled patterns on his chest. 'Anyone who sees you with Sarah for more than a minute can see that.'

'Even if she has been known to knock people flying head over heels?'

'Yes, even then.' Liv laughed, and the sound vibrated through his chest, and he hugged her closer.

'So, then I'm not a horrible person for being glad that she's sleeping over *all night*?'

'If you are, then I am too.' She nuzzled against his chin and slipped her leg between his, sending his blood racing south and bringing things to attention far earlier than he would have thought possible.

'Bloody hell, Liv, you make me feel like a teenager again.'

'Well, it would be a shame not to take advantage of that,' she purred against his ear.

'You're right. We've already wasted too much time.' He grabbed her by the hips and rolled her beneath him, leaving her giggling as he pinned her to the bed. But he soon hushed her laughter with his lips, working hard to make up for lost time. He hated that there was already a limit on how much time he had with Liv, and he intended to enjoy every second possible of their new "adult" friendship.

CHAPTER TEN

Liv glared at the clock in the corner of her computer screen and willed the seconds and minutes to speed up and tick by just a *bit* faster. Even if they just returned to their usual, reliable pace, it would be better than the speed they were currently crawling by at. She usually loved her work, and found the interactions with patients fascinating and rewarding, but today, she'd struggled to focus and had been forced to call on every bit of her professionalism to make it through the afternoon.

It had only been a few weeks since she and Callum had stopped being friends in favour of . . . well, whatever you called it, it was good fun. And distracting, in the best possible way.

She tried to focus on her notes, and the barrage of emails that had built up during her afternoon surgery, but her mind kept wandering. And it really didn't help that the source of her distraction was wandering around the building, flashing sweet and sexy smiles her way at every opportunity.

As if summoned by her thoughts, he knocked at her door and slipped into the room. In a few short steps, he covered the space between them and pulled her into a warm embrace, then stole her breath with a searing kiss. 'Is it bad that I've been thinking about this for half the day?'

'I hope not, because I've been struggling to concentrate too,' Liv admitted as she rested her head against his shoulder.

'I'm going to pick Sarah up from her netball club, and drop her off at Jake and Evelyn's. But I promised we'd go via the store so she can pick out marshmallows and sweets for her camp out.'

'Is she looking forward to her sleepover?'

'Yeah, she's been talking about it for days. She's adored Summer since they met, and is so excited that they're going to be "officially, properly family".'

'Tell her I said hello.' Liv planted a kiss on the tip of his nose. 'And hurry back.'

'Oh, I will,' he promised fervently. 'I haven't got much food in. We can order takeaway, or I can pick something up?'

'I really don't mind, but I wasn't planning on spending lots of time cooking this evening.' She blushed as she realised what she'd implied.

'Understood.' Callum grinned. 'I probably won't be more than an hour or so.'

'You know where I'll be.'

'I can't wait.'

* * *

Liv allowed herself a moment or two to catch her breath and check that her make-up wasn't too obviously smudged, before hitching her bag onto her shoulder and sauntering down the corridor. She waved to Millie as she left and walked home through the village, enjoying the sun on her back and the peace of her commute. Within minutes, she was back at her cottage, and toed off her shoes at the door before heading to the kitchen. A few minutes more and she was padding barefoot down the garden path, a steaming cup of tea in hand as she headed for her favourite spot.

She perched on the edge of the well and sighed happily. The evening light turned the garden golden, and the ancient stones were warm beneath her. Everything about the little cottage and its garden was cheerful and welcoming, and made her feel safe. As her fingers traced the almost invisible patterns in the stones, she found herself wishing this feeling could fill her always.

* * *

'I really think two packets of marshmallows, biscuits, chocolate raisins and chocolate is enough.' Callum stood in the middle of the crisp aisle, not wanting to give in to Sarah's demands, but not wanting to argue with her either. 'And you know Evelyn is going to make you dinner too.'

'We're having cheesy, sausage pasta.'

'So you probably don't need crisps then, do you?'

'No, but I like them.' Sarah pouted, her bottom lip sticking out and starting to wobble dangerously. 'And the raisins are for Uncle Jake.'

'All right, all right.' Callum lobbed the crisps in the basket while internally cursing his weakness. He didn't really want Sarah eating so much junk food, but it wasn't something that happened very often, and the last thing he wanted was a meltdown in the middle of the shop.

'When I'm seeing Summer are you going to be seeing Livvy?' Sarah tucked her hand into his, almost skipping along by his side and making him wonder if he'd just been rather expertly played.

'Yes, is that OK?'

'Yup. I like Livvy.'

'I like her too.'

'I know that.' Sarah rolled her eyes at him, reminding him — yet again — just how quickly she was growing up. Sometimes he really wished he could just hit pause for a bit.

'And are you OK about me liking Liv?' He didn't know why he'd suddenly felt the need to ask. He and Liv had both been careful not to let Sarah see them as anything more than friends. They were both well aware that their situation was only temporary, and neither wanted to confuse or upset the little girl.

He might have imagined it, but he thought for a moment that Sarah had given him a strange look, before her face lit up happily. 'I like Livvy, you like Livvy, and Livvy likes me and you. It's all good.' She'd got the American accent down perfectly.

'I'm assuming Summer taught you that phrase?'

'Yuppers.'

Callum shook his head, smothering a smile as he hustled her through the checkout and into the car. A few minutes later he waved to her as she skipped up his brother's garden path, clutching her midnight snacks. He felt a slight pang as she raced through the open door, without even looking back. A few seconds later she and her soon-to-be step-cousin appeared at the window, waving and blowing kisses. Even from the car and through the window, he could see they were giggling as his brother leaned in the car window.

'I can't believe you let her bring that much sugar.' He shook his head and laughed.

'I'd apologise, but I know you'll probably be sharing it with them. She made me buy raisins especially for you.'

'Hope they're chocolate-dipped.'

'Of course. You've trained my daughter well to smuggle in your treats.'

He laughed. 'Not my fault she's such a willing accomplice.'

'Thanks for having her tonight. And say thanks to Evelyn for me again as well.'

'Are you kidding? We love having Sarah to visit. She and Summer are "BFFs", which is apparently the single strongest bond two girls can have. And you know there's nothing I wouldn't do to see Summer happy.'

'I know, bro.' Callum clasped his hand through the window. 'But I still appreciate it.'

'Then bugger off and enjoy your free time. And give Liv our regards. Evelyn wanted to invite you all over to dinner, but said she seemed reluctant. Any idea why?'

'It might be a bit much.'

'How do you mean?'

'Well, Liv and I are just friends. At least, as far as Sarah's concerned.' He tried to explain what he didn't fully understand himself. 'It's one thing to go to a work party or something together, or grab food as friends . . . but an intimate family dinner? Just feels a bit wrong.'

'One, I'd hardly describe any meal including two little girls as intimate, and two, I don't know who you think you're fooling. We can all see you're crazy about Liv. And frankly, I can see why. If I wasn't a happily engaged husband and dad-to-be, I might have invited her out myself. And your daughter's no idiot.'

'No, she's not.' Callum drummed his fingers on the steering wheel, not really sure what to say. 'I should be going. Thanks again.'

'And again, it's no problem. We'll drop Sarah back after lunch.'

'OK. Thanks.'

* * *

Liv sighed happily and flopped back into her pillows. Though they'd had to be really organised to plan their time around responsibilities to the community, and Sarah, they'd still managed to find more than a few moments of time together. Alone together.

'Do you think Evelyn is more of a chocolate or lemon person?'

The question was so random that Liv laughed out loud. 'Why on earth are you thinking about that?'

'I was thinking maybe I should bake her a cake or something, as thanks for having Sarah over again.'

'She has been having her over a lot.' Liv rolled over to study him. 'Can you even bake?'

'Yeah, Mum taught us all. She considered being able to cook, clean and work a washing machine basic life skills — and made sure we all learnt before we left home.' Callum laughed.

157

'She wasn't wrong. Do you think Evelyn's trying to push us together?' Liv wasn't sure how she felt about that.

'Maybe a bit. But I think she's just happy for me. For us.' He grinned and pulled her closer. 'Have to admit, I'm pretty happy about this too.'

Liv laughed and snuggled against him for a few moments, before throwing the covers back with a sigh.

'Where are you going?'

'Bathroom. And then to get dressed. We can't lie around here all day.'

'We could.'

'You said you wanted to get some shopping done, and pop to the surgery before Sarah gets home, and I wanted to get in early and sort out some paperwork.'

'You must have a terrible boss, making you work at the weekend,' he deadpanned.

'Oh, he's just the worst.' She stifled a grin as she wrapped his shirt tightly around herself. 'A complete slave driver.'

His teasing smile morphed into a frown as he watched her. 'Why do you do that?'

'Do what?'

'Hide from me. After what we've just done . . . what we've been doing for a couple of weeks now . . . why do you hide your gorgeous self from me?'

'I'm just cold.' Liv pulled the shirt tighter, fumbling to do up some of the buttons and give herself some semblance of protection.

'Liv, it's roasting in here. You're not cold. What's going on?'

The sudden lump in her throat was choking, and her eyes prickled with painful tears. 'It's nothing.' She didn't even want the thoughts to form into coherent words, even in her mind.

'Liv, please don't push me away.' The bedding rustled behind her as he threw back the covers and pulled on underwear. A moment later he was behind her, wrapping his arms around her. 'Talk to me. Tell me what's wrong. Please?'

'I just . . . sometimes . . . I feel a bit . . .'

'Liv, you can trust me.'

'Damaged.' She choked the word out, and tightened her arms across her abdomen.

'This is about your ex, isn't it?'

She nodded.

'From everything you've told me, he was a first-class moron.'

'Yup.'

'But his words still hurt you?'

She nodded and angrily dashed away a hot tear which scorched its way down her cheek.

'You know he's not worth a millisecond more of your time, or a single thought. He's already had more space in your head than he ever deserved.'

Liv shrugged. It was so much easier for Callum to say it than it was for her to do. Mike's words had left their puckered, angry marks across her mind, much as the scalpel had left its scars across her skin. Every time she glanced in the mirror, or caught sight of the scars along her arm, she was reminded of how broken she was. She tried her hardest to avoid looking, but she couldn't keep her eyes from dropping to the damage that was still stark against her skin.

'Liv, you're not really hearing me, are you?'

Her throat constricted against the tears trying to choke her. 'I'm trying. It's just really hard.'

'Come here.' He gently turned her to face the large wardrobe that sat snugly in the alcove formed by the old chimney. He hugged her tightly from behind, drawing her against his warmth before cupping her chin in his hand and lifting her head.

She sighed against his palm.

'Open your eyes, Liv.'

When she met her own gaze in the mirror, she winced and tried to shy away, but he held her firm.

'Callum . . . I don't . . .'

'Please, Liv.' He placed a kiss against her temple. 'Give me a few more moments of your trust?'

'OK.' She forced the word out past the lump in her throat and nodded against his hand.

'You can be so harsh on yourself, and you let cruel words that deserve to be buried in the past change the way you look at yourself. And that breaks my heart.'

'I'm sorry.'

'I don't want you to apologise, I want you to listen to me. OK?'

'I'll try.' She owed him that much.

'If you really want to use someone else's words to define yourself, why choose his? Why do you let him hurt you even now?'

'I . . . don't know,' she admitted.

'If you want to use someone else's words, why not use mine? I wish you could see yourself the way I see you. Even if it's just for a few moments. You are beautiful.' He gathered her hair in one hand and smoothed it over her shoulder, while keeping his other arm firmly around her waist. She was glad he kept hold of her; his solid warmth was the only thing holding her in the present and giving her the strength to not hide from her reflection.

'You are smart, and kind . . .' His hand trailed a path of goose pimples down her neck, and into the V of the shirt that hung loose to her thighs. His warm fingers teased the edge of the fabric as he spoke. 'And you are one of the sweetest and loveliest people I've ever met.'

'I'm really not.'

'You really are,' he argued as his fingers slipped lower, teasing the sensitive skin between her breasts. 'You are a brilliant doctor, a visionary planner, and everyone adores you.' He flipped open the buttons she'd done up, leaving his shirt hanging open over her. '*I* adore you.'

Her breath caught in her throat — for a far more pleasurable reason than it had earlier — as he pulled the fabric aside and warmed her body with his hands.

'And you are so fucking gorgeous you make me ache.'

'Callum.' Her voice was a gasp as his hand slid lower.

'Look at yourself, Liv.' He kissed her neck, making her back arch against him as she squirmed against the sensation of his hot lips against her neck. 'You are brave, and sweet, and wonderful. And on top of it all, you are stunningly sexy. From your hair to your toes and everything in-between, you couldn't be any more perfect.' He breathed the words against her ear as his fingers gently traced her scars.

She flinched, wanting to argue, but his fingers stayed gentle and brushed her complaints away. 'These are nothing. They mean nothing. You are stunning. About half the time I'm with you, I want to pinch myself because I can hardly believe it's real. The rest of the time I'm terrified I'll wake up and find you were all a dream. Because some days, I struggle to believe that this — you — are real. That you're choosing to be with me. Most people wouldn't have the strength to overcome the things you have, and yet you're still one of the most loving and open people I know.'

She watched as the mirror version of him slid the soft cotton from her shoulders down to her elbows, and for a moment she barely recognised herself. The sun had caught in her hair, making it glow and shimmer as she moved, arching against her lover. Her cheeks were flushed and pink, making her eyes seem all the brighter. The shirt gaped, and the same light that played in her hair dusted her skin golden, and her eyes followed the path of his hand as it moved over the planes and shadows of her body, leaving her gasping.

'You don't see it, Liv, but you're beautiful. You're an inspiration.'

She almost wished he hadn't spoken and broken the spell. She shook her head. 'You're just saying that to try and make me feel better.'

'Look at me.' He met her gaze in the mirror. 'I promise you, I'm not saying anything that isn't true. I wouldn't lie to you, Liv.' He chuckled and drew her hips more firmly against his. 'I couldn't, even if I wanted to. You can feel what you do to me. You're amazing.'

'You're pretty amazing too.' Liv smiled at him in the mirror and reached up to draw him in for a kiss.

'You know, I meant what I said. I really do adore you.' His mouth traced a trail of heat down her neck as he guided her gaze back towards the mirror where her eyes traced the movement of his fingers that flooded her body with heat.

* * *

A few days later, Liv winced in sympathy as she examined the swollen foot resting on a stool in her office. 'Sorry, this might hurt a bit.' She gently rotated the foot and palpated the soft tissues under the ankle bone.

'What do you think?' Her patient watched her with worried eyes.

'I think you're going to be off your feet for a while, Mr Davies. It doesn't appear to be broken, but you might want to get it x-rayed just to be sure. I'd say it's a nasty sprain, but as you're going to have to get to the hospital for crutches — and maybe a brace — I can give you a referral for radiology.'

'Damn it! Will I be back on my feet before the big Christmas party? I'm supposed to be on one of the floats.'

'It could have been a lot worse,' Liv reassured him. 'You said you fell down a flight of stairs? A couple of minor bumps and a sprain is a good outcome. You could have been seriously hurt. You should be fine in a few weeks. Just rest up now, and I'm sure we'll get you carnival fit and ready.'

'Good. I would have hated to miss that.' He leaned forward conspiratorially. 'Not sure if I'm supposed to say too much, but the jive might be featuring on our float this year.'

'It's OK, I won't tell.' Liv grinned. 'Is that how you did this? Jiving too much?'

'No. Tripped over my dog. He's fine, though.'

'Glad to hear he's OK. I like dogs.' Liv nodded.

'Me too, usually.' He laughed. 'But my doctor visits are less expensive than his!'

Liv tried not to laugh at that, and had to fight to retain some semblance of professionalism. 'Well, like I said, I don't think it's broken, and I'll wrap it up now. But you'll need to get some proper crutches. That stick you're using is really only any good as a temporary measure. And may I suggest that maybe your dog should sleep downstairs, at least for the time being?'

'Yes, Doctor.'

'Good.' Liv wrapped the bandage around his swollen ankle in quick, gentle moves. 'Now, keep an eye on it to make sure it doesn't swell any more. If it does, you might need to take the wrapping off.'

'OK. Thank you.'

'I'll write up your notes, and have our receptionist call ahead to the hospital. Hopefully it'll reduce your waiting time. Make sure to elevate your foot as much as possible, and ice it — but keep the ice packs wrapped in a towel so you don't damage your skin. If the pain gets too bad, you can use over-the-counter painkillers.'

'Much appreciated.' He shook her hand and made his way slowly, and painfully, back to reception.

She hadn't even finished washing her hands when there was another knock at her door, and Callum slipped into the room.

'Hi, I thought you could do with this.' He held up a steaming cup. 'I hear it's already been a long morning.'

'I am so glad to see you.' She gratefully took the cup and buried her nose in it to inhale the rich, rejuvenating fragrance.

'Me, or the coffee?'

'You . . . as the bringer of my coffee?'

'Oh, so now you're a comedian.' He grinned as he stalked her and slid his arms around her waist. 'I've missed you.'

'It's only been a couple of days.' Liv laughed.

'I know, but it feels like longer though.' He slipped the coffee from her hand and placed it on the desk.

'It really does,' Liv agreed. 'Between our patients, Sarah, and all the paperwork the commissioners have been asking for, there's barely been time for anything else.'

'I'm really sorry.'

'I wasn't complaining.' Liv wrapped her arms around his neck and pulled him down to her lips. 'Just agreeing with you. Still, at least we get to see each other here. And tonight.'

'About that . . . How annoyed would you be if it wasn't just us for dinner?'

'You know I'm always glad to see Sarah.'

'Not just Sarah,' he admitted. 'Jake, Evelyn and Summer too. My sister Kimberly, and a family friend, Nick, who was basically the mastermind for the first Summer's Christmas fundraiser. And . . . we've been invited to Jake's.'

'It's a family thing, then.' Liv withdrew, already planning her excuses. Obviously she had no place at a meal like that.

'No, and even if it was, you'd still be invited. There'll be some ladies from the WI there. Some of our other fundraisers, and probably Millie and whoever else can make it from the surgery.'

'So, not quite half the village.' Butterflies started their twisting dance in Liv's stomach at the thought of a polite dinner with strangers. 'It's fine, you should go. I'll probably just get an early night.'

'Liv, I really want you there.' His words washed over her, and the butterflies slowed their anxious quick step to a smooth waltz as her heart soared. She was amazed at how easily he soothed her worries, and involved her in his plans with genuine, open invitations without obligation or expectation. And she found herself wanting to say yes — not because he would sulk or glower like Mike would have if she'd turned him down — but because she really wanted to be around Callum. And Sarah.

His hand slid down her arms to grasp her fingers in his. 'Please, Liv. I really want you to be a part of this. It's your concept, your plan, your hard work that's given us, *given me*, a chance to save the surgery. I want you to be part of it . . . with me.'

'OK.'

* * *

Callum watched Liv from across the room. She was laughing with Jake and Kimberly as they pored over photos from the original Summer's Christmas fundraiser. Nick, who was as good as an extra brother to the three of them, was there in the thick of things — watching over the plans. It was only fair. He'd come up with the original concept and designed the first fundraiser, and if anyone other than Summer owned the event, it was Nick.

He'd welcomed Liv with one of his usual warm hugs and shot a thumbs-up to Callum as soon as Liv's back had been turned.

He knew he shouldn't care about what his friends and family thought of Liv — not when they both knew their time together was limited and futureless and they had both agreed to keep things casual — but it did matter to him. And seeing her laughing together with some of the most important people in his life did something to his heart. When Sarah wriggled her way onto Liv's lap she automatically wrapped her arms around the little girl, then looked up and caught his eye. The smile she gave him slammed realisation into him like a punch to the stomach: he didn't want her to leave. Not tonight, when the party was over, and not in a few weeks or months when his parents returned from their latest adventure.

'Callum?' Evelyn waved her hand across his vision and he started guiltily.

'You've barely heard a word I've said, have you?'

'I'm sorry, I was just . . . thinking.'

'I'd offer you a penny for your thoughts, but it would be a waste of money.'

'Gee, thanks.' Callum rolled his eyes. 'Nice to know what you think I'm worth.'

'Rotter.' She gave him a gentle shove. 'You know I don't mean it like that. I know I'm relatively new to the family, but anyone who's known you for ten minutes can see what's on your mind right now.'

Callum closed his eyes, hoping that she was bluffing, or wrong.

'Or should I say *who* is on your mind?'

'Can you read all men like we're open books, or is it just us Macpearsons?' he grumbled.

'That would be telling.' Evelyn grinned. 'But it might be a new trick I'm adding to my repertoire. But right now, if you were a book, you'd probably be one of the easy-read ones Summer used to bring home from school. With easily understood text and lots of pictures.'

He stayed quiet, not knowing what to say.

She nudged his shoulder with hers. 'Look at me and tell me that I'm wrong, Cal. Or tell me it's none of my business. Or tell me that you don't want to talk about it.' She smiled when he opened his eyes, and Callum could see the kindness and warmth that made her such a good nurse. And friend. 'Or, tell me how I can help.'

'I don't think you can help.' He sighed. 'I don't think anyone can.'

'Tell me.' She kept her voice low. 'Is it what I think?'

Callum glanced over to the corner of the room again, to where Sarah bounced excitedly in Liv's lap as she pointed things out in the photo album. He watched as Nick inclined his head, listening to something Liv was saying, before nodding and scribbling something in his sketchpad.

He looked back at Evelyn, who was watching him closely. 'Did I do the wrong thing, encouraging you to get together?'

'No. Yes. Maybe. I don't know.' He ran his hands through his hair.

'I'm sorry. I thought you liked her.'

'I do. That's the problem.'

166

'She doesn't like you back?' The sympathy in Evelyn's eyes made him cringe.

'I think she does.'

'Then what's the problem?'

'There's no future. She's not going to stay in Broclington.' He knew it was true, but saying the words aloud still hurt.

'And she's told you that, has she?'

'She's told me she's not looking for anything serious.' He tried to shrug the pain away, but it was getting harder. 'I thought I felt the same but . . .'

'But now you want something more?'

'I think I might.'

'Have you asked her if she feels the same?'

'There's not much point. She's made her feelings clear. And you know she's only on a locum contract. It's obvious she'll be leaving.'

'Maybe.' She pursed her lips. 'But maybe not. When Summer and I moved in with my mum a few years ago, I hadn't really planned on staying. Now, I can't imagine wanting to live anywhere else again. Broclington is a bit funny like that. It catches you unaware and wraps such a warm welcome around you that you never really want to leave.'

'But you did leave. Originally.'

'I was a kid.' She laughed. 'And I didn't leave, so much as just didn't come back.'

'It's not the same.' Callum shook his head sadly. 'She's here on a temporary contract.'

'That's a shame.' Evelyn frowned. 'I really like her. And I'm clearly not the only one.'

Callum followed her gaze back to where Sarah leaned happily against Liv. Her small fingers twirled in Liv's silky blonde hair that he knew smelt like a summer evening. The happiness he felt when she curled against him in a private — albeit temporary — world eclipsed almost everything. Which scared him. But what terrified him more was how happy and open Sarah was when she was with Liv — more so than with anyone else outside his immediate family, which meant she was going to be hurt when Liv left. He cursed himself silently as he watched them together, realising for the first time how badly he'd screwed up. He could handle pain, but Sarah didn't deserve to be abandoned again. He could only dread the damage that would be done by another woman walking out on her.

Evelyn sighed. 'You've barely heard a word I've said, have you?'

He was saved from having to answer by the rap of the door knocker.

'You'll have to excuse me.' Evelyn grimaced. 'I should go see who that is. But don't think this conversation is over, Cal.'

* * *

Sarah leaped out of Liv's lap and raced out of the room, squealing with excitement, with Summer and Tilly hot on her heels, yipping and shouting their own excitement.

'So this is where you all are.' The familiar voice echoed down the hall, tinged with laughter. Within moments, every-one was on their feet, crowding the new guests.

As the cacophony of joyous greetings bounced off the old cottage walls, Liv retreated further and further into the corner, feeling more and more awkward. Despite what Callum had said, and the colleagues who were present, this was very much a family event and she was reminded that she was very much an outsider. However warmly she'd been wel-comed, she was only too aware that she was a temporary addi-tion to the group, and didn't have any real place within it. Unlike everyone making up the loud, noisy welcome party. She shrunk further into the corner, wishing the ground could swallow her up.

'Liv, is that you hiding in the corner? Get over here and say hello properly.'

She'd always listened to Tom in the past, and didn't want to argue now, so stood and let him fold her into a quick hug.

He stepped away after a second or two and held her at arm's length. 'You're looking much better than the last time I saw you. I'm glad. It looks like being in Broclington suits you.' He turned her hand in his. 'And I'm glad to see you're out of the cast. Are you fully recovered?'

Liv hesitated before answering as honestly as she could when surrounded by people. 'Yes thank you, as well as can be expected.'

Tom's eyes narrowed, and she knew her former mentor wasn't going to let the comment slide easily. But her recovery, incomplete as it was, wasn't something she wanted to discuss right now. Or ever really. But she was saved from the medical interrogation by an older woman who stepped forward, her arms outstretched in welcome.

'I'm Julie. I know we've never met, but I've heard so much about you for so long that I feel like I know you. I've been so looking forward to meeting you.' The older woman beamed.

'Really?'

'Of course.' She embraced Liv quickly and firmly. 'You've been one of Tom's favourite students for years. I was so sorry to hear about what happened in London, but I'm glad it brought you to us. I know I said it in my email, but I want to say it again. Thank you. For so much.'

'I've really not done anything special,' Liv asserted, embarrassed by all the eyes on her.

'We had a horrible time getting reliable cover before. It was so bad last time, Tom wasn't sure we could take another sabbatical.'

'Really?' Without seeing his face, Liv knew Callum's eyebrows would be raised in surprise, his blue eyes widening and smoothing out the laughter lines around them. 'You didn't say.'

'Your father didn't want to worry you,' Julie soothed. 'And it wasn't necessary, because Liv has been just perfect.'

'That she has,' Tom agreed, and Liv found her cheeks heating again. 'Not only have you fitted into the surgery brilliantly — and I know because I've been hearing stories about you — but you've also saved our family business.'

'It was just the idea . . .'

'The idea that's turned into a proposal that will save the surgery,' Nick argued.

'If we can raise the money.' Liv was still worried that too much hope was being pinned on an idea that might not come to fruition.

'We will. Have a little faith in me.' Nick shot her a wink.

'I wish you'd told us you were coming back early,' Jake grumbled. 'We'd have met you at the airport.'

'We weren't expecting you for a couple more weeks,' Callum agreed. 'Is everything OK?'

'Of course,' Julie reassured them all. 'We always planned to be back in time for Summer's Christmas, but when we read the proposal, we decided to come back early and help.'

'You still could have told us.'

'We could have.' Tom grinned. 'But if we did, it wouldn't have been a surprise, would it?'

'I'm glad you're back, Grandma and Grandpa. I missed you.' Sarah wriggled her way between them both.

'We missed you too, fairy.' Tom tousled her hair.

'I should be going . . .' Liv headed towards the door.

'Nonsense. This just became our welcome home party!' Tom grinned.

'You should stay,' Evelyn insisted. 'It won't be the same without you. You're part of the surgery family now. You have to stay.'

* * *

Callum struggled not to agree as Sarah bounced up and down by Liv's side, pleading with her to stay. He watched as his family enveloped her, and he found himself wishing again that a locum contract could last forever. After a moment of wallowing, he shook his head to try and banish the thought: he and Liv were just friends who were enjoying each other's company for as long as possible. And he had to be happy with that. And he *was* going to be happy with that.

Resolution made, he pushed himself back into the middle of the party and draped his arm around his mum's shoulders. She smiled up at him, squeezed his waist and placed a fond kiss on his cheek. 'I'm so proud of you.'

'Of me? How come?'

'You've looked after things so well. You always do. Your dad and I wouldn't be able to keep travelling and supporting the communities we work in if it wasn't for you. We know it's a lot harder for you to pick up in our absence than Jake: he doesn't have to take responsibility for running the surgery while looking after a rambunctious six-year-old. Who I'm convinced has grown four inches since I last saw her.'

'Well, she has cost me new shoes, so she's definitely growing.' He laughed.

'Seriously, your dad and I don't say it often enough, but thank you for everything you're doing. For all the times you've taken over at the surgery, and for everything you've done with the proposal to save it. It really is quite inspired. We couldn't have left the place in better hands.'

'You're welcome.' Callum dropped a kiss onto her cheek. 'But the proposal was mostly Liv's idea.'

'Her idea, but you — and Nick — have put in the hard work. I can see your work throughout it.'

'It's good, isn't it?' Callum had to ask.

'Yes. It really is something special. Just like you.'

'Awww, Mum.' He was reduced to being Sarah's age again.

'What? I can't make a fuss of my son when I've not seen him for months?' She reached up to tousle his hair like she'd done for most of his life.

'I've missed you, Mum.'

'I've missed you too. We both did. We missed you all, and especially Sarah.'

Callum's eyes automatically tracked back to where she sat in Liv's lap, still happily laughing and chatting with the woman who had so effectively slipped into his life and turned his world topsy-turvy.

'She's changed a lot,' his mum added.

'I know. I feel like I'm buying new shoes or clothes every other week.'

'Children grow. It's one of the things they're best at.' She laughed. 'But she's a lot more confident too. And she seems really happy.'

'Yeah, she is.'

'Our new doctor seems to have had a lot to do with that.' They watched as Sarah whispered something to Liv and they giggled together. As if feeling his eyes on her, Liv glanced up and their gazes locked, and the rest of the room faded away. He was vaguely aware that his mum was still talking to him, but he couldn't focus on anything but Liv's smile. When she looked away, he found himself smiling.

'Sorry, what was that, Mum?'

'I was just saying you seem happy too, and I asked if Liv had anything to do with that. But I think I've got my answer.'

'We're just friends.' Despite how many times he'd said them, the words felt wrong.

'If you say so, love. If you say so.' Her sharp eyes watched him, and darted back to Liv. 'But if you were something more than "just friends", would it be such a bad thing? It's been a long time since Trixie. It might be good for you, and Sarah, to have someone in your life.'

'She's not going to be here permanently. You know that as well as anyone: you and Dad hired her.'

'But with the surgery expanding, you'll need more staff. There's no reason Liv couldn't be one of them. Have you thought about asking her?'

'More than once. But she's never intended on staying in Broclington long-term.'

'Because she doesn't want to, or because her contract was initially temporary?'

Callum sighed, wishing he didn't already know the answer. 'She said she views Broclington as a bit of a break from her life. Just a temporary role while she figures out what she wants to do with herself. She was thinking of private practice. She's certainly skilled and driven enough to do it. Who am I to stand in her way?'

'People change their plans all the time, just look at me and your dad. Our first sabbatical with the medical mission was only supposed to last a matter of weeks, and now we spend as much time abroad as we do here at home.'

'Don't I know it.' Callum pulled a face.

'You are happy for us, aren't you?'

'Of course. We just miss you. And you enjoy it, don't you?'

'More than that. We love it. We hadn't expected to fall in love with the African continent and people, and the work we're doing out there, but we did. And that's the thing, there's no limit to the things people will do for love. There's no obstacle that can't be overcome, and no change you won't make for love. It's the most powerful force in the world.'

'I know, there's nothing I wouldn't do for Sarah. Just like Jake raised hundreds of thousands of pounds and travelled across continents and oceans for Summer and Evelyn.' He sighed. 'You know, I never really felt that way for Trixie, maybe that was the problem.'

'Maybe. When love is there, and true, it can heal and soothe great wounds.'

Callum's mind drifted back to the recent morning he'd spent with Liv, and he felt a smile spread across his face. Liv had given him her trust, and let herself be vulnerable as she displayed her scars and pain. The fact that she trusted him so deeply touched him, and made him feel ten feet tall.

'But when that love is missing,' his mum continued, 'its very absence can cause those wounds.'

'I learned that the hard way.'

'I know you did, love.' She squeezed his hand. 'But don't let your past experiences dictate your future, or ruin your chances of something special.' Her eyes flicked to Liv again, and Callum followed her gaze. He wished he could take his mum's advice, and take a chance, but he couldn't — *wouldn't* — risk Sarah's happiness too.

CHAPTER ELEVEN

'Hey.' Liv looked up as Callum peered into her office. 'Busy?'

'Just finishing up some admin. Nothing too urgent.' While she was glad about that, she'd definitely seen an increase in the gaps between her appointments in the last couple of weeks — and she wasn't entirely sure how she felt about that.

'Good, because I need your help with something that is. Urgent, I mean.'

'What?' Liv was on her feet in an instant.

'You, me, lunch.' He held his hand out to her. 'Come on, I can guarantee what I've got planned is better than whatever sandwich or leftovers you've got in the fridge.'

'What did you have in mind?'

'Something fun.' He tucked her hand into his. 'I think we deserve to spend some time together, away from here, away from funding bids and worries, and — if you'll forgive me for saying it — away from Sarah too.' He looked down into her eyes. 'Just you and me, Liv, what do you say?'

'It's the middle of the day,' she pointed out.

'Exactly. The perfect time for a picnic.' He stepped closer to her. 'Tell me, Liv, when was the last time you had a picnic in the countryside? Here's a hint: if the answer is that you don't know, then it's been too long. Your paperwork will still be here this afternoon. Or maybe even tomorrow.'

'Tomorrow, huh?' She reached down and grabbed her bag.

'Yeah, I hear the surgery manager can be a real pushover.'

'Oh, can he, indeed?'

'Apparently so. Especially when it comes to smart, beautiful blondes. Come on, what do you say?'

'Nice walk, get some vitamin D, and then some shade and lunch. Might be just what the doctor ordered.'

'I can write it up as a 'script if it convinces you,' he offered.

'What's for lunch?'

He gave her a cheeky grin and held up a rucksack. 'Falafel and hummus salad wraps, raspberries picked freshly from the garden this morning. And cake. What do you say? Come have a picnic and laze in the sun with me for a bit?'

'Depends . . . What type of cakes?'

'Brockle cakes, of course.'

'Next time you should lead with that.' Liv grinned and tucked her hand back into his. 'So, where are we going?'

'Not too far. I'm not expecting anything to come up, but . . . just in case there's anything the others can't handle, I thought we should stay close by.'

'Makes sense. Even on a quiet day you can't really trust it will stay that way.' Liv knew neither of them were off duty.

'Nope. So, how about the recreation ground? I've got a blanket we can spread out under one of the trees.'

'Sounds perfect.'

* * *

Callum polished off the last of the chocolate, vanilla and cherry Brockle cake and leaned back, tucking his hands behind his head. 'Well, that was delicious. Even if I do say so myself.'

'It really was. And this is lovely.' She looked around the park. 'Thank you for thinking of it.'

'I'd like to pretend it was entirely altruistic, but in reality I felt like we both deserved a bit of downtime.' He rolled

175

onto his side and propped himself up on an elbow to look at Liv. 'This was one of my favourite places growing up. I spent hours here.'

'Right here?'

'Well, maybe a few feet to the left.' He laughed.

'You know, I think I can picture it.' Liv turned to face him. 'You, Jake and Kimberley sat under here, planning your lives out and dreaming great things.'

'Don't forget the squabbling, tormenting of the sister, and chasing our dog.' He grinned. 'Don't look so disapproving. Tormenting little sisters is what big brothers are supposed to do. Worms and all.'

'Worms? I don't want to know, do I?'

'Probably not.' He chuckled. 'In fairness, it wasn't always me. Sometimes Bouncer helped.'

'Bouncer?'

'Our dog. A proper Heinz fifty-seven mongrel — part lab, part beagle, part goodness-only-knows what else. Jake always said he thought there was some spaniel too. He could be really screwy.'

'Sounds wonderful.' Liv sighed wistfully. 'I always wanted a dog when I was younger. But Mum preferred cats, and said a dog would be too much work. She was probably right.'

'They are a lot of work, but can be really rewarding.' He smiled nostalgically. 'It was probably easier because there were three of us kids, and it taught us a lot about responsibility. I think he probably influenced Jake's career at least a bit too. The patients used to love him.'

'He was a regular with patients?'

'Yeah, had a basket in reception. Way more fun for our littlest patients than the toy corner, and he was good for calming down people who were a bit nervous.'

'Sounds nice.'

'It was. I was very lucky with my childhood. So . . .' He grinned at her. 'This was one of my favourite places. Where was yours?'

Liv took a moment to think about the answer. 'I used to love being in the kitchen with Mum. I wasn't always the best of cooks or bakers, but we always had good fun. She used to lift me up on the work surface when I was tiny, and I'd steal raw pastry out of the bowl. It's one of my earliest memories. For a while, I even thought about becoming a chef.'

'Why didn't you?'

'Well, that was my plan when I was probably about Sarah's age, and thought I'd just get to eat lots of lovely things all the time. But, like I said, I'm not exactly the best of cooks all the time. Plus I think I saw too many TV programmes with shouting, swearing head chefs. It looked pretty stressful.'

'So instead you chose a nice calm, stress-free, low-pressure career in medicine,' Callum teased.

'I know, when you put it like that it makes no sense.'

'Well, I for one am very, very glad you chose medicine, and ended up here.' He leaned over to brush a kiss against her lips. 'Even if I would have preferred you'd ended up here through a less stressful route.' He stroked her wrist, fingers brushing over the scars that were still dark against her skin.

'Enough about me.' Liv squeezed his fingers. 'Did you always want to be a doctor?'

'Well, obviously with it being the family practice there was always a focus on medicine in the family. It worked for me and Jake — albeit with animals. Kimberley definitely went the path-less-trodden route.'

'Never any question then?'

'Well . . .' He hesitated. 'You have to promise not to laugh.'

'OK.'

'Well, there was a period when I was probably about nine or ten when I thought about a different career.'

'What?'

'Remember, you promised not to laugh.' He waited for her nod. 'A Ninja helicopter pilot.'

'Awww, that's sweet. And only a little bit funny.'

'You don't know the best bit yet.'

'Go on . . .'

'I hate heights.'

* * *

A few days later, Liv closed the door behind her and leaned against it with a sigh. She dragged her overly tight ponytail down, and massaged her scalp tiredly. Try as she might, she couldn't keep tears of disappointment from prickling at her eyes. While Tom wasn't officially back working, word of his return had spread through the village quicker than chicken pox through a playgroup, and the villagers who he'd been treating for years were eager to see him.

It wasn't that she felt put out that "her" patients were choosing to wait for longer to see Tom instead — but it did serve a stark reminder of how temporary her role was. Broclington, and the surgery, had been a place for her to heal and take a break from the pressures of her former life while she figured out if she could still have a future in medicine. And it had given her exactly that. And now Tom was back, they didn't need her. She needed to make plans, and she'd avoided them for too long.

Taking a deep breath, she opened up her laptop and tapped in the address for the site she had been avoiding. She told herself that she wasn't making any commitments or decisions, that she was just having a look around. She fired off a couple of emails that she didn't really want to send before shutting the laptop down.

That would have to be enough for now.

* * *

The next few weeks were swallowed up by a blur of meetings and organisation, and Liv watched in amazement as the local Women's Institute swung into action to transform the village into a shimmering snow globe of possibility that glistened in the summer sun. A huge marquee sprung up, swooping out from the cricket pavilion and grazing the top of the bandstand as it cocooned part of the park, turning it into a magical venue that looked like it belonged on the pages of the most glamorous and glossy magazine. The trees edging the path that led away from the marquee sprouted tiny lights encased in what looked like snowy globes, and ribbons that twisted back and forth as if they'd been dropped there by over-excited fairies.

The decorations spiralled out from the park and spread across the village, with those fairies leaving their sparkling mark everywhere from shop fronts to lampposts, and even the hedgerows grew brightly coloured yarn baubles and snowflakes overnight. The tree in the village square stood proudly, topped off with a beautiful star. Around the tree, tables and stalls stood patiently, waiting for stallholders to arrive the next day and unload their wares.

The whole village looked amazing, and Liv was shocked and overwhelmed at the amount of attention attracted from reporters from local and regional news and papers. She couldn't believe how many people were interested in what was happening with the little village surgery, and how many donations had already been made. Everything was falling into place as perfectly as anyone could have hoped — led by the local WI and Nick who marshalled, cajoled, pleaded and organised a team of volunteers from the village into a veritable army of decorators, organisers and planners. They were even supported by local businesses who, as part of their corporate social responsibility and in exchange for some positive media coverage, were donating phenomenal amounts of time and goods.

It seemed to Liv that half the county had fallen in love with Broclington and their surgery. And she couldn't blame them. She was more than a little bit in love with the place herself.

The only downside, as far as Liv was concerned, was that the arrangements and organising had been so all-encompassing that she'd barely seen Callum outside of work or preparation meetings since his parents had returned from their sabbatical. So she struggled to keep from skipping as she headed up the path to knock at Callum's front door. His bright smile matched her own as he leaned forward to brush a quick kiss against her lips, before reluctantly pulling away when small feet pounded down the stairs.

'Hi Livvy!'

'Hi Sarah!' She was forced a step back under the weight of the little girl's excited greeting. 'Are you excited for tonight?'

'Yeah!' She bounced on the spot, propelled into the air by excitement.

'I hope you're ready for this, Liv. Sarah's really excited about you being here. She's been talking about it most of the week, and has planned the whole evening especially for you.' He ruffled his daughter's hair. 'Haven't you, munchkin? Are you going to let her in, Sarah?'

'Yup.' As usual, her smile was contagious to Liv. 'First we're going to make milkshakes like they have in America that Summer told me all about, and then we're going to watch her and Uncle Jake and Grandpa on the TV. And maybe Evie too. I don't know. But definitely Summer. It's so exciting!'

'Wow, it sounds it.' She shot Callum a quizzical look. 'You didn't fancy being on the local news and being the face of the "Save our Surgery" campaign?'

'No. We want to raise money, not scare people.' He chuckled good-naturedly. 'Jake and Dad make much better spokespeople than me, and Summer's practically a celebrity round here.'

'Yup. She's got nearly a million likes.' Sarah nodded solemnly.

'Do you even know what that means?' Callum looked horrified as he took Liv's coat.

'Yes. Obviously. It means lots of people are glad she's better, and will come help us to save the surgery.'

'Hopefully. And do you know how she got so many likes?'

'She makes videos so people can see how much better she is. Tilly is in them too. She gets more likes for Tilly's videos.'

'You . . . don't want to make videos like that, do you?'

Liv watched as Sarah tilted her head and pursed her lips in thought. 'No.'

Liv let out a breath she hadn't realised she'd been holding.

'Cancer isn't much fun,' Sarah said. 'Talking about it doesn't sound fun either. And Summer said sometimes, if Tilly is naughty, they have to make the same video over and over and over again. That sounds boring.'

She could almost feel Callum's relief as Sarah launched herself into the sofa cushions. 'She's growing up too fast as it is,' he murmured. 'I don't think I could handle the idea of her being a social media starlet.'

'I don't think you've too much to worry about. She's got her head screwed on straight and clearly knows her own mind.' She grinned as Sarah glared at them both.

'Come on, it's nearly time for Summer to be on TV. Livvy, you can sit here next to me, and Daddy can sit on the other side. And Dr Cuddlington can sit on my lap. And after Summer's been on TV and they start talking about boring stuff then we can have pizza for dinner.'

Liv pressed her lips together to keep from laughing when she caught Callum's eye. 'See what I mean?'

'Shhh, shh. It's starting! I helped Summer pick her dress. Do you like it, Livvy?'

'I think you have very good taste. It's a lovely dress.' She smiled as Sarah snuggled against her.

* * *

'Don't just stand there, Daddy. Summer and Evelyn and Uncle Jake are on the TV.'

'Yes, don't just stand there,' Liv teased.

'It's all right, I'm recording it.'

'But you need to watch it too!'

'OK, OK.' He stretched out on the sofa with them and let his arm fall over the back to brush against Liv's bare

181

shoulder. She shot him a smile that was so filled with warmth and promise that he had to drag his eyes away from her to focus on what his soon-to-be-niece was saying on the screen.

'. . . and that's why we want everyone to come out this weekend and help us have lots of fun celebrating Christmas in summer.' Summer grinned happily at the camera.

'Summer's Christmas.' The interviewer leaned forward.

'Yes.' Summer giggled. 'My Christmas. But it's not for me this year.'

'No, because you're all better now.' Evelyn's happiness beamed across the airwaves. 'The first year we ran "Summer's Christmas" was so we could raise the money needed to take Summer to America for life-saving cancer treatment. And last year, we raised money to help other children, and families, who were living with cancer.'

'And do you want to tell us about the cause you're raising money for this year?' The presenter nudged the conversation forward, looking expectantly at Summer who responded like a pro.

'It's to save the village surgery. And it's really, really important.'

'Maybe your mum can tell us a bit more about why that is? You're a nurse there, aren't you, Evelyn?'

'Yes, I am.' She nodded. 'I've been working as part of the surgery's team — which includes Jake's parents and brother as well as other staff — since I moved back to Broclington. It really is a vital part of the community.'

'She's not wrong,' Liv agreed with the digital image of her colleague and friend.

'Without the surgery,' Evelyn continued, 'members of our community wouldn't have any immediate access to medical help. They'd have to travel into the next town.'

'Which I suppose isn't good when you're not feeling well.' The reporter prompted again.

'No, it isn't, especially when a lot of our community don't drive, and buses run in and out of the village twice a day. On a good day. But it's not just about the impact on our village. Truthfully, the other surgeries near us don't have the space to take on extra patients without damaging the services they offer to their patients. It would be a disruption for everyone. But what we're proposing is about more than just keeping our little surgery open. It's also about improving things for everyone by offering more services. This would mean we could treat a lot of people in the community and offer minor procedures here that would relieve the pressure on our local hospitals. And we could discharge people from hospital sooner so we could lead their recoveries at home, which frees up hospital beds and is better for everyone.'

'The surgery really is a vital part of the village.' Jake now leaned forward. 'We all know it can be really stressful when you, or someone you love, is sick. But imagine how much worse that would be if you didn't have a doctor nearby, who you could get to easily, who knew you to help treat you. I'd already fallen head over heels in love with Evelyn and Summer when we found out Summer's cancer had returned.' He gulped visibly and Callum could see the tell-tale twitch in his brother's jaw that always gave his stress away. 'It was one of the most painful situations anyone can imagine. And it would have been worse without the support of our village surgery, and medical team.'

'I would have died.'

Summer's bluntness was brutal and shocking, and Callum automatically reached out to comfort Sarah. He was surprised to see her looking up at Liv.

'Is that true? Did Summer nearly die?'

He watched as Liv's tongue darted out to wet her lips, before she nodded slowly. 'The type of cancer Summer had was very, very serious. Not everyone gets better from it.'

'That's so sad!' Sarah ignored the TV and her dad to bury her face in Liv's shoulder.

'It really is.' She brushed Sarah's hair from her face. 'But Summer's all better. So that's a happy thing, right?'

'You're sure?'

'That's what her mum and your grandad say.'

'OK then.' Sarah settled back happily, and Callum let his eyes be tugged back towards the TV while he mulled over Sarah's reaction and how she'd automatically turned to Liv for comfort and reassurance. Again. The thought both thrilled and terrified him. He was so glad his daughter had someone other than him to turn to, but he wished it was someone who was a bit more . . . permanent. And yet, even knowing that, he couldn't resist the same magnetic pull that Sarah clearly felt too.

As if feeling his eyes on her, Liv turned and smiled at him, and his worries vanished almost immediately, blown away by the butterflies that had taken up residence in his stomach.

* * *

Liv groaned and pushed away the pizza box. 'That's it.' She waved her kitchen-roll napkin as if it was a white flag. 'I'm stuffed. I couldn't eat another bite if you paid me to.'

'I can!' Sarah laughed and reached for the box.

'You've already had three slices. You'll turn into a pizza!' Callum pulled the pizza away from her. 'And you need to go upstairs and start getting ready for bed.'

'Can I really turn into a pizza?'

'Do you know for sure that you can't?'

Sarah screwed up her mouth in thought. 'Liv, can I really turn into a pizza?'

Callum's eyes creased with amusement as he caught Liv's gaze over the top of Sarah's head. 'Well, I've never heard of anyone turning into a pizza. But I haven't read every single medical journal that has ever been written. And I do remember reading about a little girl who turned yellow from too much of her favourite drink. So it *could* be possible.'

'What was she drinking?' Sarah's eyes were wide.

'Some type of juice.' Liv laughed. 'But I can't remember the name.'

'Maybe I should have ice cream instead of pizza,' Sarah mused. 'Just to be safe.'

'Maybe you should go and get your things ready for school tomorrow,' Callum argued. 'And if you're still hungry then, I will consider dishing you up a small bowl of ice cream.'

'But Liv's here . . .'

'And I'll still be here when you're done.' Liv's words popped out before she'd even thought to check with Callum. She cringed inwardly at her presumption. 'If it's OK with your dad.'

Callum nodded, and she felt herself having to bite back a sigh of relief. While they still hadn't — officially — spoken about their relationship being anything more than "friends with benefits" or whatever the phrase was, it was becoming more and more obvious to her that they were behaving in a way that was a lot more than "just friendly". And that Sarah and Callum had become hugely important to her, and probably her favourite part of being in Broclington. So much so, that she neither could, or wanted to, picture a future without them as part of her life.

Oblivious to her thought process, Sarah gave her a bright grin. 'Then Livvy can read me my bedtime story.'

'Only if it's all right with Liv.' Callum raised his eyebrows in question. 'She might have to get home. The next few days are going to be really busy for everyone. It's getting late. Did you think about that, fairy?'

'Nope,' Sarah admitted with a small frown. 'But I'm not tired yet, and you say kids need more sleep than adults.' She grinned as a thought occurred to her. 'Maybe Livvy could sleep over. Then she could read me my bedtime story but still go to bed whenever she wanted.'

'Erm . . .'

'Ah . . .'

'What?' Sarah glanced between them. 'It's a good idea. Best friends have sleepovers all the time, and you *are* best friends.'

'What makes you say that?'

'Well, it's obvious. You see each other all day at work and still want to see each other after work. Like me and Summer. And she's my best friend.'

'Right.' Callum looked as panicked as Liv felt. This was rapidly racing towards the exact conversation they'd both agreed to avoid having with Sarah.

If it hadn't been for years of experience in emergency situations, Liv didn't think she would have been able to keep her racing pulse hidden. 'I'm sure I can read you a story. But only if you hurry up. I think your dad said you were supposed to be getting your school things ready, didn't he?'

'Ugh.' Sarah sighed as though the weight of the world was on her young shoulders, and Liv had to bite back a smile. 'OK. But it had better be a good story.'

'Fair deal.' Liv watched as Sarah trailed out of the room, dragging her feet with every step.

'I'm sorry she put you on the spot like that.'

'It's OK.' Liv shrugged. 'I'm happy to read her a story.'

'I didn't just mean the story.'

'I know.' Liv forced herself to meet his gaze. 'Talk about "out of the mouths of babes" and all that.'

'So, what do you think about it?' Callum's face was unreadable.

Liv took a deep breath. The truth was, she didn't know what to think about everything. She'd been doing her best to avoid thinking about the situation, because that was less painful than facing reality, or thinking about the future. She had barely even admitted her feelings to herself, unable to contemplate them because if she didn't think about them, it felt like they might be less real. And that they would be able to hurt her less. At least, that was what she kept telling herself. It was easier that than admitting how she felt, and risking tearing her heart open for the sake of the few days or weeks that she might have left in the village.

'Liv? Did you hear me?' His eyes burned into her and flooded her with his usual warmth.

'I think we need to talk.'

Callum nodded.

'But if it's all right, I'd like to read Sarah her story first.'

'Of course.' Callum nodded again. 'Then, when she's asleep, we can talk.'

Liv nodded, and headed towards the stairs, wondering if Sarah was too young for *The Complete Works of Shakespeare*. At least if she read a few rounds of the bard, she'd buy herself a bit more time to think.

* * *

Callum tiptoed along his own landing, feeling silly and sneaky as he did so, but he was drawn down the corridor by soft murmurs and giggles. As silly as it was, even in his own head, he didn't want to miss anything or feel left out. So he stepped carefully over the creaky floorboard and leaned against the doorframe. Sarah was tucked up in her bed, and Liv sat beside her, with her feet tucked under Sarah's duvet, and her arm around the little girl. The scene was so cosy that he held back, not wanting to disturb them.

He listened as the story came to its end, and the beautiful princess headed off into the sunset with her new best friend — the dragon who had realised the error of its ways and apologised to all — leaving the prince to return to his castle. While Callum appreciated the sentiment and idea of encouraging little girls to stand on their own feet instead of waiting for a prince to sweep them off them, he did always feel a bit sad for the prince: instead of heading off to happy ever after, he was left standing alone. It was just a little too close to his own life for comfort.

After a few moments, Liv closed the book and carefully wriggled her arm away from Sarah, leaving the little girl resting on her pillow and apparently asleep. With gentle movements, Liv pulled the covers around Sarah, and leaned over to turn off her lamp.

'Goodnight, Sarah.' Liv's voice was hushed and low. 'Dream sweet.'

'Night, night, Livvy.' Sarah's voice was thick with sleep. 'Love you.'

Liv froze for a second before she leaned down and placed a gentle kiss on the top of Sarah's head. 'I love you too, Sarey-fairy.'

Callum froze as the words washed over him, flushing adrenaline through his veins that made his fingers tingle. He wasn't sure what worried him more: that Sarah had clearly gotten so much closer to Liv than he'd realised, or the way Liv had replied.

He watched as Liv's shadowy form reached out to smooth Sarah's hair, and tuck her in more tightly. Callum backed away, hating that he felt like he was intruding in his own house, and with his own daughter, but at the same time he didn't want Liv to see him and think he was spying on her. He stepped back hastily, but his haste and the semi-darkness combined to disorientate him and he creaked across the loose floorboard.

He looked up, and Liv's eyes met his and pinned him to the spot as she smiled softly at him, her features picked out in shadow against the gentle glow of Sarah's nightlight. His breath caught in his throat as she stepped towards him, pausing to pull the door closed to the exact position that Sarah preferred. Had Liv really been there so often as to notice, or was it just coincidence? It was basically that thought which tortured him most of the time; there were so many moments, so many gestures that could be interpreted as her really caring. But at the same time, he could just be seeing what he wanted to see, and setting himself and Sarah up for more hurt.

And it would really, really, really hurt.

But he didn't have any choice. 'Liv, we need to talk. Downstairs?'

She nodded and followed him to the living room.

'You know, there's not many good conversation topics that start with the words "we need to talk", don't you?' She still kept her voice low, but even the soft whisper carried her worry to him. His heartbeat stepped up at the look on her face. He didn't ever want to cause her worry or pain, but her concern gave him hope that maybe, just maybe, he wasn't alone in struggling to keep things casual.

'Come on.' He held out his hand, hoping that she was wrong, and that it would be one of the rare, good conversations.

* * *

Liv let him lead her down the stairs, unsure of what to think. Her mind raced as her feet dragged. Callum had obviously seen her when she was in Sarah's room, but had he heard her too? She had replied to Sarah without thinking. The words "I love you too" had slipped out before she'd even realised that she'd thought them: her automatic reply to Sarah's sleepy declaration.

The words surprised her, but less than the realisation that she wouldn't take them back, even if she could. She really *did* love the little girl who dressed as a fairy, brought her cupcakes when she was upset, and taught her about fairy magic and wishing wells while leaving trails of sequins and glitter across her floors. But it was more than that, Liv realised. Sarah's glitter and love for life had helped patch over the cracks in her heart. And, if it was true that Sarah had patched her up, then Callum was certainly the one who had zapped her heart into beating properly again.

The thought thrilled and terrified her in equal measure. She hadn't come to Broclington intending to find anything other than a rest, and a chance to escape and plan for her new life. She hadn't expected . . . whatever it was she and Callum had become. She didn't want to even *think* the word: it was much easier to love a bright, happy, innocent little girl than it was a grown man who could hurt her so badly. But, whether she liked it or not, now the thought was in her head she didn't know how to bury it again.

And if she was honest with herself, she was already so far into the summersault of falling head over heels that there was no way she could abort the twisting aerobatics and land without pain, and with her dignity intact.

Her heart pounded so loudly she was amazed Callum couldn't hear it. Medically, she knew it was impossible, yet

189

the racing beats were so deafening in her own ears that it seemed impossible that he wouldn't hear them.

His hand brushed the small of her back as he guided her into the living room. It was the tiniest of gestures, yet sent shivers through her and she could still feel the ghost of his touch as she perched nervously on the sofa.

He cleared his throat. 'Can I get you anything? Coffee? Glass of wine?'

'No, thank you.' She took a deep breath and tried to calm her churning stomach by will alone. 'Let's just get this over with.'

Confusion clouded his face and darkened his eyes. 'What do you think this is, Liv?'

She shrugged, not really wanting to make things easier for him by saying the words. 'Like I said, "needing to talk" conversations aren't usually ones people look forward to.'

'I'm hoping this is an exception.' He sat next to her, but left her space to still easily move away. Even though it was the last thing she wanted.

'I'm listening.'

'I don't really know how to say this.'

'Well, I don't know what it is you're trying to say, so I can't really help.' She tried to laugh, but the sound choked in her throat.

'This . . . what we have between us . . . I don't think it's working for me, Liv. I know we talked about things, and agreed we'd just be friends and keep anything else casual, but . . . I don't think I can. I'm sorry.'

Liv's heart felt like it redoubled its efforts, thundering in her ears as she went cold and fought to keep her hands from shaking. She didn't want him to see how upset she was — not after so little time together. And he hadn't promised her anything. So she had no right to be upset. And yet, she felt as if something inside her had broken with his words, so she bit the inside of her cheek hard, not wanting to get upset in front of him.

* * *

Liv refused to meet his eyes, making it so much harder for him to even guess at what she was thinking. His stomach was twisting in knots, and he felt like he couldn't quite catch his breath. He was about to put everything — his happiness as well as Sarah's — on the line, the one thing he'd promised himself that he would never do again. But when he'd seen Liv and Sarah upstairs and, more importantly, heard their goodnight, the thought he'd been trying to avoid for weeks crystallized into sharp, unavoidable focus: it was already too late. He was already too far gone.

'Liv, will you say something, please?'

'Like what?' Her voice was clipped and choked. He reached over and slid his fingers beneath her chin, forcing her to look up at him. The unshed tears and anger in her gaze pierced his heart.

'I don't think I'm doing a very good job of making myself clear.'

'I understand you fine.' She shook off his touch. 'Oh, so you really are still seeing all of this—' he gestured around hopelessly trying to encompass himself, Sarah, Broclington and everything else important in his world — 'as just a place and a phase you're passing through?'

'No!' Her eyes flashed angrily. 'Do you really think I'm that heartless? That I care about you and Sarah, and Broclington so little?' She shoved him away and started gathering up her things in sharp, angry movements.

Panic rose in his throat, and he reached out to her, seizing her hands. They shook in his, and his stomach clenched painfully. 'I don't want you to go, Liv. That's what I'm trying to say.'

'I'm just a locum.'

'But when we've raised the funds to save the surgery, which we will, there's going to be new roles. One of them could be for you, if you wanted. If it wasn't for your ideas and your hard work, there wouldn't even be a future for the surgery. It *should* be your job.' He smoothed a strand of hair away from her face and cupped her cheek in his palm. Her skin was warm against his, and familiar in a way which he wanted to repeat again and again, countless times. 'I want it to be your job. I want you to stay, Liv.'

'Why?'

'Because I think I've broken my promise to you.'

She shrugged and shook her head, still not understanding what he was trying to say.

'I promised we'd be friends, Liv. That we wouldn't be anything serious. Because we both knew you'd be leaving. But...' He forced a deep breath into his lungs. 'I lied to you. I don't think I can be just your friend. And I'm not sure I ever could. I think I'm falling in love with you. And I know I have no right to expect you to feel the same, but... would you consider staying? And maybe giving us a chance?'

'I don't know what to say.'

He could see her hands starting to shake, so he pulled them into his.

'What do you *want* to say?'

'I think I'm scared to answer that,' she admitted, her voice so quiet that he strained to hear her.

'You think I'm not scared? Liv, I'm terrified. But... I have to ask. I might be wrong, but I really think — I really hope — that I'm not. Is there something more here than friendship and... casual enjoyment?' He swallowed hard. It was now or never. 'Because, for me, I think there might be. And—' he took a step towards her, squeezing her hands more tightly — 'I really would like to find out.'

'I...' She stared at him, her eyes wide and overly bright, and he felt like he'd been sucker-punched in the stomach by the knowledge that he'd caused her distress.

'Liv.' He pulled her towards the sofa and sat down. 'I'm not asking you to promise me forever. I can't promise you that either. But I can, and will, promise that I wouldn't ever hurt you the way your ex did. Do you know that?'

'I want to believe you,' she admitted softly. 'I really do.'

'But after everything you've been through, it's hard for you to trust anyone.'

She nodded and pulled away from him, leaving him feeling bereft.

'I don't want to put any pressure on you, Liv, and I'm sorry if this has. If you tell me you don't want anything more, then we can go back to just being friends. Or colleagues. Whatever you need, I will do. And if that means pretending the last few minutes haven't happened, and that I haven't said any of this, then I'll figure out how to do that. OK? But if you think there might be something here, I'm just asking you to try and let your guard down and give us a chance.'

'I don't think I can do that.' She shook her head.

'I understand.' And even though he meant the words, they were still agony to say. Whatever it was that she needed, he'd work out how to be it. Even if it was just a friend.

'I mean, I think you're right. And I don't think I can pretend this conversation never happened. As much as I'm terrified, I think there might be something more here. Between us. And that really, really scares me.' She took a deep breath. 'But, if I'm honest, I think pretending you've not said anything scares me too. Maybe more.'

'Maybe more?' He tried to keep the hope out of his voice.

'Maybe.' Liv's gaze fell to study her nails.

'Look at me, Liv. Please.'

* * *

As much as Liv was terrified, she couldn't ignore his plea.

'So, what if we stopped pretending, and gave this . . . us . . . a chance?'

'You make it sound so easy.' Liv tried to force back the tears threatening to choke her.

'Why can't it be that easy?' He squeezed her hands gently.

'Because it just isn't.'

'Because you've been hurt and let down?' Even though his tone was gentle, his words still hurt.

'Yes.'

'You're not the only one.'

'I know that.'

'Be honest with me, Liv, is that all that's holding you back? Being scared?' His eyes searched hers.

'Yes, but it's a pretty big "all", isn't it?' She had to force the words out.

'It is. Yes. But isn't there a part of you that wants to try?'

She couldn't keep a smile from teasing the corner of her lips. 'I think there might be.'

He brought up a hand to caress her cheek. 'You think, or you know?'

She nodded, slowly. 'Yes. There's a part of me that really does want to try. I just don't know how to.'

'Liv, I can't promise not to hurt you . . .'

'I know that. That's the problem.'

'Will you let me finish? Please?' He waited for her nod. 'I can't promise that I'm not going to hurt you, but I can promise to really try. I care about you, Liv. And I think you care about me too. And I'm trusting you not to hurt me, or Sarah. At least, not deliberately. You're not callous or unkind. And I think what could be between us is worth the risk. And I'm really hoping you might agree.'

'I can't make you any promises, Cal.' She shook her head.

'And I'm not asking you to. But I am asking you to try and trust me, and give us a chance to see if this . . . if we . . . could be something really amazing.' The gentle stroke of his fingers against her cheek sent shivers racing over her skin. 'What do you say, Liv?'

Her voice caught in her throat, and she couldn't manage to get the words out past the lump of emotion that had lodged itself firmly there.

'Liv?'

She could see his throat convulse as he swallowed hard, and worry darkened his eyes.

She nodded, still struggling to speak.

All of the cheesy, romantic clichés suddenly made sense to Liv as a smile spread across his face and warmed his eyes, lifting the weight from her chest that had made it so hard to breathe or speak. In the perfect, made-for-TV, stereotypical moment, the world around Liv seemed to slip into silent slow motion as Callum gently traced the line of her chin with his fingers to cup her cheek and run a gentle thumb across her lips. Heat raced across her skin and flooded through her body.

'When I kiss you this time, it's going to be about a lot more than just attraction and chasing a spark between us. You know that, right?' The intensity in his eyes was scorching as he studied her.

'Yeah, I do.' She looped her arms around his neck and tangled her fingers through his hair before pulling him gently down to meet her lips in a kiss that sent shivers all the way down to her toes.

He teased her lips gently, his hands sliding around her waist to pull her more firmly against him. The room seemed to swirl around them, and she was dizzy with his taste, smell and presence, and the feel of him holding her tightly — safe and protected from harm. When she was almost completely breathless, he pulled back slightly, leaving her gasping, and she felt his smile against her lips.

'Is that a yes?' His breath was hot as it mingled with hers. 'Will you take a chance with me?'

'Yes.' For the first time, in she didn't know how long, Liv felt safe and protected, and free to be herself.

CHAPTER TWELVE

Liv sighed as she tucked the last bauble into place at the bottom of the tree, and leaned back to admire the scene around her, and how well her work blended in. The whole village square looked like it had been plucked out of a fairy tale or Christmas movie, and sparkled with hope as much as it did tinsel and glitter. Most of the decorations didn't match, and a hefty percentage of them were clearly handmade — sometimes with more enthusiasm than skill. Reindeer jostled for space on the tree with robins, next to angels and elegant baroque style decorations that wouldn't have looked out of place in the poshest of London hotels. Tinsel wound throughout branches across dozens of trees, and lights of every colour and size looped around and between them to light the entire square.

It couldn't have been more different to the perfectly coiffed, painfully elegant and expertly designed tree that Mike had insisted on a few seasons earlier. And she thought it couldn't have been more perfect.

Much like her beautiful designer shoes, Liv had never been completely enamoured with Mike's perfectly managed approach to Christmas that had been perfectly beautiful in every way, complete with everything prepared. Right down to the shop-bought, already constructed and perfectly iced gingerbread cottage that was invariably thrown in the bin by New Year's Eve. Perfect, elegant, soulless, and more than a little uncomfortable after a while.

She wriggled her bare toes in her garish plastic flip-flops and wondered whether the local store would have everything she needed to make gingerbread. She was sure there would be a video somewhere online that she'd be able to follow.

'You look hot.' Callum offered a large glass filled with amber liquid — already frosting in the summer heat. 'In both senses of the phrase.'

'Thanks.' She took the glass and rested it against her cheek and neck for a moment, before grinning cheekily. 'For this too.'

'You're welcome.' He plonked himself down beside her, and chinked his glass against hers before kissing her on the cheek. 'It looks really good here. If ever you get bored of doctoring, you could decorate instead.'

'I hardly think so.' She took a deep swig from her glass, ridiculously pleased at the praise — whatever she said. 'This is good. What is it?'

'Spiced apple. There's an alcoholic version too, but . . .'

'But we're never really not on call.'

'Exactly. Especially when there's so many people up and down ladders today, and opportunities to trip over cables, fake snow, staging and whatever else. Not to mention dehydration and sunburn.'

'No. Please don't mention it.' Liv raised her eyes to the heavens.

'Besides, imagine how embarrassing it would be for you to topple head over heels and smack your head. Again.'

'Hey! I did have some help falling over last time.'

'True enough.' He reached over to brush loose strands of her hair from her face. 'But I don't want you getting hurt again. And anyway, the only falling you should be doing is for me. So you'd best be keeping your feet firmly on the ground, unless it's because I'm sweeping you off them!'

Liv pursed her lips, trying not to laugh. 'Sweeping me off my feet, huh? Is that what you're planning?'

'It sounded better in my head. But I still say it's a good idea.'

'You do, huh?'

'Yup. Don't you agree?' His eyes sparkled, almost the same colour as the summer sky above them.

'Maybe.'

'Maybe yes?'

'Maybe yes.'

* * *

Callum wrapped his hand tightly around Liv's and squeezed. He knew that, fortunately, it wasn't actually possible for a person's heart to burst from joy or pride — but the phrase had never meant more to him as he watched her with Sarah.

'My hair is too hot, Livvy.'

Callum bit back a sigh of exasperation. He'd argued with Sarah that morning, telling her she should let him put her hair up — but she'd wanted it to stay down so she "could look like a princess".

'Oh dear, we'll have to see what we can do about that.' Liv let go of his hand to rummage in her large bag. 'So long as it's all right with your dad.'

'It's not his hair. It's mine.'

He shrugged at Liv when she caught his eye. Even if he had minded, it was very clear his opinion didn't count for much.

'Can you make it look like yours?' Sarah pointed to the complicated looking braid that twisted Liv's hair up like a halo, with just a few soft strands escaping to caress her neck. He was convinced it would have taken ages, and wasn't possible to recreate in a crowd of people eagerly awaiting the start of the parade in a few minutes. Which meant there was a high possibility of a small foot being stamped and Sarah becoming very, very grumpy. It was what often happened when he couldn't deliver one of the complex hairstyles that Sarah's friends often sported. Or worse, like one of the princesses from her favourite films.

'Hmmm. It would take quite a bit of time to do that.' Liv pulled out a folding brush, and flicked it open. 'But I'd love to braid it another day, when we have more time. We can probably even add some sparkly bits too. Maybe, just for now, we could just tie it up prettily and enjoy the parade. What do you think?'

'OK,' Sarah agreed before spinning around.

Callum watched in mild amazement as, in less time than it would have taken him to convince his daughter to sit still, Liv deftly brushed her hair and pulled it into a neat, bouncy ponytail.

'Thanks, Livvy.' Sarah span round, and hugged Liv round the neck and placed a quick kiss on her cheek.

'You're welcome, Sarey-fairy. And don't forget, I'll braid it like mine another time.'

'With sparkly bits. For both of us?'

'Of course.' Liv's easy laugh made Callum's stomach twist in a delicious way. And when she picked Sarah up, all the breath rushed from his lungs as if he'd been punched. The noise and crowd around him seemed to disappear as all of his attention focussed on Liv, who stood with his daughter balanced comfortably on her hip, laughing with the little girl as they pointed out different parts of the Christmas decorations and celebrations.

They looked so happy and utterly perfect together that any doubts he had melted away as quickly as real snow would in the summer heat. When they turned to look at him, joy sparkling in their eyes, the realisation hit him that this was exactly what he wanted: Liv as a permanent feature in his and Sarah's life. The thought that should have terrified him — that would have a few weeks ago — was far less scary than the idea of her leaving. There was nothing else he could do, he would just have to do everything possible to convince her to stay. Forever. And if that meant getting over his fears again, it was something he'd just have to figure out. But any thoughts he might have had on that matter were drowned out by the fanfare from the local silver band, loudly announcing the start of the parade.

'Dad, *Dad*! Look, it's starting!' Sarah squealed and started to wriggle excitedly. '*Oooh*, is Uncle Nick being an elf?'

'I think Nick would be a little bit tall to be an elf.' He peered at the male elf who was leading one of the reindeer and burst out laughing. 'You're right. It *is* Nick. I can't believe he didn't tell me he was dressing up this year. Oh, I need to get some pictures of this!'

'And you wonder why he didn't tell you.' Liv laughed.

'What are friends for if not to take the . . . mick.'

They *oooh*'ed and *awww*'ed together, cheering along with the crowd as the local dance school — dressed as snowflakes — twirled and pirouetted through the street, closely followed by Santa's sleigh, which was followed by a team of elves cheerfully jangling buckets and fishing nets already full of donations along with the bells stitched to their costumes.

Behind them came the first of the beautifully decorated floats. This one was dressed as an icy throne room — complete with the village's elected Snow Queen bedecked in finery, and the Christmas Princess waving healthily and happily from her right-hand side.

Seeing his soon-to-be niece so full of life and joy, after they'd come so close to losing her, filled him with gratitude and utterly thrilled him. He was sure he was grinning like a loon as he jumped up and down, waving and whistling, but he couldn't have cared less. Summer, the mini-miracle that she was, was recovered and thriving in her new life — he'd seen the test results to prove it. He was so pleased he'd been able to be a part of making it happen, even in a small way.

Soon, she'd be a Macpearson, and officially part of his family. And she and Evelyn were already utterly adored by them all. They had both just fitted in so easily, that it seemed as if they'd always meant to be a part of the Macpearson clan.

He glanced at Liv, now dancing with Sarah, bobbing up and down in time to the silver band's rendition of "Frosty the Snowman".

'Daddy, dance with us.'

'Yes, come on, Cal. Come dance with us.' Liv's outstretched fingers were warm as they wrapped around his, and drew him close. He couldn't help but marvel at how easily, and well, the three of them fit together — dancing along and laughing as more floats drifted by in a riot of colour. Each one filled with people he knew, all of them raising money to help save the surgery. And help keep Liv with him — although they didn't know that yet. Even so, knowing how well she'd settled in and hearing what the Broclington community said about her, he knew it would be a popular decision.

All around him people cheered, and the warm sun glinted off coins as they were dropped into the rattling noisy buckets and nets that were already weighed down by the generosity of countless thousands of people.

He was overwhelmed by the rush of emotion — the gratitude he felt to everyone around him donating money to save his future, and the futures of the people he cared about the most. But it was more than that: it was the sense of peace and just complete . . . rightness . . . he got when he looked at Liv. Everything just felt better, and a bit more *right*, when she was near him, and it was obvious that Sarah felt the same way too. It was exactly what he'd never realised was missing in his life.

* * *

Liv laughed as the floats meandered past, with people she recognised on almost every one. The offering from the local primary school was done up like a pirate ship — and someone had seen fit to arm the children with squirt guns.

'Hey, Dr Emery,' Timothy called cheerfully from the lorry bed — his blow-up parrot lopsided on his shoulder as he brandished his pistol. 'Cash or splash!'

'Don't you think it's hot enough some people might like that?' Callum shouted back.

A hook-handed pirate who Liv thought was probably the school's headteacher under the hot-looking wig, hat and make-up leaned down and whispered something.

Timothy grinned. 'In that case . . . pay for a spray? Either way, hand over the treasure! Yo, ho, ho!'

'All right, all right.' She dropped some change in the brandished fishing net, and pointed surreptitiously at Callum, who received the full blast of water. The "ship" carried on through the village centre, closely followed by a 1950s float on which the residents were dressed in poodle skirts or leather jackets and jeans. Half of them were boogieing away while the rest gleefully heckled the crowd loudly for donations, enjoying being "too old to be told off", as one of her patients had cheerfully informed her when she'd tried to get him to abstain from his nightly brandy. She waved extra hard when she saw Mr Davies dancing away, despite the ankle she'd strapped up for him a few weeks earlier.

As the heckling village elders rounded the corner, their float was replaced by a lorry dressed as a stage from which the local drama group acted out scenes from their latest show. She grimaced as Romeo clambered up Juliet's balcony, lurching slightly as the truck moved. She really hoped she and Cal's professional services weren't going to be needed!

She smiled as another float rolled past, and another, each filled with members of the community — and her patients — and as they recognised her and waved, she was filled with a deep sense of peace and happiness. She felt more like a member of the community here in Broclington than she ever had anywhere else.

She grinned down at Sarah, excitedly throwing change into as many buckets and nets as she could reach, and realised what the feeling was: she'd finally found somewhere she could call home. And maybe, even people she could call family.

The thought didn't scare her as much as it would have a few weeks ago, and she took it as a good sign.

As the last float meandered by, Sarah dragged her into the road to follow. 'Come on!'

'What are we doing?'

'Joining in.' She laughed, holding tightly to Liv's hand as the street filled with people.

By the time they reached the car park at the cricket pavilion that had been transformed into a stage and the entrance to the fete, the crowd was as thick as any she'd seen at even the biggest event in London, and spilling out into the closed roads. After a few moments, Summer and "Santa" appeared on the stage, where they were joined by a vaguely familiar woman brandishing a microphone.

'Is that . . . ?'

'Miss Natalie from the news? Yup.' Sarah grinned cheerfully.

* * *

Callum felt his stomach clench as he watched Summer wave to the countless number of people gathered around them. All their work, all their hopes, and his future in Broclington, were pinned on what was going to happen in the next few hours and days. And there was nothing else he could do to influence the outcome, which was terrifying.

As if sensing his worry, Liv's fingers wrapped around his and gave a reassuring squeeze.

'Well, hello Broclington. Merry Summer's Christmas!' A cheer rang round the crowd as Natalie started to speak, and she waited a few moments for it to settle. 'Can you believe this is our third Summer's Christmas?'

She played the crowd like an expert, building them up and up, and waiting for the lull again, before speaking so quietly that almost everyone fell silent to hear. 'When we first met here two years ago, it was because we'd all heard of a cause so vitally important that we couldn't not be a part of it: raising the money to save Summer's life. And look how much better she is! All thanks to this amazing event, and you truly wonderful people!'

This time the crowd cheered each other and themselves for long moments, and she had to wait for nearly a minute before she could speak again. 'All right, all right, thank you so much for your incredibly kind welcome. But, as it should be with this event, we all know it's not really me that you want to hear from. Is it?' She knelt down, throwing her arm around Summer's shoulders, and offering the microphone to her. 'Tell us all, Summer, how are you doing now?'

'I'm all better.' She beamed and the crowd roared their approval while Summer blew kisses and waved to everyone, and Callum once again sent thanks to whatever angels watched over the little girl that it had worked. He just hoped those same angels were still feeling charitable, and looking over his family and the surgery. It was going to take a miracle to save them.

When finally the crowd settled, Natalie spoke again. 'By now, you all know how Summer's Christmas started, and what it's achieved. The first year, we raised money to make sure Summer got the treatment she needed to get well. Last year, we raised money to help extend the local hospice. And this year, we've come together, family, friends, community members, to raise money for something so very important that it's part of the very heart of our community.

'It's the place where people go when you don't feel well, when you have questions and worries. It's the team who help look after you and the people you love the most when they're vulnerable or hurting. They deliver babies, and help welcome them into the world and make sure they thrive.'

As she spoke, Callum felt someone clap him on the shoulder from behind. He turned to see Harry grinning broadly, his other arm firmly around his wife who held their newborn, snuggled against her chest.

'And when you've needed the hospital, they're the ones who help welcome you back home safely. And it's the same team and surgery who helped get Summer the treatment she needed, and now make sure she stays well.

'The team are your first point of contact for help and care, and the ones who are with you throughout. No matter what you're going through, they're there offering a kind ear, friendly smile, expert advice and compassion and support.' Natalie paused as a murmur of agreement rippled through the crowd.

'Well, it's about time we supported them to make sure we can keep them, right here where they belong, in the heart of your community. Summer, why don't you tell us what we're all raising money for this year?' She handed the microphone back.

'We're going to save the doctor's surgery! So give us lots of money!'

'I don't think I could have put it better myself.' Natalie laughed. 'For years, the Macpearson family have looked after you all, digging deep and working hard to give the best possible care for this community, whether it was the middle of the day, the weekend, or the middle of the night. So let's repay the favour, and dig deep to give as generously as we can, and make sure they can stay here, continuing to care for us for years more to come.'

The cheer that echoed around him was so full of emotion that he had to look down at the ground while he took a few deep breaths to regain his composure.

When he looked up again, the microphone was in the hand of Santa. 'Ho, ho, ho! Merry Summer's Christmas!' He waited for the applause to wane. 'You've all heard what these two lovely ladies have had to say, and you all know how important this weekend is. So, as the expert on all things Christmas, I now declare the third Summer's Christmas officially open! Ho, ho, ho!' He waved his hand, and the park gates were opened by volunteers, to another huge cheer from the crowd who streamed through the gates, through the avenue of sparkling, decorated trees, and into the waiting fete grounds.

'So, what do we think, Sarey-fairy? Shall we do a quick lap of the fair and maybe get some snowman snow cones before I go and check in with the first-aid tent?'

'Can I go in the giant snow globe too?'

'I think we can manage that.' Callum hoped everyone else was as eager to spend money. 'But Liv and I both need to take our turn in the first-aid tent.'

'I know.' Sarah pouted. 'Doctors are never really off duty.'

'I guess you hear that a lot.' Liv shot Sarah a sympathetic look.

'Yeah. But it's an important job.'

'Yes, it is.'

'But we can still have some fun first, right?'

'We absolutely can.' Callum grinned before taking off towards the fun. 'Come on, race ya!'

'Cheat!' Sarah raced after him, leaving Liv to laugh at their silliness.

* * *

'You've got another bit, right here.' Liv tried not to shiver as Callum leaned over and pulled another lump of "snow" from her hair. When Sarah had begged her to join her in the giant, bouncy-castle snow globe, she hadn't been able to resist. And right now, as Callum stood too close to her, plucking fake snow off her, she was finding other things much harder to resist.

'Snowmen snow cones now?' Sarah pleaded.

'All right.' He plucked a final clump of fake snow from Liv's hair. 'Fancy a snow cone, Liv?'

There was something else she fancied a lot more than that, but in public she'd settle for ice cream. 'Sure.'

Callum grimaced as his phone vibrated and burst into demanding chirrups and jangles that Liv recognised only too well. 'Surgery line?'

'Yup.' He glanced at Sarah as her face fell. 'Sorry, but you know I have to get this.'

'I know.'

'Maybe you can stay with Liv for a few minutes.' He waited for Liv's nod. Of course it was fine, she adored Sarah, and understood better than anyone. 'I'll be as fast as I can.'

'OK.'

He swiped the irritating intrusion and headed away from the crowd. 'Dr Macpearson speaking. How can I help? Sorry, I'm struggling to hear you. Can you speak up please? I'm just trying to get to somewhere a bit quieter.'

Liv held her hand out to Sarah. 'What do you say we go find those ice creams?'

'OK.' Sarah's fingers wrapped around hers, and Liv found herself once again hit by a wave of love for the little girl.

'Try not to worry. Most calls aren't emergencies, or anything bad.'

'But everyone is here and knows not to call.'

'Maybe it's about today.' Liv did her best to reassure Sarah. 'Maybe it's another journalist or something else good that could help?'

'Maybe.'

* * *

Callum stared down at the now blank screen, reeling in disbelief. He'd been polite, and professional, and answered every question as he should have: fairly, honestly, and with a level of professional detachment that he really didn't feel. But what the actual hell? How could she do this to him?

He turned back towards the fete, to where he could see Liv laughing with Sarah and a torrent of pain slammed into him. He couldn't believe he'd been so stupid as to let her into his life — into his home and Sarah's life — and fallen for her pretty lies.

Again, he'd let a woman take him for a ride. That, in itself, was unforgivably stupid — but to let his precious daughter get sucked into the web of betrayal. It made him feel sick to think that he'd actually believed her act. And the worst thing was, she'd warned him from the start that she hadn't wanted anything serious. That it was just sex.

But why the fuck had she treated Sarah like this?

A dark cloud of misery and suspicion rolled over him, blocking out all the hope and joy of the day. He stalked towards them, fury slamming his feet hard into the ground.

But as he saw Sarah's face, filled with joy and excitement, he forced himself to shove the feelings down. He had no idea how he was going to manage this, but he did know he'd do anything to keep his daughter from any more pain than was already barrelling towards her. So, as much as he wanted to yell, he forced himself to project an air of calm that couldn't be further from how he really felt, and pasted on the professional smile that had served him so well over the years.

She greeted him with a sunny smile, holding up an already melting ice cream. 'Sorry, it's not the best weather for a snowman, but it'll probably still taste good.'

She must have seen past his polite, professional smile, because her face fell.

'Is everything OK?'

'Actually, Liv, no, it's not.' He ground out the words, before taking a breath and forcing the rest out calmly. 'Could I have a moment, please?'

'Of course.' She smoothed down the fabric of her skirt.

'Sarah, stay right here, please. I just need a quick word with Liv. All right?' He waited for her nod before pulling Liv a few steps away. Close enough that he could still keep an eye on Sarah, but far enough that he was sure she couldn't hear. Enough things were about to be ruined, he wasn't going to take away her happiness of the day too.

'Do I need to grab my bag? Are we wanted somewhere?'

Oh, the irony of how she'd phrased it. He tried to force down the lump of raw emotion that threatened to choke him. How he'd been so stupid as to trust her he didn't know.

'Cal? What was the call? Who needs help?'

'Apparently one of the West London NHS Clinical Trusts.'

'What?'

'Congratulations, Dr Emery. You got the job you wanted. That call,' he spat the words out angrily, 'was a reference request. Don't worry, I didn't fuck it up for you. I wouldn't want you to be stuck here in this backwards village with me for any longer than strictly necessary.'

'Callum, I . . .'

'In fact, now Dad's back, you needn't hang around any longer. You can consider your contract terminated. Effective immediately. I'm sure it won't take you too long to gather your things. It's not like you ever planned to stay here.'

'Callum, will you please let me '

'Let you what?' His anger overwhelmed him and he had to force his voice to a low growl to keep from screaming all that anger at her. But if he did that, Sarah would be hurt even more than she was already going to be. 'Let you tell me more lies? Lead me along another of your stories just to make your stay here a bit . . . what? Less dull?'

'That's not what happened. I would never . . .'

'So it's all a mistake, is it? You didn't apply for another London job? The reference call was for a different Olivia Emery, was it?'

'No. I mean, yes. I did apply for another post but . . .'

'I really am an idiot. You told me yourself you couldn't make me any promises. You've been telling me all along, haven't you?'

Liv started to speak, but he cut her off again.

'I'm sorry, but I just don't want to hear it.' He paused. 'Actually, no I'm not. I'm not sorry about that at all. I'm sorry about trusting you, believing you when you said you were willing to give us a chance. My God, Liv, no wonder you held back so much. You never had any intention of staying here. And I'm sorry for believing that the connection I thought we had was real. And I'm sorry for thinking you were someone you're clearly not — someone who was kind, and who I thought meant something to me. But most of all, I'm sorry I let you anywhere near my daughter. And I'm really, really sorry that she's going to be hurt by you.'

* * *

She stared at him in horror, shock freezing her limbs and numbing her tongue. She wanted to explain, but his harsh tone and words slammed into her and knocked the breath from her lungs. 'Callum, please . . . I wouldn't . . .'

He held up a hand, looking more tired than she'd ever seen him before. 'Liv, just stop. I don't want to hear it. I'm done. I thought we had something, but was obviously mistaken. I'm not making any more mistakes.' He stared at her, pain etched across his face. 'I just don't understand how you could do it. How you could tell a little girl like my Sarah that you loved her, while all along you were planning on leaving.'

That was enough to loosen her tongue. 'I *do* love Sarah. I'd never want to hurt her. Or you.'

'But you still planned to leave.' He shook his head and looked away from her, more closed off and distant than he'd ever been to her. He couldn't even look at her, and clearly wasn't interested in listening. That he wasn't even willing to give her a chance to explain hurt Liv beyond words. He'd asked her for his trust, to bare her pain and scars to him, and she'd given it willingly, knowing that he wouldn't hurt her. But it seemed he couldn't return that faith. He couldn't even trust her to be a decent person who told the truth. And knowing he thought so very little of her left bitter, angry bile in her mouth.

'I'd like to ask a favour of you. I know I have no right, but if you ever really cared for Sarah or me, even a little, I hope you'll consider this.'

'Anything.' Liv grasped at the chance to make things right, to wind time back to before the phone call.

'Sarah adores you, Liv. This is going to hurt her badly enough as it is. If you ever really cared for her, even a little, please don't destroy this event for her. Or the community, if you cared about them too.'

'Do you really think so little of me?' Liv could barely get the words out. It didn't matter. He was past listening.

'Just make your excuses, Liv. I don't care what they are. But please, just make your excuses to leave and don't break Sarah's heart today. Or ruin our . . . my . . . chances of saving my family's surgery.'

And there was her answer. Obviously he really *did* think that little of her. Numbly, she followed him back to where Sarah was still happily licking ice cream from her fingers. She muttered some empty, placating excuse, gave the little girl what she knew would be the last hug, and picked up her bag with fingers that shook.

She stood for long moments, watching Callum, praying he would show her some sign of encouragement or hope. But instead he sat by Sarah and stared resolutely at the floor. But she had to try. It was too painful not to. 'Callum, maybe tomorrow we could talk?'

'Nothing to talk about.' His words were quiet, calm and even, but they shook her to her core. Nothing. After everything he'd said, everything she thought they'd shared, she was nothing to him. The pain seared her into movement, and she forced herself to turn and walk away.

She bit the inside of her cheek hard, and tasted the coppery tang of blood as she forced herself to keep her pace calm and measured, and fought back tears. If anyone saw her upset, they'd wonder why — and maybe try to intervene — and she couldn't handle that right now. If anyone was kind to her, she would break into a million pieces. And she didn't think she would be strong enough to cope.

Somehow — probably the years of training to deal with trauma by segmenting and compartmentalising her feelings at work — she made it all the way back to her street before her tears started to fall. By the time she made it to the cottage door, the tears were blinding and she shook so badly that she couldn't get the key and the lock to connect properly and work together to let her in.

Just like she couldn't get Callum to connect with her and listen to her for long enough to explain. After goodness knows how many failed attempts, she gave up and staggered around the side of the cottage, and let herself into the small back gate. She dropped her bag by the back door and stumbled up the garden path to collapse on the edge of the well.

She let her fingers dig against the ancient sun-warmed stone as her tears splashed against it and darkened its surface, and she tried desperately to hang on to the happiness that had seemed so close to becoming hers less than an hour ago.

* * *

Sarah bounced up and down in the first-aid tent, making the already small, hot, canvas room feel a lot smaller and a lot hotter. Callum checked the refrigerator again for cool packs and water, and then flicked through the first-aid kit. He wasn't expecting anything more than sunburn, overheating and maybe a few bites and stings in this heat. That and some upset tummies from too much sugar and excitement. But then, it always paid to try to be prepared for anything. That was part of the training — prepare for the worst and hope for the best.

If only he'd learned from Trixie's betrayal, he might have been better prepared for Liv's. He slammed the box shut, still seething with anger. How could she have done this, when she'd made so many lovely-sounding promises? Pie crust promises was what his mother called them: easily made and even more easily broken. He rubbed his forehead, trying to dispel the headache growing there. The anger and disappointment was so strong he could taste it. Bitterness and bile filling his throat and mouth. He was *stupid* to have let her get so close — to Sarah as well as himself. And he was *stupid* for believing in second chances and that there was any chance of him playing happy families. He'd already learned that the hard way, and yet he'd been dragged into fairy-tale thinking by Jake and Evelyn's happiness. He'd actually thought he might be lucky enough to have a chance at something like that — and with Liv.

But they were the exception, and his life wasn't one out of Sarah's story books. There wasn't going to be any happy ever after for him — or Sarah. His stomach churned again as he watched Sarah kicking her feet happily from the chair while she licked at her rapidly melting ice cream, innocently making a horrible mess and splattering herself with sticky sweetness. But even though it was her second one of the day, he couldn't bring himself to deny her it.

He hated that her happiness was going to be demolished so completely and so soon.

He'd never forgive Liv for that. And he'd probably never forgive himself either.

'Do you think Liv will be back soon?'

'I don't know.' He ground out the words, not wanting to tell Sarah the truth just yet.

'I want to get my face painted like a princess. Or a butterfly. Or a princess butterfly. Do you think Liv will get hers painted too?'

'No. I don't think she will.'

'When she's back, I'm going to ask her.'

'Sarah, she won't do it.'

'I think she will for me.'

Callum sighed, feeing his temper fray. He could have cried with relief when a familiar face sauntered past the open tent door. 'Mrs Turner!' He waved as she turned.

'Hi, Dr Mac. Hi, Sarah. Are you enjoying the fair?'

'Not as much as we'd hoped. Listen, I know it's a huge imposition, but Dr Emery has been called away.' He winced inwardly at the lie. 'And I'm stuck here. Do you think you might be able to take Sarah for a couple of hours? Or perhaps find her uncle and Evelyn? I tried calling them both, but it's going through to voicemail.'

'Probably can't hear their phones with all the fun and noise going on.'

'Maybe,' Callum agreed.

'Tell you what, why don't we go for a quick walk around the fair, and see if we can't find your uncle? I was planning to get something for lunch.' She knelt down to Sarah's level. 'Have you eaten anything other than ice cream today?'

'Sweets.' Sarah grinned, and Callum felt like the worst father and doctor in the county.

'Well . . .' She grinned. 'If we don't find Jake or Evelyn, we'll have some lunch together. All right?'

'You're sure you don't mind?'

'Not at all.' She held out a hand. 'Come on, Sarah. Let's go find something more fun to do than sitting in a tent.'

'OK. Can we maybe get some face painting on the way?'

'Maybe.' Mrs Turner laughed.

'Thank you,' Callum told her earnestly. 'I owe you.'

'Yup, but I'm sure you'll pay me back sooner or later.'

CHAPTER THIRTEEN

Liv had thrown open the window at the surgery in her office — her soon-to-be former office — almost as soon as she'd gotten there. Her head ached fiercely from crying so much, and though she was tempted to bury herself under a duvet, she knew it wouldn't help. She also knew she couldn't bear to see Callum again, to watch him avoid meeting her eyes while acting like she and everything they'd shared meant nothing.

So, rather than leave it until next week, when he was bound to be in, she'd decided to pack up her meagre belongings immediately and get out sooner rather than later. After all, he'd been the one to end her contract so abruptly. She'd just stick the surgery key through his letter box or something, and she wouldn't have to see him.

And that was fine by her. If he really thought so little of her, and that she would be capable of such unkindness, he didn't deserve her. She just wished he'd given her a chance to explain. But she'd tried, and he'd made it clear he wasn't interested in listening. Which meant she had been wrong about him, and he wasn't really who she thought: someone she could trust, who cared for her. Someone she could maybe even love. Far better to learn that now, rather than wait until she was so deeply committed that it would be agony to leave.

Her hand hovered over a picture Sarah had drawn for her, and she knew she was kidding herself. It was already agony. She wondered what Callum would tell Sarah, and whether the sweet little fairy would hate her. She hated to think of her crying, and knowing that, at least indirectly, she would be the reason for Sarah's tears.

Her resolve crumbled and hot tears scorched a pathway down her cheeks as her sobs mingled with the Christmas cheer filling the village and floating in the window. She'd been hurt before; what Mike had done had been so much worse — on paper at least. But Callum's lack of trust in her, his belief that she could be so unkind, cut her far more deeply than anything she'd experienced before.

Suddenly, she couldn't catch her breath between the sobs, and the stream of tears turned into a blinding flood, so she gave in and put her head down on the desk and cried out all the hurt and anger that was trying to suffocate her.

* * *

When she finally stopped crying, it was much later, and the sun was low and streaming through the surgery windows to paint the room with golden light that did nothing to improve her mood. She had just leaned over the sink to try and wash the burning sandy feeling from her eyes when she heard the screech of tyres followed by a muffled crunch and the electronic scream of a car horn.

She didn't stop to think as she raced to grab the emergency bags from where they lived under the reception desk, and raced out of the surgery, hoping it was nothing more than a fender bender and the contents of the bags weighing down her shoulders wouldn't be needed.

* * *

Callum stared in horror at the mangled wreck that used to be the front of the café. The driver had been going far too fast, and had somehow mounted the kerb, launched over the pretty flowers lining the small car park and smashed through the front wall, window and door of the café, wedging itself at a strange angle that left one wheel spinning in the air. The car horn was blaring, and the front section of the vehicle was crushed beneath part of the café's roof which had come crashing down. It was like something out of a disaster movie, and so out of place in his village that, for a moment, he was frozen to the ground, in a bubble of shock.

It was the groans coming from the car that snapped him back into reality and action.

'Hi, I'm Dr Macpearson, please try not to move.' He checked over the rubble quickly, before climbing over it to peer through the open car window. 'Can you tell me where it hurts?'

The man peered back at him blankly through swollen, reddened eyes. Clearly the airbag had hit him hard.

'Can you tell me your name? Do you know what happened?' Callum persisted as he gently pinned the man back against his seat.

He mumbled something, and Callum just about made out the word Rick.

'All right, Rick, it's really very important that you don't try to move.' He stabilised the man's head against the head-rest. 'Do you have pain anywhere?'

The man mumbled again, and Callum leaned closer to try and catch what he was saying, but instead got a strong whiff of alcohol. The idiot was drunk. He forced down his anger and tried to focus on his job. He didn't have time for judgement, and if it wasn't medically relevant, he couldn't care about it right now. He had to focus on his job.

'All right, Rick. You've got to stay very still now.' He tried the handle, and sighed in relief as the door swung open a bit. He had to force it to open fully, and the metal fought and complained, but at least he had decent access to his patient now. He focussed on that, and tried to ignore the noise behind him.

* * *

217

Liv glanced at the chaos filling the car park and spilling out into the road, taking it all in quickly as she dropped the bags to the floor. People were milling around, helping each other, struggling in the mess of rubble and injuries. Callum was already half in the car that had caused all the damage, and she could see multiple walking wounded patients. But she knew, from the sheer sound of the accident and position of the car, that there could easily be more serious injuries inside. A hand on her shoulder made her turn, and she half-smiled at Millie. She was miles from an A&E, and didn't have even a tenth of the equipment she would want in a situation like this. But she did have caring medics around her, and the training to manage emergency situations.

'Right, Millie. Can you get anyone who is walking away from this area, and set up a triage? Stay near enough to call for help if it's needed, but far enough away from this—' she gestured to the mess in front of her 'to make sure it's not a danger. I assume help is on the way?'

'Yup.' A small crowd of people eager to help had gathered around her. 'I've got the emergency dispatcher on the phone. First responders are maybe ten minutes away, and we've got more being routed towards us.'

'Good,' Liv nodded decisively. 'Evelyn?' She spotted the nurse amongst the small crowd. 'Can you help Millie with triage and walking wounded, and Julie, gather up anyone with enough first-aid knowledge to help them until the cavalry arrives. And can someone make sure the gas and electric in the café is turned off? Last thing we need is complications from that!'

She waited a moment for the agreement to be shouted out, then moved on.

'Tom?' She called the older doctor, her mentor, over. 'This is your community, do you want to take the lead?'

'You're doing fine, Liv.' He shook his head. 'Keep doing it. I'll see if Callum needs help with his patient.'

She nodded, then looked around. 'Jake, Nick, Harry.' She beckoned to them. 'As much as I know people are wanting to help, we've got to be careful and make sure we don't do anything to compromise what's left of the building. We have to assume people might be inside still, but I'd hate for a would-be rescuer to get hurt, or make things worse. Can you create some sort of cordon to keep people back while we try and understand what's happened here?'

'Consider it done.' Harry headed off in full police sergeant mode, pleading, nagging and ordering people back from the damaged building, closely followed by Jake and Summer.

'We have to assume there's people inside.' Nick looked over to the café.

'I know.' Liv nodded. 'But the first rule of an emergency situation is to make sure you don't make the situation worse by anyone else getting hurt. I'm hoping there's a back way in.'

'Fire door that opens out into the courtyard,' Tom confirmed. 'But it's enclosed and the wall is pretty high. We're getting some ladders now.'

'Don't really want to wait.' Liv had already shouldered her first responder's bag and was heading around the side of the building.

She stared at the wall, looking for purchase when Nick knelt down next to her, steepling his fingers. 'I'll give you a boost. Careful on the other side, now.'

'Thanks.' Liv nodded before finding herself shot up in the air. She lowered herself carefully before reaching up for her bag which Nick was already dropping over the wall.

'Dr Emery, thank goodness.' She was folded into a quick hug by Margaret, the café owner.

'Good to see you're still upright. Are you OK?'

'Dusty and a bit shaken, as you'd expect, but none the worse for wear. Unlike the Badger's Paws. Part of the roof came down. Thank the angels it was a few seconds after the car hit, so I don't think anyone was under it. But I can't get to the front of the shop. There could still be people in there who are hurt.' She swallowed hard, clearly fighting back

219

tears. 'And I couldn't get to my first-aid box, so we had to make do with tea towels and aprons.'

'Plenty of supplies here.' Liv hefted the bag up.

'Good. It's mostly just bruises, and a few lacerations out here. But some of them are quite deep and probably need stitches. Sammi Feathers knocked her head pretty hard and was out for a few seconds, so we got her outside — carefully — and into the recovery position, but she's awake and complaining so we think she's fine.'

'You're first-aid trained?' Liv was impressed — and relieved.

Margaret nodded. 'Dr Macpearson — your one, not his dad—' the words cut through Liv, but she forced herself to ignore them 'sorted it a while ago. Kitchens can be pretty dangerous places, so he arranged it for anyone who wanted to learn.'

'Thanks, Margaret.' Liv gave her shoulder a squeeze. 'I'll take a look at Sammi, and can you point out to me who you think needs my help the most? We've got paramedics and the fire brigade on their way, but no reason to wait when I'm here and well equipped. Feel free to borrow whatever you need from my bag. And . . .' She hesitated and looked back at the dusty building. 'Can you get someone to go round and talk with your guests, and we'll try to put together some sort of list to make sure everyone is out and safe?'

* * *

Callum sighed in relief as the fire brigade and paramedics took over, sliding the bright orange spinal board behind his patient and securing the man firmly to it. With the equipment and experience they had, their victim come perpetrator would be safely extracted and on his way to hospital in no time. And, as unprofessional as it was of him, Callum couldn't wait to get away from the drunken idiot who had caused so much damage to his village.

He stripped off his apron and gloves and dropped them in the first bright yellow hazmat bag he saw, before dousing his hands liberally with sanitiser and making his way over to where Evelyn and Millie had set up their triage and were patching, strapping and plastering up the walking wounded.

His dad joined him, dumping his own gloves and holding his hands out for cleanser. 'Once I'm done here, I'm thinking of heading over to the surgery and opening up there. If we grab the golf carts from the parade, and some volunteers, we can shuttle people to us and clean out the glass and debris and stitch or glue the lacerations that are primary care level. Obviously some of the injuries will need the hospital, and any eye injuries will need checking out, but if we can avoid a hospital trip for some people, I think it will be appreciated. Maybe you can stay here, help with the triage, and send anyone over to me needing a bit more than first aid, but a bit less than a hospital visit.'

'Agreed.' Callum nodded.

'Make sure Liv doesn't need any help either. My old knees wouldn't thank me for clambering over walls. Even with a ladder.'

'I'll check in with Jake first, then will get started. Are you OK here for a few more minutes?' Callum just needed to give his daughter a quick hug — reassure himself she was OK, then he could concentrate again.

'Yeah, we're good,' Evelyn replied. 'He was heading over to the Brockle's Retreat to try and keep people calm and out of harm's way.'

'Fair enough.' Callum jogged over the road, pausing to let another set of blue lights pass and pull into the car park. When he swung open the pub door, he was greeted by a wall of noise as people sobbed and comforted each other, and sadly gossiped, about the accident.

It took him a few long minutes to spot his brother, squished into a corner with Summer on the floor by his side with her dog. Jake's head was down as he and one of the

221

local police community officers tried to take down everyone's contact details.

'Hey, good to see you in one piece.' Jake gave him a relieved look from behind his stack of papers. 'How are things?'

'Not great,' Cal admitted. 'But far from as bad as they could be. Paramedics and fire brigade are with the driver now, and should soon have him out and on the way to the hospital, and Dad's heading over to open up the surgery to handle the glass wounds that we can. I just wanted to give Sarah a hug before I joined him. Where is she?'

'What do you mean? I've not seen her all day?' The words slammed into Callum's chest with the same amount of force that it must have taken to bring down part of the café.

'She's not with you?' He looked around, desperately hoping to see the edge of a sparkly pink fairy wing.

'No. I said I've not seen her.'

Callum could see his own panic reflected in his brother's eyes.

'Liv had to . . . go . . . earlier. I was in the first-aid tent.' He scrabbled around for his phone and had to force his fingers steady before he could unlock it. 'Cathy Turner was supposed to bring her to you.' The call went straight to voicemail. 'She didn't find you?'

'No . . .'

The phone rang once before his sitter's voicemail answered again. 'Shit!' He wracked his brains to remember what she'd said. Something about getting food? 'Fuck. I don't know where they are. She said if she couldn't find you, Sarah could have lunch with her.'

'They didn't find us.' Jake shook his head.

'Is Sarah all right?' Summer looked up at Jake, her face filled with the worry Callum was already feeling.

'Yes, I'm sure she is.' He tousled her hair. 'Probably just having fun at the fete. But will you please stay here with Tilly and Rosie—' he waved to the bar maid 'while I help Callum find her?'

'OK.'

'Good girl.' He placed a quick kiss on her forehead before squeezing towards the door as fast as he could. 'I meant what I said. It's probably fine. I mean, there's loads of other places they could have had lunch today. Lots of food stalls.'

'That sell Brockle cakes?'

'No. Shit.' He raced across the road, struggling to keep up with his brother's panicked pace.

CHAPTER FOURTEEN

'Shit,' Liv swore under her breath, trying to keep calm as she listened to the café customer. She wasn't from Broclington, she was just visiting for Summer's Christmas, but she seemed sure about what she was saying, and Liv had no reason to doubt she was being anything but honest. She'd been sat in the corner of the café, waiting for her husband and son, when the car had hit. She'd gotten away with only a few cuts from the breaking window, and had managed to move before the roof came down. But that wasn't what had sent ice running through Liv's veins: it was that there had been people at the table next to hers. Closer to where the car had hit, and café collapsed. They still had people trapped inside.

'An older lady, she seemed friendly, and smiled at me. And what looked like her granddaughter. A sweet little girl who said hello to me. They were joined by another lady, with brown curly hair and a rainbow dress. That was why I remembered them, because I commented on the lady's dress. And the little girl was so sweet in her fairy wings.'

'Sorry, what?' Liv could have sworn her heart skipped a beat or two. 'What did you say the little girl was wearing?'

'Sparkly wings. You know, like a butterfly or fairy.'

'Oh no, please God no.' She darted away and shot up the ladder and over the wall faster than she could think. 'Please, please no.'

She peered around the car park wildly, before running up to one of the firemen. 'Stand back please, Miss.'

'I'm Dr Emery. I've been helping with the injured round the back.'

'Right, they're our next priority,' he reassured her. 'But you've got paramedics with you, right?'

'Yes, but that's not the problem,' Liv tried to explain. 'We've got confirmation there are people still inside. Or, at least there were. I'm really hoping they came out this way.' She scanned the crowd hopefully.

'I don't think anyone has. We've not been able to get in yet. We had to get our patient out the vehicle, and we've got structural engineers on the way in. We want their view before we move the car. How sure are you about people being in there?'

'Pretty certain.'

'Do you know who they are?'

'We think so, yes.' Liv thought the woman in the rainbow dress with curly hair was Angela, and she was pretty sure it would have been her mum, Cathy Turner, looking after Sarah. And she knew, deep in her darkest fears, that Sarah was the little girl described.

'Have you tried calling them?'

'Idiot. No, I haven't.' She shook her head at her stupidity while reaching for her phone. 'No, Angela's not answering. It's just ringing.' She scrolled rapidly through her phone, before looking around and shouting. 'Anyone got Cathy Turner's phone number?'

'She's not answering either. Straight to voicemail.' Jake ran up to them.

'Are they in there?' Callum grabbed her hands. 'Please tell me they're not in there.'

Liv could feel her eyes burning with tears as she forced her jaw to unclench. 'They were definitely there before the car hit. And no one remembers seeing them leave, or has seen them since.'

'Do you know where they were?'

'In the booth nearest the corner window. We think.' It was the very last place she wanted anyone she cared about to be.

Callum ran towards the café, screaming his daughter's name, only to be grabbed and pulled back by the fireman and Jake. 'She's in there, Jake! Let me the hell go!'

'Callum, no.' Jake stood firm.

'Sir, I understand you're upset . . .' the fireman began.

'You understand? Really? That's my daughter in there, and *you're* telling *me* you understand?'

'I do. You're scared, and want nothing more than to get to her and make sure she's OK. But, and I promise you this, tearing in there like this, now, won't help anyone. The building isn't stable. Let us do our work, and get everyone out safely.'

'And you expect me to just stand here and *wait*!'

'You're one of the doctors here, right?' The fireman indicated the stethoscope around his neck. 'What would you tell me if it were one of my crew who had been injured and I was in your way?'

'It's not the same,' Callum tried to argue.

'What would you say?' The fireman got in his face, forcing Callum to look at him.

'You'd ask him to step back, get out of your way, and let you do your job,' Liv answered the question quietly.

'She's right.' The fireman kept his hand on Callum's shoulder. 'So please, do as your colleague says. Step back, keep out of our way, and let us do our job and get in there and bring everyone out safely.'

Callum visibly deflated before Liv's eyes. All his anger gone and replaced by agonising worry.

* * *

226

Liv tried to concentrate on the patient she was patching up, and gently pick out the fragments of glass from her arm. She flushed the wound with saline, before carefully padding it with clean gauze. 'You are going to need a bit more attention, I'm afraid, and maybe a few stitches. But it should heal up nicely.'

Her attention was pulled away from her patient's thanks by Callum pacing by for the hundredth or so time while waiting for the firemen to reappear. She longed to reach out and comfort him somehow, to make it a bit better, but she knew there was nothing she could say or do right now. And he'd made it clear that he had no interest in anything she had to say.

So she made herself as useful as she could, going from one patient to the next and patching up their wounds, falling back into the compartmentalisation she'd used in emergency medicine for so many years.

But she wished, so much, it was different, and that they could support each other right now. The wait was interminable. And pointless. When eventually the firemen came out, blinking in the bright sunshine, it was to shake their heads apologetically. They hadn't been able to get far enough inside, the building was too unstable, and there just wasn't room to work safely. They had to wait for the structural team and their equipment.

She could see the tension in Callum's back, and feel his frustration building from across the car park. Not that she could blame him. She didn't care that she wasn't going to be a part of their life going forward, or that she and Callum had broken up, all she wanted was to see Sarah, safe and well, sparkling in the sunshine. She loved that little girl so much it physically *hurt* to think that anything might have happened to her.

Unable to focus, and not having any real hope for a response, she unlocked her phone again and redialled Angela's number which rang and rang and rang. Just as she was about to hit end, rather than listen to the cheery answerphone message for Angela and the animal rescue centre for the umpteenth time, there was a quiet click.

'Hello! Angela? Can you hear me?'

'Livvy? I gotted Angela's phone from her bag.'

'Oh my God, Sarah!' Liv's heart rushed into her throat as she looked around for Callum and beckoned to one of the firemen. 'Are you all right? Where are you? Let me put you on loudspeaker and find your dad. Sarah, are you OK? Are you still in the café?

'Uh huh. Livvy, I'm scared.'

'I know, sweetie. But it will be all right. I promise you, we've got lots of people out here who are working really hard to come and get you safely. OK?'

'OK.'

Finally, she spotted Callum, emerging from down the side of the café. She waved and beckoned, pointing at the phone while trying to stay calm for Sarah. 'Can you tell me where you are?'

'Kinda in the booth where we sitted, but it's upsy topsy.'

'Oh my God, Sarah.' Callum grabbed Liv's hand around the phone. 'I'm so glad to hear your voice, baby girl. Are you OK?'

'I'm scared. It's really dark in here. I don't like it.' Her voice dissolved into tears and great sobbing gulps.

'It's all right, it's going to be all right.' Callum tried to soothe her, but Liv could see that he was getting more and more upset as Sarah cried harder and harder.

After wrestling with herself for a few moments, Liv took a deep breath and placed her hand on Callum's shoulder. 'Let me try?' She kept her voice low, and forced calmness into it.

He nodded, his jaw clenched. 'But stay close. I want to hear.'

'Of course.'

'Sarey-fairy, it's Livvy. I know you're upset and scared, but I want you to try and take a deep breath for me, OK? I'm going to count to three, and when I get there, you're going to take the biggest breath you can, and hold it until I say to

228

let go, all right? A really big, big breath like you're about to blow up a big balloon. OK? One, two, big breath remember, three.' Liv felt her own breath catch as the sobbing abruptly ceased. 'Now, slowly, slowly let it out. Then, when you've done that, take in another big, big breath, and blow it out slowly for me again. OK?'

'Like when we blow bubbles?'

'Yes, sweetie. Exactly like when we blow bubbles. You're doing so good.'

'Is Daddy still there?'

'Yes, munchkin, I'm still here. And you'll be out here with me soon, I promise. But for now you've got to be brave, OK?'

'K.' She started coughing and spluttering.

'All right, Sarah,' Liv continued. 'Now, like your daddy said, you're going to have to be super brave now. Like super Disney princess brave.'

'Like when Anna has to save Elsa?'

'Exactly like that. And that's a really, really good comparison, because Anna was scared too, but she did what she had to and saved Elsa, and it was all OK, wasn't it?'

'Yup.'

'And this will be OK too, right? You believe me when I say that, don't you?'

'I always believe you, Livvy.'

* * *

Callum looked up at his daughter's words, and really studied the woman opposite him. Her eyes were red and raw from crying, and tears still tracked down her cheeks. But she wiped them away and kept her voice calm and reassuring for Sarah, and he admired her for that. Even with everything going on, she was still putting his daughter first, which made him wonder if he might have been wrong in his assumptions.

'OK, Sarah, can you tell me who else is with you? Are Angela or Mrs Turner there?'

'Yes.'

'OK, where are they?'

'Mrs Turner is here in the topsy upsy booth, but she's not talking. And Angela is more outside. But it's really dark.'

Liv glanced up at Callum and he could see the worry in her eyes.

'OK. That's really good, Sarah.' She paused, clearly thinking. 'Can you remember how to turn the torch on, the one on the phone? Don't worry, if you accidentally hang up on us, I promise we'll call right back. The same second, all right?'

'OK.' There were a few seconds of muffled rustling before Sarah came back to the phone. 'I can see now.'

'All right, can you see Mrs Turner?'

'Yes.'

'How is she?' Callum asked gently.

'I think she's sleeping,' Sarah replied. 'But she's got a big bump on her head.'

'OK, you're doing really well,' Callum reassured her. 'If you touch Mrs Turner's hand, does she feel warm? Will she respond?' He heard the older woman groan. 'OK, tell her not to move. Can you see Angela?'

'Yeah. But she's out of the booth.'

'Can you reach her? *Safely?*'

'I think so.' The was another bout of rustling. 'Uh oh.'

'What's "uh oh", Sarah?' Callum leaned forward, wishing they were on a video call and able to see what was happening.

'I think she's bleeding. And her leg is bended funny.'

'OK, you're doing great, Sarah. Have you got your bag with you? Do you have a jumper in it?' She waited for her to reply. 'OK, that's great. Can you tie it around you nose and mouth?'

'Like a cowgirl?'

'Exactly like a cowgirl! That would be perfect. It sounds like it's kind of dusty, and you don't want to be breathing in dust.'

'OK.'

She hit the mute button on her phone while Sarah followed her instructions. 'I've had enough of this.' She hit the button again. 'Sarah, I'll be right back. Keep talking to your dad.'

She stormed away, and Callum couldn't help but track her movements across the car park.

* * *

'I don't care about your rules.' Liv threw her hands up in frustration. 'There are people in there who need help, and you need to get a medic in there *NOW!*'

'We can't get in safely . . .'

'I know, I know. You're waiting for the structural engineers.' Liv shook her head. 'How long before they get here?'

'Maybe another half-hour to an hour.'

Liv shook her head. 'And then they'll need time to assess the situation and do their jobs. We don't have that long.'

'We have patients in there.' Callum joined her, backing her up. 'Sarah's talking to Jake.' He added in response to her unanswered question.

'And from the information we've been able to gather, one of them is likely concussed, and the other might well be haemorrhaging,' Liv explained, her temper fraying.

'And the other is my daughter. She's only six and terrified. We have to get in there.'

'I've told you, it's not safe. I can't ask my men to go in there.' The fireman shook his head. 'We don't have any choice but to wait.'

'You might not have any choice, but we do.' Liv glared at him with such ferocity that even Callum wanted to take a step or two back.

'I can't let you go in there.' He blocked her way.

'I'm not actually sure that you can stop me.' She stepped around him.

'Miss . . .'

'I already told you, it's *Doctor*,' she snapped back. 'And emergency medicine happens to be a specialism of mine. Now, we need to get to our patients, with or without your help. Personally, I'd prefer it to be with your help as it would be safer with your backup and your equipment. But either way, I need to get in there.'

'It's too dangerous. You could get hurt.'

'I'm volunteering. I understand and accept the risk.'

'I'm sorry, but it's not your decision.' The fireman did look genuinely sorry.

'Liv.' Callum rested a hand on her arm. 'Maybe we should listen.'

She wheeled on him, forcing him backwards. 'If it's too dangerous for me, then you can be sure as anything it's too dangerous for them. For Sarah. You heard what she said. Neither Cathy or Angela are properly conscious, and at least one of them is bleeding. If you think I'm going to stand here while people are in trouble — while Sarah is in trouble — you don't know me at all!' Her gaze softened as she looked at him. 'I'll be careful, Callum. You know I won't do anything to hurt Sarah.'

The honest pain in her eyes ripped through him. Deep in his heart, he did know that. He probably always had. 'I do. But if you're doing this, you're not doing it alone.' He squeezed her fingers tightly. 'You'll probably need help anyway.'

Liv gave him a tight smile and nodded, before grabbing her bag.

'Under section forty-four of the Fire and Rescue Services Act, I am formally restricting you access to this premises.'

'Good for you.' Liv carried on loading up her bag. 'Not sure if "doctor" trumps "fireman", but we can argue about it later. You either find a way to get us in there as safely as possible, or get out of our way.'

'I really am sorry. And I do promise we'll do our best to get everyone out safely, ASAP. But if you keep pushing, I'll have to involve the police.'

'Yeah, good luck with that.' Callum shook his head and shouldered his kit. 'Harry?' He shouted across the car park to the police sergeant. 'You the ranking officer here?'

'Yeah, why?' He jogged over to the three of them.

'Fancy trying to arrest me or Liv?'

'Uh no, why would I do that?'

'Fire chief here wants to bar us entry to the café.'

The man took off his helmet. 'I just want you to wait until we get the experts and proper equipment here.'

'Sounds sensible.' Harry followed them round the side of the café and to the courtyard wall.

'Harry.' Liv rested her hand on his arm. 'Sarah's in there. Along with Cathy and Angela Turner, who we think are hurt and possibly unconscious. We might not have time to wait.'

'Are you sure about this?'

'Yes.'

'And you both understand the risks?'

'We do.'

'I'm not happy about it, but what can I do?' He shrugged. 'I trusted you when Marie needed help to bring Oliver into the world. How can I not trust you when it's your Sarah?' He turned to the fireman. 'I suggest you come up with a plan to get them in as safely as possible. Because with or without your help, I'm pretty sure there's nothing that will stop this from happening.'

The fireman nodded abruptly and spoke into his radio briefly, a quick, crackly conversation with other members of his team. After a few moments, he beckoned for the two doctors to follow him. 'All right, we have something . . . not much . . . but something approaching a plan. We think the car is holding up what's left of the main support wall. When that came down, part of the ceiling did too. We're going to try to clear the worst of the rubble from under the car, get the hydraulic jacks on the beam resting on it, and try and get access that way.'

'You mean crawling under the car?' Callum gaped.

'I did say it wasn't much of a plan. But access from the rear is even more compromised since the roof collapsed.'

'Let's do it.'

* * *

Callum watched as they raked out the worst of the rubble, and helped Liv step into the thick, heavy trousers that were supposed to protect her from the shards of glass everywhere. The jacket they handed her, despite being worn by a female firefighter, still dwarfed her, and he suddenly wondered what the hell he was doing, letting her put herself in danger like this. She looked so small and vulnerable, peering out at him from underneath the too big helmet and over the top of the mask they hoped would protect them from the worst of the dust. For a moment, she looked like a child playing dress-up.

He struggled to shake the thought as he pulled on his own jacket, and accepted the thick leather gloves offered.

'Liv.' He caught her by the arm. 'You don't have to do this.'

'Yeah, I do. I've already argued enough with them. Don't make me argue with you too.' She tied her bag firmly round her waist before donning her own set of far-too-big gloves. 'Come on. Our patients have waited for too long already.'

'Fine, but I'm going first.' He knelt down to peer underneath the car.

'Actually, I think I should.' Liv shrugged. 'It makes more sense. If I get stuck at any point, you're a lot more likely to be able to pull me out than vice versa.' She flicked on the light on the top of her borrowed helmet and flattened herself against the ground to wriggle through the gap that had been created for them.

'Liv, I . . .' Callum wanted to say something, but he wasn't sure what. Somehow, he needed to apologise and try and make things right between them. Even if she was still planning to leave.

'Not now.' She turned to look at him, half-blinding him with the torch. 'This isn't about us.' With that, she wriggled between the wheels of the car, and disappeared into the dark rubble.

He sent a quick prayer to anyone who might be listening that they would be safe, and able to bring out everyone safely, before diving into the darkness himself. It was only a few feet, a distance he would have crossed in a heartbeat on any other day, but it felt like it took an eternity or two of careful wriggling and crawling on his elbows while dragging himself through to reach the area where his daughter would have been sitting. Liv came to a stop ahead of him, forcing him to a halt as well. He tried to keep his breathing calm, focussing on the task rather than the tonnes of building resting on top of a poorly balanced beam, scrap car and much-smaller-than-you'd-really-expect pneumatic jacks that the firemen had forced into place.

'Is everything OK?'

'Yeah, just . . . hush for a minute. I thought I heard something.' Liv went completely still and silent ahead of him. 'There it is again. Sarah, can you shout for me?'

'Livvy?' The little voice was muffled, but clearly her.

'Thank God. We can hear you, munchkin!' Callum shouted back as well as he could while on his chest with part of a car or building pressing him into the floor.

'Daddy!' The voice cut through him.

'Just stay where you are, and keep talking to us! We're coming to get you all.' He lowered his voice so only Liv could hear him. 'We *are* able to get to them, right?'

'Let's find out.' Her voice was steady and determined as she pushed forward, following Sarah's calls.

After another brief eternity of shifting rubble out of their way and slowly, slowly crawling forward in the devastation of what used to be the cosy, welcoming café, Liv came to a halt in front of what looked like a wall beneath the rubble.

Sarah's voice was much louder now, but in the chaos of stone, metal, beams and dust, it seemed to echo all around

235

him. He stared at the wall in frustration, completely disorientated and trying to figure out where they were in relation to where they needed to be.

Liv sat back on her haunches, holding herself awkwardly to avoid banging her head, and knocked gently on the barrier. 'It's wood.'

'Wood?' Callum repeated, confused. His breath caught as an answering knock echoed around them. '*Sarah*?'

'I'm here, Daddy.'

But where was "here"?

'Sarah.' Liv's voice was muffled by her mask, but still calm and strong. 'We're so close to you right now, but we're just trying to work out how to get to you, and we need a bit more help. Can you shine the torch around a bit, please?'

They waited for long moments, before seeing a flicker of something in the darkness, far above their heads. 'It's not strong enough.' Liv reached up to her helmet and clicked off her light. Callum did the same, and they disappeared into darkness. 'All right, Sarah, can you do it again? Just a bit more slowly.'

They waited, both holding their breath until they saw a pale patch of light flicker again. 'Sarah, stop! Hold it right there.' Callum tried to work out what he was seeing as the light danced around. 'Where it is doesn't make sense,' he muttered to Liv.

'I think it's reflecting off something,' Liv murmured back as she snapped her light back on and started forward again, crawling along the side of the wooden "wall", following it with her hand. After a few feet, she stopped again.

'Everything all right? Well, as all right as it can be under half a building.'

'I think we're heading in the right direction.'

'What makes you say that?' As much as he needed to concentrate on what he was doing, at the same time he didn't want to think about what was happening, and what still could happen.

'I think this "wall" we're following is really the side of a booth.'

'Well, that's good. Sarah said she was in the booth still.'

He looked down as the radio he'd hooked onto his jacket spluttered into life. 'Docs, it's Harry. Can you hear me? Over.'

'Yeah, we've got you Harry. Over.'

'Just thought you'd like to know the structural specialists are rolling up as I speak. Confirm, structural engineers have arrived. Over.'

'Received and understood. That's good news. Thanks, Harry. Over.' Callum let the radio fall back against his chest.

'Well, that's good timing.' Liv looked back from where she was exploring. 'Because I've got bad news. I've run out of wall, or booth, or whatever just ahead, and we have a problem.'

'Go on.'

'It's getting a lot narrower.'

'Do you think we can get through?'

'Honestly? No. I think I might be able to wriggle through, but I don't see how you can.'

'Let me see.' He squished himself alongside her to peer into the narrowing space. He could have cried with frustration to be so close to getting to his daughter, only to be forced back now. 'It doesn't look like it's this narrow for very far. I'll make myself fit.' He knew it was stupid as soon as he'd said it.

'Do I need to tell you how stupid that is?' He couldn't see Liv's face beneath the bright glare of her head lamp, but he was pretty sure she was scowling as she kept her voice low. 'One wrong move and we could unbalance this mess.'

'We can't give up.' He fought the despair that was choking him as much as the dust.

'We're not,' she replied calmly, before rolling into a sitting position and stripping off her gloves. 'Here, give me a hand with this.' She struggled out of the heavy coat and undid the belt she'd been using to drag her bag along.

'What are you doing?'

'Making myself as small as possible. I don't want to get snagged on something in borrowed clothes.'

'Liv, I can't ask you to do this.'

'No, you can't. But you can't ask me not to either.' She sighed as she dragged the gloves back on. 'You don't get to ask anything of me anymore.'

* * *

She knew it didn't really make any different to the size and shape of her shoulders, but Liv couldn't help but hold her breath as she wriggled through the very narrow hole in the rubble, terrified of disturbing something important. She didn't breathe again until her feet connected back with the ground. Wincing, she brushed painful shards carefully off her elbows before peering back at Callum. 'Bag please.'

'Liv, please be careful,' he begged as he handed the bag through to her.

'I am. I promise.' She crunched a few feet further.

'I can hear you!' Sarah's voice was excited.

'I can hear you too, fairy, I'm nearly with you,' she called back, before looking around the mess in front of her. The front section of what she now realised was one of the large café booths had been crushed by a falling beam and rubble. It looked like the whole thing had been picked up and shoved sideways, before being toppled over, and its heavy, old table had been thrown with it, blocking part of the entrance to leave just a small gap. While it was going to be difficult to get in, somehow it must have protected the people inside.

The weak light from the phone flickered out of the gap and bounced off the mess behind her.

After a few seconds, Sarah's face appeared in the small space. 'Livvy!'

'Hi, Sarey-fairy.' She held out her arms and tried not to squash the little girl in her relief at finding her alive and well. She rubbed her back gently, letting Sarah sob against her. 'It's all right, Sarah, I've got you.'

'I knew you'd come save me.'

The trust she had in her was painful, but Liv didn't have time to think about it, so instead she shouted back. 'I've got her, Callum. She's fine.'

'Thank goodness.' His voice echoed back, bouncing around eerily.

'Hello?' A shaky voice called out from beneath the table. 'Who's there?'

'It's Dr Emery,' Liv called back as she tucked Sarah against her side. 'Good to hear you're awake, Mrs Turner. How are you feeling?'

'I'm fine. Just a bit sore, and I can't really move. But . . . Angela's not answering. Can you please reach her?'

'Of course, I'll check on her now.' Liv hoped she sounded more confident that she felt. 'Sarah, I need you to wait here while I check on Angela, all right?'

'Do I have to?'

'Yes.' If things were the worst they could be, she didn't want Sarah to see them. The poor girl was going to be traumatised badly enough as it was. They all were. 'You'll be able to see me, and I might need an assistant to pass me things from my bag.'

'I don't like this,' the little girl admitted.

'I don't blame you.' Liv crawled towards her patient. 'There's a big torch in the front, top pocket. It will be brighter than the phone.'

She blinked a few seconds later when high-strength, halogen light pierced the dust around her. Sarah was right, there was blood, but it wasn't as bad as she'd feared, though she could immediately see the problem. Poor Angela's right leg was badly twisted, and she could see the pale bone of the femur sticking out through the top of her leg. There was blood around her, but not so much as to suggest she had damaged the femoral artery. She breathed a sigh of relief when she saw Angela's chest rise and fall steadily. It was bad, but it was far from as bad as it could have been.

'Angela, can you hear me?' She thought she saw the woman's eyelids flicker. 'I'm just going to check you over.

239

Sarah, can you tell Mrs Turner that Angela . . .' She paused, not quite sure how to phrase the next bit. 'Tell her that Angela has a poorly leg, but that she's OK.' She prayed she was telling the truth as she started her clinical examination. A few minutes later, she was satisfied that, although severe, Angela's injuries weren't immediately life-threatening. 'Right, you've got a badly broken leg, Angela, but you probably already know that. I'm guessing you've been in quite a bit of pain, so I'm just going to grab some things from my bag, and get you patched up. The emergency teams are on their way, but there's no need to make you wait.'

She crawled back to Sarah and her bag. 'You still all right in there, Mrs Turner?'

'Yes. How's Angela?'

'She's got a bad break to her leg, and is experiencing a bit of shock, but I think she's all right otherwise. I'd like to give her some pain meds. Is there anything she's allergic to?'

'No. Nothing I know of.'

'OK, let me get her patched up and I'll give her some fluids and pain meds, then I'll come and check you out properly.'

Her radio crackled into life just as she'd finished placing the IV line for Angela. 'How are things going in there, Liv?'

'Sarah, can you come here and give me a hand, please?' She tucked the radio into the little girl's fingers. 'Press this button when I'm talking, OK, then let it go when I say "over". Got that?'

'Uh huh.'

'Now, press the button for me. Hey, Callum. I've got Angela here with an open fibula fracture but thankfully no, I repeat NO, apparent damage to the associated artery. Some blood loss, but minor for the injury and typical shock reaction. Wound is dressed, patient warming up, and I'm pushing fluids and meds now. Over. You can let go now.' She winked at Sarah.

'Good to hear. How's her mum?' His voice crackled back to her.

'Button, Sarah. She's awake and coherent. Not reporting any major injuries. Over.'

'Good. I'll pass the reports on to the rescue team. They're going to be starting with more props and things in a few minutes, so it's going to get loud. You should come out.'

Liv held her hand out for the radio. 'Two minutes, Callum.'

* * *

Those two minutes lasted far, far longer than he could have imagined, but when he finally saw Liv appear, with Sarah tucked carefully beneath her, the tears that had been threatening for ages finally won out. As she crawled through the hole and into his arms, he snatched her up and swore to never let her go again.

'Daddy, you're squashing me.'

'Sorry.' He forced himself to loosen his grip, then looked up to Liv. 'Thank you so, so much.' He held a hand out to her.

She shook her head. 'Get Sarah out of here. I've still got patients who need me.'

He watched as she turned, and disappeared back into the darkness.

'Daddy?'

'Yes, fairy.' He buried his face in her dusty hair.

'Do all superheroes wear masks like on TV? Coz I think Liv might be a superhero.'

'I think she might be too.' He gave her another squeeze. 'Come on. Let's get out of here and give the experts space to work.'

'Livvy's going to be OK, right?'

'Of course she is. You're right. She's a superhero.'

CHAPTER FIFTEEN

Liv gave Cathy's hand a final squeeze, and hopped out of the ambulance, promising to check in on her soon. She waved to the paramedics and stretched, trying to ease the kinks of the last few hours out of her back. She couldn't believe how much had happened in such a short space of time. She caught sight of herself in the hospital doors, and laughed at her reflection. Her dress was creased from being stuffed into borrowed clothes, she was streaked with dirt and stained with blood, and her hair looked like she'd rubbed half a pound of dirt through it.

She turned her head upside down and dragged her fingers through her hair, shaking out a cloud of dust. It wasn't even close to enough, but it was the best she could do. A quick stop by the toilets to scrub off the worst of the dirt and smears, and she was done. At least, as best she could manage. All she really wanted to do was go back to the cottage and soak away the dirt and stress of the day, and finish packing. But first, she needed to see Sarah, and reassure herself that she really was fine, and hadn't been hurt by the events of the day.

She followed the staff route through to the children's wards, and checked the board for Sarah's name, before knocking on the door it indicated.

'Hey, Sarey-fairy. How are you feeling?'

'Bored. I want to go home.'

'Not until you've been checked out properly,' Callum argued.

'But I feel fine,' Sarah complained.

'But you were in a building collapse. And I need to know that you're fine.'

Sarah sighed and rolled her eyes at Liv, who smothered a smile.

'I just wanted to check in before I . . .' She trailed off, not quite knowing how to finish the sentence. 'I just wanted to make sure you're OK, Sarah. Angela's already in surgery, and her mum's just been taken in for assessment. She's suffered a concussion, and they want to make sure she didn't breathe in too much dust. Like you, little fairy.'

'She'll be out before the end of today,' Callum confirmed. 'Just a few hours of observation.'

'That's good.' She smiled at Sarah.

'Livvy? Can I have another hug?'

Liv's eyes flicked to Callum, who gave her a crooked smile, which she took as agreement. 'Of course, you can.' She sat on the bed and held out her arms. 'But I'm pretty mucky still.'

'Don't care.' Sarah snuggled against her and placed a kiss on her cheek. 'Thank you for coming to get me when I got stucked. You're braver than all the Disney princesses all together and my hero! Thank you, thank you, thank you!'

'You're more than welcome, Sarah. I was always going to come and get you. I'm glad you're safe. That's the most important thing.' She found herself tearing up, and had to bite the inside of her cheek to keep from sobbing all over the little girl in her arms. It was just too painful.

After a while, she reluctantly pulled away, and placed a gentle kiss on Sarah's forehead. 'You were so brave today, and you really are a very special, very wonderful, very sweet and clever little girl. And you are so, so very loved. Whatever happens, promise me you will remember that?' She smoothed

Sarah's hair down and tugged the covers more tightly around her.

'All right.' She nodded sleepily.

Liv felt Callum behind her as she stepped back into the corridor.

'Liv, you were incredible back there.'

She didn't really know what to say. Regardless of what had happened in the last few hours, the pain from their argument was still raw, and feelings of betrayal and anger still burned in her chest. 'I'll clear my things from the surgery and drop the key through your letter box.'

'Liv, that's not necessary.' Callum reached out to her, but she stepped back, knowing nothing had changed. Or, more accurately, everything had changed from a few days ago and the promises they'd made to each other. He didn't trust her, and without trust there wasn't really any hope of a future.

'I'm sorry, but I think it is. I'm glad Sarah's going to be fine, I really am.' Her voice broke under the strain of unshed tears. 'But I don't think anything has changed. The surgery, Broclington, the community . . . it's your home. Not mine.'

'Liv, it could be your home too.'

'For a while, I thought maybe that was true. But . . . I'll be gone in a few days, Callum. I'll take the job they rang you for the reference for. It's only another locum position, but it will give me enough time to sort myself out and figure out what it is that I really want to do.' All the feelings of safety and security that she'd felt around him, all the hopes for the future had melted under the heat of his anger, and she didn't know how to get them back.

'Liv, please don't do this.'

'It's already happened, Callum. You made your feelings very clear.' She turned away while she still had the strength. She'd already been in a relationship where she'd had to convince herself that she was happy, and she'd promised herself that she'd never settle again. So she focussed on putting one foot in front of the other and trying not to burst into tears. She only made it a couple of dozen steps before something occurred to her, and she span on her heel. 'But just so you know. I applied for that job before we'd talked. Before we'd made any promises. It doesn't make any difference now, but I just wanted you to know that. I'd never set out to hurt you, or to betray your trust. And I would never, ever, ever have hurt Sarah. I just needed to say that.'

* * *

The events of the day slammed into Callum, rendering him speechless. The huge argument with Liv, the car crash, nearly losing his daughter, crawling through the debris of the café, and the relief of her being all right was just too much.

His knees gave way and he slowly slid down the wall behind him, unable to make sense of what was happening, and certainly not able to respond or chase after Liv. He wouldn't have known what to say even if his legs had worked enough to follow her.

* * *

Liv folded another jumper and sat it amongst the others in the overly-full suitcase. True to her word, she'd finished packing up her things, and returned the surgery key that night, and had rapidly packed her Broclington life in a few short days. She dumped the last jumper into the case and squished it down, trying to force the zip closed while wondering why she seemed to have so much more stuff to pack than when she'd moved here just a handful of months ago. Had she really bought so much in her new life here? Not that there had been any point in it.

Finally, the zip gave in and moved and rushed around the corner of the case, only to split open. Liv looked at the gaping hole and burst into tears. Angrily, she shoved the case off the bed and collapsed onto it. She wrapped her arms tightly around her pillow, and cried into it, overwhelmed by sadness, anger and embarrassment. And betrayal. She'd honestly thought that Callum had cared about her, and wanted to help mend her broken heart, but instead of helping her heal, he'd let her down at the first obstacle and left her feeling shattered.

She'd trusted him and opened her heart to him, believing him when he'd said they could be something serious. Something *real* and permanent to each other. And that was what hurt the most. That despite all his lovely words, his sweet gestures and what she'd thought they shared, when it came to the first obstacle, their first challenge, he hadn't cared enough to fight for them, to give her the chance to explain, or to listen to her.

She'd started to let herself dream about a life where being snuggled between Callum and Sarah would be a nightly event. Where she'd help brush Sarah's hair, tuck her into bed with a story and favourite bear, before sharing Callum's bed and everything he had to offer.

She'd even thought — hoped — that one day the little girl might call her "Mum".

She dashed away the tears that scorched her cheeks, angry at her foolishness. She wanted to be angry at Callum, but he'd done nothing wrong. This time it wasn't a man who had broken her heart. The only person she could blame for the current burning ache in her chest was herself.

She wrapped her arms around her waist, helplessly trying to comfort herself as she stared around the empty room. The cottage that had been so warm and welcoming, so full of promise, when she'd arrived, now seemed stark and cold.

Her phone buzzed in her pocket and Liv morosely pulled it out and glanced at the glowing screen: Callum. Resolutely, she pressed ignore on the last person she wanted to talk to. Almost immediately the phone buzzed again. This time she hesitated. She really didn't want to talk to him, and she thought she'd made that more than clear at the hospital, and every time he'd tried to contact her in the few days since.

But, there was always the chance it could be something medical. There were only limited medics in the village, and after the last couple of days it was clear that anything could happen.

But she hesitated for too long, and the call ended. She shrugged and threw the phone on the bed. If it *was* something urgent, he'd call back or leave a message. She stared at the phone as, sure enough, it lit up again, flashing and bouncing with its eagerness to be answered.

With trembling fingers, Liv answered the call, hoping that her voice was steadier than her hand. 'What is it?'

'Livvy!' Sarah's voice was too high-pitched and Liv's heart squeezed painfully. She hated herself for upsetting the little girl she'd fallen as much in love with as her father, but Callum had made it clear she had no place in either of their lives.

'Hi, Sarey-fairy.' She tried to keep the sadness from her voice. If she could just make it through this call, then she could climb into bed, pull the covers over her head, and let herself cry until some of the hurt escaped. She'd had enough of being brave. Then, tomorrow, she could drive away and hope that the pain wouldn't follow her back to London.

'Livvy, you have to come.'

Liv's blood ran cold at the panic in Sarah's voice. 'What is it? What's wrong? Where's your dad?'

'He fell, Livvy. Off the ladder.'

Liv's heart leapt into her throat as she scoured the room for her keys. 'Where are you, Sarah? Are you at home?'

'No. The surgery. Livvy, please come. Please. Daddy won't open his eyes. I think he might be very very hurting.'

'I'm on my way.' She grabbed the keys from where they'd landed on the floor. 'Now, are you near your dad?'

'Yes.'

'This is very important.' Liv raced down the cottage stairs. 'Is Daddy breathing? Can you see his chest moving?' She held her breath and silently prayed as she waited for the vital answer. The world couldn't be so cruel as to hurt Sarah again, not after what she'd been through already. But, Liv was a doctor, and knew only too well how unfair things could really be.

'Yes.'

Liv's breath exploded in a rush as she pulled the cottage door shut behind her and zapped her car unlocked. 'That's good, Sarah. That's really good.' She slammed the car door, shoved the key into the ignition, yanked the handbrake off and rammed the accelerator down. 'Is there any blood you can see?'

'No.' Her voice was incredibly small sounding to Liv.

'Daddy's going to be fine, Sarah, I'm sure of it. You're being so brave right now. I'm on my way.'

'You promise you're coming?' Sarah begged. 'Promise promise?'

'Yes.' Liv took a corner too fast and had to force herself into a level of calmness and focus. It wouldn't help Callum if she dumped her car in a ditch or had an accident herself. 'I'll be there in a couple of minutes. That's no time at all, OK?'

'K,' Sarah's voice sounded muffled and seconds later the call was replaced with static.

Liv swore, cursing the poor signal in the area. She longed to call Sarah back, but she didn't dare take her hands off the wheel long enough to unlock the phone on the windy country roads, and she couldn't pull over either. Instead she gunned the car harder and screeched around the next corner, her heart thumping in her ears. She'd been in plenty of emergency situations before and knew how important it was to stay calm under pressure. Usually the adrenaline that was sending her heart into overdrive was useful to her — it sharpened her reactions and senses — but today, when it was Callum in trouble, her hands shook and white-hot panic clouded her mind.

She had to stay calm, get to him, and make sure he got whatever help he needed. Nothing else mattered. She could go back to being hurt and angry after that.

She screeched to a halt in the surgery car park and raced to the door, not even bothering to turn the engine off. She flung the door open and came face-to-face with Sarah, waiting in reception . . . and giggling nervously.

'Please don't be angry, Livvy.'

'I'm not angry, sweetie. Where's your dad?' Now that she could see Sarah was OK, her focus was entirely on Callum.

'I didn't want to fib, but Daddy said it was OK, just this once.' Sarah giggled again, and tried to hide the laughter behind the huge bunch of flowers she was holding.

'What are you talking about, Sarah?' She looked down at the little girl, and finally took in the pretty princess dress she was wearing and the flowers cradled carefully in her arms. She looked around the room, and stared at the petals on the floor in confusion. 'What's going on? Is your dad OK?'

'Yup.' Sarah nodded cheerfully, and pushed the flowers into Liv's arms. 'These are for you, and I'm sorry for fibbing. Wait here, K?'

'But your dad's really OK?'

'Yes,' Sarah replied with a small huff and a level of complete exasperation that only a six-year-old could manage. 'Promise to stay here.' She stared at Liv in wide-eyed expectation.

Liv nodded, utterly confused as Sarah span on her heel and ran down the corridor leading to the consulting rooms, her fairy wings flapping and bouncing with every step.

Liv buried her nose in the bouquet, and inhaled the delicate scent of roses. She had no idea what was going on, or what to think, but if this was Callum's way of apologising, and saying goodbye, then at least she'd be leaving with a few happy memories instead of the hurt she'd been nursing for the last few days.

She looked around the waiting room, and allowed herself a moment of sadness. She was really going to miss it here. But with Tom and his wife back, they didn't really need a locum right now. The fundraising had been a success, but the refurbishments the surgery needed would take months, so they'd have plenty of time to find someone else. Someone more permanent. And with her new job starting in less than a fortnight, she wanted time to settle in at what would be her new home.

The bell that usually called patients through to the consultation rooms pinged, and Liv looked up and smiled as her name appeared on the screen instructing her to go to Callum's room. Apparently, she could now find out what was happening without risking incurring the wrath of her favourite fairy.

She gasped in amazement as she opened the door into the corridor, and found it lined with rose petals and flickering candles. She swallowed hard, suddenly feeling incredibly nervous as she walked through the familiar space and slowly pushed open the door to his office.

* * *

Callum licked his lips nervously as he heard Liv's footsteps in the corridor, and the door swung slowly open. He scrubbed his suddenly clammy hands against his trousers, and tried to force a smile to his face.

He looked at her as she stood in the doorway, clutching her flowers and looking confused. At least she'd accepted the flowers — that had to be a good sign. But then again, even though she might have thrown them back in his face, he knew she'd never reject Sarah like that.

As usual, Liv looked stunning to him. In jeans and an oversized jumper that moulded itself softly to her curves, and with her hair in a scruffy knot on the top of her head and without a scrap of make-up, she was still breath-taking. Possibly even more so than when she was dressed up, because she looked softer, younger, and more like the version of herself who crawled around the floor playing with Sarah, and curled up happily next to him on a couch. He had to convince her to stay. He loved her far too much to let her go, and he loved who she was, and how she was, with Sarah.

Then panic hit him. He'd been so busy making sure Sarah was OK after the car crash, and planning this and getting the flowers, candles and himself and Sarah ready — not to mention hatching the plan to get Liv here and practicing

Sarah's phone call with her — that he suddenly realised he didn't know what to say. He hadn't planned the most important words of all. Blind panic filled him, and he could feel the sweat start to prickle at his temples.

'So.' Liv gave him a smile that warmed his heart. 'As farewell apologies go, this one is certainly up there with the best.'

'That's not what this is.'

'It's not?'

'No, I mean it is.' Callum fumbled his words. 'I mean, an apology. It's an apology. I owe you that and so much more. But it's not a farewell. At least I hope it's not.' He ran his hands through his hair. 'I'm not doing a very good job of this.'

'Of what, exactly?'

'I'm trying . . . very badly . . . to ask you to stay, Liv. I'm asking you to forgive me my unforgivable behaviour, and give me another chance. To give us another chance.' He ran his hands through his hair. 'It seems like me apologising for terrible behaviour is something of a theme for us.'

'You could say that.' She bit the inside of her lip. 'You hurt me really badly, Callum.'

'I know, and I really am so, so sorry. But will you hear me out? Please?' He waited for her nod. 'I felt like we'd started to create a family. You, me and Sarah. And I want that back. These last few days without you have been . . . well, they've been the worst of my life.'

'All you had to do was listen to me. That's all you ever had to do.'

'I know. And if you let me, if you can forgive me enough to give me another chance, I promise I'll do my best to always, *always* listen to you.'

'I don't know what to say.' The cellophane around the flowers rustled as her hands started to tremble.

'You don't need to say anything if you don't want to. I'm just going to ask you to do the one thing that I didn't manage for you. I just want you to listen. To do better than I did.'

She nodded.

'I don't know if this is the right time, or if it's premature, but it's what I really want, and how I really feel. But, I promise, whatever you say, whatever you need, I'll do my best to give it to you. And I'll do my best to be patient for as long as you need. Even if it drives me crazy. I'd do anything for you, Liv.'

'Oh my God.' Liv's voice was breathy as Callum produced a small box from his pocket.

'I-I'm sorry it's not a real ring yet,' Callum stammered nervously. 'I didn't have a chance to get one. Or properly work out what to say to you. But if you say yes, it will be. A real ring, I mean. Any one you like. We can pick it out together. And it can be whenever you like. Whenever you're ready.'

'I can help,' Sarah exclaimed from behind him.

'Sarah.' He rested a restraining hand on her shoulder. 'She hasn't said yes, yet.'

'You haven't asked me anything.'

Callum winced. This was not going the way he'd imagined at all. 'Liv, this is not the ring, or the proposal you deserve. I'm not even sure I'm the man you deserve — I certainly haven't been lately. But, if you agree, I'll spend the rest of my life making it up to you, and trying to be everything that someone as amazing as you should have in your life. Please, Liv, give me another chance and I swear I'll never let you down again. I'll never not hear you. If you agree to stay with me, and Sarah, we'll build a family together. However and whenever you want.' He took a deep breath, and prayed she would say yes. 'Liv, will you do me the greatest honour I've never deserved, and maybe consider marrying me? If not now, then whenever you're ready?'

He opened the box, revealing a sparkly fairy ring.

Liv laughed, and for a moment Callum doubted his choice and wondered if she'd understand the gesture.

'This might be the craziest thing ever.'

'I know. But I feel like letting you walk away would be even crazier. What do you say? Will you at least think about it?'

Liv took the box gently, her hand shaking as she held it out to Sarah. She couldn't believe she'd gone from being about to leave, to being offered a dream come true. But as much as she loved Callum, she had to be sure it was what Sarah wanted too. She was just as important in this decision as he was. So she held out a hand to Sarah, and pulled her a few steps away from her dad. 'Is this one of yours?'

'Yup.' Sarah grinned proudly. 'It's my bestest and most favourite. It's magic too. It fits everyone. Even Daddy's fat fingers.'

Liv pressed her lips together, trying not to smile. She wanted to be completely serious for this conversation — it wasn't just her life that was about to change forever. 'Do you know what this means?'

Sarah nodded, equally serious.

'Tell me?' Liv asked gently, needing to be sure.

'If you say yes, it means you and Daddy get married, and I get to be a bridesmaid in a pretty dress. And we all live happily ever after. And you will be my mummy.'

Liv sniffed, and had to blink back tears. She was already desperately in love with this little girl, and hearing the name "Mummy" from her filled her heart with joy and hope. 'And is that what you want, Sarah? For me to be your mummy?'

Sarah nodded reverently. 'Yes!'

'Do you know that before I came here, I got hurt. And it means I probably can't have my own babies, so if I become your mummy, then you won't ever have a little brother or sister.' She met Callum's eyes over Sarah's head, and he gave her a reassuring smile, telling her without words what she needed to hear: that she was everything he wanted, and having her complete his and Sarah's family was already more than enough for him.

'Daddy told me you might not be able to have babies. But I think it's OK. My friend Chrissy has a new baby brother and she says all he does is cry and poop and be sick on people and isn't any fun. So I thought who would want a baby?' She paused for a deep breath. 'And it's like a fairy story. Daddy loves you, and I love you too. And I think you really like me. I thought maybe I could be your little girl as well as Daddy's and then you wouldn't need a baby and smell of sick all the time, and maybe we could get a dog instead 'coz dogs are cool. What do you think?'

'I think that sounds amazing. But you're wrong. I don't just "really like" you, Sarah. I already love you too.' Liv wiped her eyes and leaned closer, and rested her forehead against Sarah's. 'So you think I should say yes to your daddy?'

'Yes. But . . .'

'But what, sweetie?'

'But you should make him ask proper.' Sarah glared at her dad, and Liv struggled not to laugh — partly in relief, and partly at the look of disgust that Callum was being given by his daughter. *Her daughter* she realised, with tears of joy threatening to spill down her cheeks.

'Properly?' He raised an eyebrow at his daughter. 'We've got candles, and flowers and a ring.'

'You're supposed to be on one knee. And say "Liv, will you marry me?", like they do on the TV.' She stuck one hand on her hip, her other still tightly holding onto Liv's.

Liv looked down at the little girl, her heart filled with love for the beautiful, precocious, bright little fairy who was about to become her daughter. She only hoped she'd be up to the challenge. She gave Callum a bright smile, and chucked the boxed ring back at him, and tried not to laugh as he fumbled the catch.

He looked at her quizzically.

Liv shrugged. 'You heard your daughter. You have to do it properly.'

Callum couldn't keep the smile from his face as he dropped to one knee, and took Liv's spare hand in his. 'Liv . . . Olivia . . . Will you please, *please*, marry me?'

'Hmmm . . .' Liv tapped a finger against her lips, apparently deep in thought. 'What do you think, Sarah?'

'Say yes!' Sarah tugged at her hand. 'Yes, yes, yes, yes, yes.'

Liv laughed, the joy bubbling out of her. 'As crazy as this is, I think you're right. It would be crazier for me to say no.'

'So, does that mean . . . ?'

'Yes. It means, yes!' She laughed as he scooped her up and held her tightly against him, and placed a soft kiss against her lips while Sarah giggled and wrapped her arms around both of their legs.

EPILOGUE

'Sarah, will you please calm down and be careful?' Callum shouted after his daughter as she raced through the garden at top speed with Summer, leaving a trail of bubbles that Tilly was trying to snap out of the air. 'At least stay away from the barbeque. I've only just lit it, but it's still hot. The last thing I want to be doing today is taking anyone to A&E!'

Sarah ignored him, zooming past the wishing well and coming dangerously close to the hot coals again.

'Young lady, if I have to tell you one more time you'll . . . you'll go to bed early without any dessert.'

'But Summer and Tilly are here!' Sarah's bottom lip stuck out with that wobble that so often warned of a stubborn tantrum. 'You're so *unfair*!'

'Sarah, will you please take your bubble game down to the bottom of the garden? It's a lot safer for Tilly down there.' Liv brought a plate of bread rolls and bowl of salad from the kitchen, and smiled as the trio raced off to do exactly as she'd asked.

Callum gaped. 'Why is it she does what you ask, but not me?'

'Novelty value.' Liv laughed. 'I'm sure when she has to put up with me twenty-four seven, she'll ignore me as much as she does you.'

'I don't believe that for a second.' Callum slipped an arm around his fiancée's waist, and pulled her in for a kiss. He still couldn't believe that Liv had said yes. It hadn't even been a full week since he'd asked her, since she'd agreed to marry him, but already Sarah was paying more attention to her than she did her own father. He couldn't really be more thrilled. 'She adores you.'

'I know. I love her too.' He watched as Liv's eyes tracked Sarah's pink, glittery dance across the garden.

'You know, you could just move in with us straight away.' He let his fingers trace a line down the back of her neck, enjoying her shiver. 'I'm not doing anything tomorrow.'

'You're incorrigible, Dr Macpearson.' She folded her arms across her chest. 'We talked about this. You agreed, remember? That's why I extended the lease here for a couple of months. So we can take our time and let Sarah adjust gradually. Besides, I'm still not sure I want to move into your bachelor pad.'

'It's hardly a bachelor pad. Not with the amount of pink and purple glitter madam spreads everywhere.'

'You know what I mean.'

She leaned against him comfortably, and Callum marvelled again at just how easily and well she fitted. Against him, in his life, in Sarah's world.

'I just think I might like a few more feminine touches.'

'And I need you to feel at home. Hell, you and Sarah can redecorate the whole house from top to bottom if you want. Just maybe leave me one small corner that isn't completely pink.'

'Well, thank you,' Liv laughed 'But I was thinking something a bit smaller. Maybe a few throw pillows. Matching towels. Things like that. And we'll need more furniture, especially in your bedroom.'

'King sized bed?' He grinned.

'Cheeky.' She tweaked his nose. 'I was thinking more like drawers for my clothes, another wardrobe. Your home is lovely, Callum, and I can't wait for it to be my home too.

But it's been yours and Sarah's home for years. *Only* yours and Sarah's. You need to make space for me, and that can't be rushed. We have to do things right by Sarah.'

'I know, and you're right. It's just frustrating. I want everything to happen right now. Or tomorrow?'

'By the time tomorrow gets here, I'm betting we have two overtired little girls on our hands, and anything more energetic than watching princess movies will be beyond us all.'

'You think it's going to be that bad tonight?' Callum shuddered.

'I don't think anyone is getting a full night's sleep, if that's what you're asking. Did you see the snack bag your brother sent with Summer? I'm pretty sure it's ninety per cent sugar.' She rolled her eyes.

'I think he's getting his own back,' he complained. 'I wasn't expecting the dog too.'

'Well, Jake and Evelyn hosted plenty of sleepovers for Sarah. It seems only fair. And Tilly's well-behaved.' She winced as the "well-behaved" dog knocked over her bird bath. 'Mostly. I'm sure Angela's little Sparks won't be any trouble.'

'You're too sweet.' He placed a kiss on her cheek. 'What time are you expecting Cathy?'

Liv checked the time on her phone. 'Any time now.' She accepted the drink Callum offered her, and sat on the edge of Sarah's fairy well. Even though she knew it wasn't a bench any more, it was still one of her favourite places to sit in the garden. She would miss it when she moved. But, as she watched her soon-to-officially-be daughter play and dance in the sunshine with her best friend, she knew she'd be gaining far more than she was giving up. She was getting a dream come true.

She sighed happily, and leaned her head against Callum's shoulder.

'Are you all right?'

'Yeah, just thinking how lucky I am.'

'We're the lucky ones, love.' He wrapped an arm around her shoulders.

Tilly raced past her to the garden gate, leaving the girls still playing a game that seemed to involve a lot of arm flapping, curtseys and bubble blowing. Smiling, Liv followed Tilly. The little Shiba Inu leaped up and down excitedly, yipping and barking.

'You know there's someone out here who you want to play with, don't you?' She knelt down to pet the little dog. 'But you'll need to be patient a bit longer. Sit. Stay.' She slipped out of the gate.

'Hi, Cathy. And hi, Angela — we hadn't expected to see you.' Liv held the front garden gate open, surprised to see Angela out and about. 'Do you need a hand with that chair?'

'No, thanks,' Cathy answered for her daughter. 'I'm getting pretty used to manoeuvring the wheelchair. Though everything takes a bit longer with it. That's why we're a tad late. Sorry. But I'm fine with this.' She pushed the chair through the front gate and followed Liv up the side of the house. It was then that she caught her first glimpse of their reason for visiting. 'I've had plenty of practice; after all I've been pushing Angela around for years.'

Liv smiled as Angela complained. 'It wasn't funny the first time she tried that joke on the hospital physios, or the occupational health team. Or the other dozen times I've heard it since.'

'It could be worse.' Cathy grinned at her daughter. 'You could be doing all this without my wonderful sense of humour.'

'You're not late at all,' Liv reassured them both. 'How's your leg healing, Angela? Getting plenty of rest after the acci-dent and surgery?'

'I feel like I've done nothing but rest all week. Rest in the hospital, rest at home. Even going for a walk is a rest because I'm not allowed out of this thing.' She rolled her eyes. 'Anyway, I'm not here as your patient, Liv. Do you want to meet him?' Angela's grin was contagious.

'Of course.'

'He's still pretty shy,' Angela warned as Liv knelt beside her. 'Come on, Sparks. Come and say "hi" to my friends.'

Liv had to suppress her excitement as a pair of pointy tan ears peeped out from behind the wheelchair, quickly followed by a snowy white snout covered in freckles and brown splodges. 'Hello, Sparks.' She held out her fingers to let the little dog sniff at them. After a few long seconds in which she held her breath, he took a couple of tiny steps towards her. Gently and slowly she patted the top of his head. After freezing for a moment, the dog relaxed and butted his head against her hand.

'Here, try these.' Angela held up a bag of biscuits. 'Would you like a treat, Sparks? Ask Liv if she has one for you.' She shook her head. 'We had the hardest time getting him to eat when he came in a few weeks ago. Poor little pup was so nervous.'

'I dread to think what he's been through.' The thought made Liv angry. 'You said Jake thought he was about three?'

'Three, maybe four. It's so hard to tell with rescues when you don't know what their nutrition and health has been previously. But someone loved this little guy once. He's house trained, but an absolute terror on the leash still. Are you sure you're OK with this?'

'It's just a few weeks, Angela.' Liv smiled as a cold nose and wet tongue hit her palm. 'Look, he's eating from my hand. We'll be fine, won't we, Sparks?'

'He certainly seems to have taken to you quite fast.' Angela grinned at the dog who was now half-standing on Liv, eagerly investigating the prospect of more treats.

'The feeling's mutual.' Liv rubbed his ears gently and fed him another biscuit. 'Would you like to join us? Cal's barbequing, and we've got extra sausages.' She laughed as Sparks yipped. 'Oh, you know that word, don't you? Come join us all in the garden. Please.'

Behind the back gate, Tilly yapped in excitement, and Sparks froze, his ears pointing towards the sound.

'Are you sure?'

'Of course. Besides, Sparks here might feel a bit happier if you're here while he settles in. I've got everything Jake sent over hidden under the stairs. I didn't want to tell Sarah I'm fostering him for a few weeks in case he didn't take to me. Let's go introduce him to the rabble, before Tilly gives us away.'

* * *

Callum looked up as the gate swung open, and shot Liv a wink. Nervously following her in was a scruffy-looking Jack Russell who seemed to be trying to hide behind Liv while also sniff at Tilly. Within moments the Shiba had cheerfully sniffed him all over, and was racing down the garden to find her human.

'Hi, Cathy, hi, Angela. I take it the introduction went well.'

'Yeah, at least to Liv. He's still pretty shy though.'

'Can't really blame him, we don't know what he's been through.' He broke off a piece of sausage, blew on it, and crouched down. 'Hey, little chap. Want to come see what I've got for you?' He grinned when the dog sidled over and snaffled the treat from between his fingers. 'You'll be fine here. And it's only a few weeks until Angela's back on her feet and back working to find you a forever home.'

The blur of ginger fur bounded past before the girls screeched to a halt next to him.

'Who's the cute doggy?' Sarah asked.

'Can we pet him?' Summer added. She looked at Sarah and sagely added, 'Did you know you should always, always ask before touching an animal? In case they get scared or something.'

'Duuuh.' Sarah laughed. 'Uncle Jake always says that. Well?' She looked at Angela, Cathy and Liv. 'Can we pet him? What's his name?'

'Well, we've been calling him Sparks. And he's very shy, but he might like to be petted if you're really gentle.'

'Is he one of your rescues?' Summer asked, quietly.

'Yes. He came in a few weeks ago.'

Sarah's eyes went wide as she looked at Liv. 'Are we going to be his new home? Am I getting a new dog as well as a new mum?'

'Don't get too excited, Sarah,' Callum warned. 'Liv's just fostering him — looking after him for a few weeks — while Angela gets better from the accident and surgery. She can't really walk Sparks as much as he needs right now, and he could knock her off her crutches too easily. Liv's just looking after him for a little while, and then he'll probably be going back to her while she looks for his new family.'

'Oh.' Sarah's face fell for a few seconds before she grinned and looked at Liv. 'So he's a borrowed dog. A bit like a borrowed locum doctor?'

'Yeah, a bit like that.' Callum tousled her hair.

Sarah glanced at Liv, then back at him, and beamed. 'OK.' Sarah grabbed Summer's hand. 'Come on Tilly, let's show Sparks your toys. C'mon boy.'

Callum watched in amazement as the shy dog hesitated, looked at all the adults, then bounded down the garden after the girls, yapping excitedly.

They hadn't made it halfway down the garden path before Sarah ran back and threw herself into Liv's arms. 'I love borrowed locums.' Just as quickly, she was off again, chattering loudly and excitedly to Summer and the dogs.

'Liv?' He folded his arms across his chest.

'Yes, Callum.'

'I thought you'd planned to be a temporary foster home for him.'

'I did.' He could see she was trying not to laugh. 'But it looks like your daughter might have different ideas.'

'Angela, when you're feeling better, do you want to start drawing up the adoption papers, just in case?'

'Sparks does seem pretty happy here,' Angela agreed as they watched the dog bounce around the garden like an over-excited ping-pong ball.

Callum threw his arm around Liv's shoulder and pulled her closer to him. 'I've got news for you,' he whispered in her ear.

'What's that?'

'It's not just my daughter with different ideas.'

'No?'

'No. It won't be long before she's officially your daughter too.'

She turned to grin up at him, her eyes sparkling. 'I can't wait.'

THE END

THANK YOU

Wonderful, lovely Reader — thank *you* for choosing *Healing Hearts in the Little Village*.

I really hoped you enjoyed your visit to Broclington — whether it was your first time, or you're catching up with some old friends — I've certainly loved re-visiting "Badger Town" and its residents, and have more visits planned.

If you have enjoyed yourself, please let others know by leaving a review — it really, really does help us authors hugely.

You can also follow me on Twitter (@ellacookwrites) for news on my next book — and maybe share some of your own magical, fairy moments. Or just pop on by and say "Hi!".

Love and light,
Ella x

THE CHOC LIT STORY

Established in 2009, Choc Lit is an independent, award-winning publisher dedicated to creating a delicious selection of quality women's fiction.

We have won 18 awards, including Publisher of the Year and the Romantic Novel of the Year, and have been shortlisted for countless others.

All our novels are selected by genuine readers. We are proud to publish talented first-time authors, as well as established writers whose books we love introducing to a new generation of readers.

In 2023, we became a Joffe Books company. Best known for publishing a wide range of commercial fiction, Joffe Books has its roots in women's fiction. Today it is one of the largest independent publishers in the UK.

We love to hear from you, so please email us about absolutely anything bookish at choc-lit@joffebooks.com

If you want to hear about all our bargain new releases, join our mailing list.

www.choc-lit.com

ALSO BY ELLA COOK

BROCLINGTON
Book 1: SUMMER'S CHRISTMAS
Book 2: HEALING HEARTS IN THE LITTLE
VILLAGE

STANDALONES
BEYOND GREY